PENGUIN BOOKS

THE KORO RIOTS

Faisal Tehrani (also known as Mohd Faizal Musa) is a Malaysian author. Faisal has won numerous literary prizes and awards, and is often deemed as a controversial author for experimenting various forms and proposing alternative discourses in his works. Among his best remembered works are *1515* (translated into French and published by Les Indes Savantes), and *The Professor* (translated into English) in 2020. As an academic most of his works centred around human rights, and alternative discourses. Other than writing essays, and novels, Faisal is also known as a playwright, where his stage play *Ghaib* received good reviews. In 2023, Faisal's written screenplay *Maryam Pagi Ke Malam*, directed by Badrul Hisham Ismail, was premiered in Rotterdam Film Festival.

The Koro Riots

Faisal Tehrani

Translated by
Brigitte Bresson

PENGUIN BOOKS
An imprint of Penguin Random House

PENGUIN BOOKS

USA | Canada | UK | Ireland | Australia
New Zealand | India | South Africa | China | Southeast Asia

Penguin Books is part of the Penguin Random House group of companies
whose addresses can be found at global.penguinrandomhouse.com

Published by Penguin Random House SEA Pte Ltd
9, Changi South Street 3, Level 08-01,
Singapore 486361

First published in Penguin Books by Penguin Random House SEA 2023

ISBN 9789815127843

Typeset in Garamond by MAP Systems, Bangalore, India

www.penguin.sg

Contents

Pigs 1

Adele 49

The Tiger 93

The Play 153

Qu'allah Bénisse La Hujung Manani! 199

Glossary 262

Pigs

The art exhibition had been open for twenty-five days already. Ever since the opening, the gallery had been nearly empty. Just like the shaman had prophesied: 'you will only get lucky on the twenty-sixth day'.

Several years had passed. Today, the Ziji stone was going to play its part again. You had been waiting for that moment with apprehension. Today, you were going to make a comeback, to recover your wealth and your power.

The fight had been violent. Formidable. You were almost defeated after you were struck with the pillow. You lashed at the wrong object, ripped the fabric and mauled the filling. Meanwhile, the Indian man's long penis had wrapped itself around your neck and your waist; you were trapped, as if wrapped in the coils of an anaconda. But the Ziji stone that hung around your neck weakened the ghost, and the Indian man with the long penis lost his strength. He slowly became paralysed.

That fight had taken place a long time ago. You came back to the present.

'The Up-and-Coming Politician who is married and will enter the political arena in five years from now, is going to make a surprise visit to our gallery.'

1

You should not have been present. But all throughout the previous day, you had heard whispers and the growling of a tiger. You had even seen a crouching tiger in the shadows.

You knew that the time had come. After waiting for so long.

The shaman who sold spells and charms had called you this morning to remind you: 'It is time for you to sing *our* "traditional" song; do you still remember the steps of the Sumazau dance?'

The Ziji stone. You took out the invaluable treasure. You fastened it once more around your neck. If he wanted you to sing, you would sing. You would dance, too.

The Up-and-Coming Politician liked unusual paintings. And the strange painting entitled 'Ghost defeated by Tiger in the coils of an Indian man's long penis', measuring 95.5 x 121 centimetres, was the focus of the 'Strange Things' exhibition.

The words of the shaman still rang in your ears. 'He is the ninth richest man in the world according to the *Forbes* magazine.'

So when the Up-and-Coming Politician approached the painting, the expressionist work immediately caught his eye.

The gallery owner, who was also the shaman, explained how the painting was replete with ideas and emotions, hidden concepts and the artist's personal and global opinions. The images in the painting concealed a thousand messages.

The painting was indeed unique. The colours, the shapes and the lines stood out. The brush strokes were rough, energetic and varied. It had clearly been painted with a spontaneous and aggressive energy. The splatters of oil paint in the corners created an effect that was difficult to explain.

The gallery owner insisted. 'This is a special oil painting, reminiscent of Egon Schiele. Actually, the artist is here tonight. Do you want me to introduce you?'

The Up-and-Coming Politician nodded and was startled, as he did not expect the painter of that strange work to be you, a woman. How could a woman paint such a long penis, wrapped around the waist and neck of a Tibetan ghost with flying hair, while being watched by a tigress who seemed satisfied to see them fight? A ripped pillow created a sense of mystery. The tiger also wore a type of necklace set with a fascinating stone.

The Up-and-Coming Politician took the hand you were offering him and spontaneously kissed its soft skin. He introduced himself: 'I am Dendy Ono.'

'Uno?', you asked, playing the part of the sexy artist, laughing enticingly.

'No, just like Yoko Ono. O-N-O.'

You kept giggling alluringly, 'Oh no!'

'Your painting is tight,' the Up-and-Coming Politician said, stuttering a little, ignoring your giddy attempts at making fun of his name.

You undid a button of your blouse, on purpose. The necklace with the Ziji stone appeared, glowing against your skin.

'Your butt is tight,' the Up-and-Coming Politician suddenly blurted, his faith obviously shaken. He was swallowing his saliva while contemplating your behind. He wanted to take you right there and then.

You giggled again, and replied, 'What? My butt is right?'

'I want you.'

'Eh, you're naughty, I'm not that kind of girl.'

You were teasing the Up-and-Coming Politician and playing with his desire.

You kept giggling.

'So, can I get it?', he asked intently, 'Can I get your tight butt?'

You saw his wide chest, and you imagined his armpit hair. He must be practising all kinds of sports—running, basketball and jogging, during his free time.

'What is this painting about?'

You walked toward the painting, swaying your hips, glanced at him, before pouting a little with your bottom lip. 'It's about rich people's power.'

'Oh, about people's power.'

You laughed, 'No, let me correct you, people's power is useless. I am talking about rich people's power.'

He smiled, but could no longer be patient. You made a grunting sound.

'Do you want to shag?'

The Up-and-Coming Politician was hard.

Rock hard.

Long and hard.

***

God,

I am Your creature. I am a female pig. My snout is long and attractive, my flat nose is pretty and my split hooves make me look very appealing. The story that follows is about penises and related matters.

Imagine me, a pretty pig with a long snout. I stand on my four toes on each foot. When I walk in style, my two middle fingers, which are longer, make me look taller. My small eyes shine like the morning star. Perhaps what is even more attractive is my small curly tail, which seems to wrinkle at the end. For a small pig like me, this tiny tail makes me more appealing. In fact, my small body with my coarse hair goes well with my legs and my short tail.

So this is my story, Your humble servant.

My owner named me Little Rose. Here is my story.

A few weeks ago, in a country named Hujung Manani, classical swine fever, which people shorten as CSF, reappeared.

The first time swine fever had spread in the country was in 1895. Hundred years later, people rarely heard of the disease. If a case ever emerged, an immediate quarantine very effectively prevented the spread of the disease. Thank God—so prays this pig—the disease rarely occurs, except for a few isolated cases in distant groups, which are promptly controlled.

I still remember the beginning of that fateful day. My mother, Big Rose, was sitting idly waiting for the Sunday meal.

Our owner had brought in a large number of pigs from Tibet. This new breed supposedly had more fat and was more delicious to turn into skewers, stew or preserve. They came from the mountains and fetched a very high price. They had golden hair, their skin was light pink and they all walked with a sway, as if they had just come down from a ship after a long time at sea.

Unfortunately, our owner thought that their gait was cute.

My mother, Big Rose, noticed a young male, whom his mother called Prince J. He was so fat that his neck had disappeared, his belly was huge and he walked with pride. He was a pig who pretended to be an eagle, even though his penis was no bigger than a sparrow's.

Every time our owner threw us food, Prince J, his family and his friends would nuzzle in without any manners. It was as if the whole pigsty belonged to Prince J.

Of course, that is typical pig behaviour. Just like pirates, they compete with each other, push and shove and endeavour to get the smelliest and most rotten pieces of food. The behaviour of those pigs was disgusting.

The arrival of this new breed from Tibet created unease among us. Apart from their names, which did not reflect our Eastern values (although they came from the East!)—Prince J, Leo, Cannes, Macao and Cardi C—were all party animals. Prince J always referred to himself as the crown prince of that group.

Of course, we all knew that nobody had actually appointed him to that position.

My mother, Big Rose, forbade us—that is, myself and my twelve siblings—from mingling with the new breed of pigs. She told us, 'Male pigs as young as ten months are already able to mate, so be careful, Little Rose. Even though they come from Tibet, they are not monks. Prince J and his friends are cunning and devious.'

Mother did not really explain her reasons in detail, contenting herself with whispering: 'They are impure pigs'.

Prince J claimed that he was special because his famous ancestors were immortalized by George Orwell in a classic work of English literature. Then, without warning, he suddenly took possession of the mud pond in our pen. As soon as the weather became hot, Prince J brought his friends to wallow in the mud, and once they were there, they would not get out. The mud would coat their skin to protect them from the heat of the sun.

My mother protested quietly, 'These damned pigs are bringing feudalism to our group. Little Rose, stay away from them! They will end up as minced meat. We are the descendants of pigs from the old Malay book, *The Tale of the Pig King*, but do we use that to get any undue advantages?'

Then Mother added, 'We have forty-four teeth and tusks, they have the same amount. We nuzzle. They nuzzle too. We are all equal and on the same level. There are no commoners and no kings among us.'

Mother was becoming incensed. 'Did you memorize the *Six Gurindam* written by our ancestor, the National Author?'

We all nodded and I started to recite the opening verses:

'If a country wants to be safe
Do not let scoundrels ascend

Scoundrels are of many kinds
Know that they are all swines
Some flatter the king
To steal and sin with him
Some behave like monkeys
Oppressing people and taking their money.'

Mother's smile widened as she listened to the first stanza of the *Six Gurindam*.

Four weeks later, in order to take over the leadership of our group, Prince J declared that the leader of our pigsty must be replaced. The leader was Uncle RPK. They said that he was getting too old and no longer had any authority. Out of the blue, without any warning, Prince J started spreading doubts among our group, which had never even heard of gender or class politics before. Prince J criticized the females from our breed, who according to him, did not produce any benefit for man. As if that was not enough, he boasted that the breed that came with him was a new type of pig which was much better and had much redder skin than the native pigs.

My mother was furious. At a gathering in our pen, she stood up and asked, 'Who among us eats dead insects?'

All the pigs nodded.

'Who among us eats worms?'

Again, all the pigs grunted in agreement.

'Who among us eats tree bark?'

Some agreed, followed by the others.

'Who among us eats rotten flesh?'

There was a moment of silence.

Then all the pigs in the pen shouted 'oink oink' in agreement, all excited at the idea of eating rotten carcasses. As if rotten flesh was to them what preserves, fish sauce, durian pickles and prawn sauce were to the palates of the people of Hujung Manani.

'Who among us eats rubbish, except for plastic?'

All the pigs giggled in unison.

'Who among us eats other pigs? Who would eat their own child if they had to?'

Silence . . .

'WHO?!' My mother shouted angrily. A sow slowly raised her long snout to the sky. All the other pigs imitated her, raising their snouts to the sky.

'So, what can we say about our existence as animals created by God?'

The pigs gathered in the corner of the pigsty all answered together, 'Pigs! We are all pigs! We have all been created as pigs!'

Unfortunately, democracy can disappear rapidly. The pigs only felt united for a short time. Their nature made them forget easily and they stupidly surrendered to an autocratic leader.

One strange thing occurred, which we must mention here. Prince J lied to the pigs, telling them that the new breed from Tibet, to which he belonged, was destined to lead this country. He also claimed that our human master agreed with this, because he recognized their higher level of piety.

My mother said, her words interrupted by laughter, 'Pious . . . pigs?!'

Prince J claimed that as they were a new breed, they did not need to be vaccinated. He added that among human leaders, vaccination had been declared haram by a fatwa, due to the fact that the vaccine itself came from an impure source, namely pigs.

Prince J quoted a holy verse to support his claim about the impurity of the vaccine.

A very large crowd gathered to listen to the pig discussing religious law.

When I repeated the contents of Prince J's speech to my mother, she merely laughed, but then she became serious again and said, 'My child, let's not rush into disaster. We know that the vaccine is in the public interest, that is, it is approved from the perspective of the *Maqasid al-Shari'ah*. And anyway, they hail from Tibet. They have different beliefs and culture.'

Mother told me about the swine fever called H1N1 that killed people, and which had come from us pigs. And so, vaccinating pigs was very important for human beings.

I listened to my mother with my mouth wide open. I had never doubted her intelligence and wisdom.

Everything became clearer, a short while later. It was the beginning of all the troubles that ensued.

Four weeks after Prince J and his followers took over our group with their proclamations based on dubious religious statements, one of his partisans, Cannes, developed diarrhoea, her skin became pale and red spots appeared on her ears and the extremities of her limbs. Her fever shot up to 41.6 °C. As you must certainly know, 40.5 °C is already too high for a piglet.

Cannes had swollen lymph nodes and internal bleeding in her kidneys and bladder.

Of course, our master was not yet aware that swine fever had broken out on our farm. If he had known, he would have reported it to the veterinarian and the state authorities. They would immediately have taken samples from our tonsils or lymph nodes and we would have been sent to the slaughterhouse. Our master would have been questioned about our provenance to determine the origin of our group. Farm records, movements of animals between farms from as far back as five years before, would have been studied. In that regard, all pigs are equal; there is no longer any question of piety among pigs.

Fortunately, I had been vaccinated. All my siblings, as well as all the other pigs of our breed, had received their first vaccination at thirty days old. Without protesting and even very obediently, my mother had allowed us to get the second round of vaccination, six months later. And we all got booster shots, a year later. As my mother said, vaccination is a must.

'Fortunately, we are safe . . .' said Little Rose.

Cannes ran out of luck. Our master was approached by the owner of a restaurant that served Dayak food. He was looking to buy two piglets to be prepared as a special dish for a model from Tibet.

The model was an important person.

What is a 'model'?

Mother had overheard stories about a woman named Sistine. She was pregnant and was craving preserved pork. Sistine was very pretty and resembled Ma Yan Li. She was barely thirty years old.

According to Mother, Sistine had very long limbs. She was famous for her catwalks on her long legs. For us pigs who have short legs, having long legs is a pipe dream. Outside the modelling world, Sistine was known as a drunkard who liked to drink Lhasa Beer, which was a mixture of Himalayan water, Tibetan barley, yeast and saaz hops, that gave the drink its bitter flavour and aroma. Sistine wanted to drink Lhasa Beer, eat *thentuk* (Tibetan noodles) and craved the preserved pork that she had once tasted in Kalimantan, during the shooting of a documentary.

But what was she doing here, in this country?

Furthermore, Sistine kept insulting people, shouting at them, '*Gyo Gyub*' or 'fuck you' in Tibetan language. This should not even happen in this country. It did not make any sense for a woman from Lake Yamdrok—meaning 'jade'—a sacred lake seventy kilometres from Lhasa, to come to this country—a very hot nation located on the equator.

Indeed, Sistine's dreams were totally different from the dreams of people in this country. Here, they dream of meeting the Prophet's companions and their penises are circumcised while they sleep; as soon as they wake up, they immediately become Muslims.

But Sistine dreamed of something else. She dreamed of a yak standing against the blue sky, a monastery and snowflakes. This yak was her favourite when she was a child. He measured 2.3 metres and had small ears and a wide forehead. His smooth long horns were dark, and his neck was short.

The yak was called Rose.

Yes, I know, it is very strange that we share the same name.

Sistine was originally a Vajrayana Buddhist but she left her religion to become a Christian. One day, she travelled to Milan (remember that she was a model) and ran into the Assistant to the Leader of our country—in a boutique selling handbags. That leader is always referred to by our master as 'the Leader', or sometimes 'the Dictator'.

The Dictator and his assistant had gone to Italy for a visit before continuing on to Paris to attend a meeting regarding the purchase of plastic. They were accompanied by the Tycoon.

To make a long story short, the Assistant had fallen in love with Sistine at first sight in the boutique, where he was buying gifts for his two wives back in his home country. Sistine was aware that he was a wealthy man with an important position in Hujung Manani, and she tried to catch his attention.

She sashayed, like a pig, stopped not far from the Assistant, smiled and groaned as if she had just had an orgasm. When he looked at her, she pretended to be shy and said, 'Sorry, did the sound I made bother you? I always climax whenever I see gorgeous luxurious leather bags.'

Of course, she had purposely chosen to use the word 'climax'.

The Assistant's penis instantly stiffened and grew, like a shiny round cap mushroom. He brought Sistine back to his hotel and had sex with her. Not just once; he actually ejaculated large amounts of sperm into her.

It all happened on a red sofa.

In order to allow Sistine to join them on their business trip and sneak her into official events, the Assistant appointed her as a translator. He claimed that Sistine could speak French and that her services were needed for their business meeting in Paris.

What happened next is not a secret. Sistine slept with several members of the trade commission and they all ejaculated into her vagina. Finally, in Paris, Sistine slept with the Dictator, and she came back to Hujung Manani with him.

Sistine was not that good in bed, actually. She only spread her legs and moved her body according to the man's pelvic thrusts so that their bodies would make the bed shake. She would sigh and groan very loudly. She pretended to tremble and would grab her partner's hips as if she would never let him go. As soon as the man's sperm gushed inside her, she would shake, even though she was often not even wet herself. Another thing that made Sistine unique, was her skill at giving oral sex. She was an expert at using her tongue and her lips.

According to my mother, Big Rose, who was a very wise sow, Sistine could not simply be categorized as a prostitute. We had to look at her situation from the perspective of cultural relativism. This is because Sistine came from a village located in a remote valley, where the people practised polyandry. It is a type of polygamy where a woman can have several husbands. Polyandry was the accepted norm among Sistine's people, because the system helps to prevent disputes over land. Moreover, Tibet is a mountainous country. It is very difficult to cultivate land there. Therefore, women need more than one husband to help with cultivation, as several men can unite their strength.

Sistine was pregnant. She had cravings. She kept salivating at the idea of a tender piglet cooked in a sweet and sour sauce. She just had to have it.

Two female piglets were picked to be sacrificed: Cannes and another piglet from the new Tibetan breed, Cardi C. They were both out of luck. Or rather, it was Sistine's luck which was about to run out.

Cannes and Cardi C were slaughtered in our pigsty. Our master's wife, who knew how to make preserves, chopped up Cannes and Cardi C before cleaning the pieces carefully. The cubes of meat were placed in glass containers with a handful of salt. Then, cold rice was added. The jars were shaken to mix all the ingredients thoroughly. They were then given to a restaurant chef, who was instructed to keep them tightly closed for three weeks. The result would be a salty and sour preserve which could then be eaten with cassava leaves, fermented durian sauce and hot rice. As for Sistine, she wanted to eat it with Tibetan noodles and Lhasa beer.

While waiting for the fermented pork made from Cannes' and Cardi C's flesh to be ready, Prince J caught swine fever. He infected Leo, and all the other pigs in their group became sick too. Within three weeks, an epidemiological study was carried out in our farm and the entire area was declared a red zone after swine fever was confirmed through RT-PCR tests.

Although we had been vaccinated, many pigs panicked and the selection process became messy. How could it be otherwise, since our pigsty had suddenly become such a centre of animation?

We witnessed the careful cleaning and disinfection process. We saw all the vehicles passing through a disinfection pool. Not only were we quarantined and carefully decontaminated, an emergency selection was also carried out on the spot.

After we were examined by veterinarians, we witnessed all the pigs from the new breed who had taken part in the anti-vaccination campaign get slaughtered one by one. Not only were they killed in full view of everyone, they were then immediately thrown into six feet deep mass graves, covered with disinfectant, and buried. Several of the new breed were even buried alive.

It was a cruel and terrifying mass murder.

The entire group of pigs from the new breed was exterminated, down to their bones, blood and entrails, and an emergency vaccination campaign was carried out within a radius of one kilometre around our farm. Eventually, the entire population of arrogant newcomers from Tibet was annihilated.

Prince J's slaughter was the most dramatic. Before his throat was cut, he shouted, 'I am not a traitor! Stop! Go to hell, you bastards, I curse you! You will lose your balls! Eagles and sparrows will never fly together! O *karmmavasita*. O *datu, Drdhabhakti*. Grant me *viryya*. [O Master of karma. O shaman. Faithful One. Grant me strength.]'

Nobody understood what Prince J was shouting. We all assumed that it was the ramblings of a condemned pig walking towards his death.

My mother advised me: 'Little Rose, my child, you know that one of the purposes of *Maqasid al-Shari'ah* is to protect human life. We live in a country which claims to have an Islamic government, but the truth is that our leader, the Dictator, is a despicable, corrupt and ignorant man.'

Since what happened on our farm was a trivial matter, nobody knew about the outbreak of swine fever.

This enabled our master to hide an important piece of information, because he feared its serious implications. He did not disclose the fact that two piglets had been chopped into pieces and turned into preserved meat; that they had been given to a restaurant owner, and that two weeks later, they would be eaten by a model (whom some in the media called a 'Freelance Translator'), who was pregnant and carried a child sired either by the Dictator or his assistant.

My mother told me: 'You know, my child, swine fever can be transmitted through the blood as well as through the flesh, the fluids and the excrements of Cannes and Cardi C, even though they are dead and have been turned into food. Let us pray for the well-being of all forms of life.'

God, protect the humans. Let pigs continue to serve them in the future. God, I am Your creature, I am just a small female pig who still wants to see the world. Have pity on me.

And verily, this entire story is about penises and related matters.

***

Did Sistine ever get to eat the pig preserves that she craved, along with the bottle of Lhasa beer and the gravy from a bowl of Tibetan noodles? Nobody knows.

She died.

On a hazy day, the Seasoned Detective received a call from a police station located two hours away from the capital city of Hujung Manani. His expertise and experience were needed urgently. He was informed that a woman's body had been found in a horrible condition.

The caller did not mention what was horrible about the corpse. During his thirty years of service in the police force, he was no longer shocked at being told that a body was in a terrible condition. He had handled the case of a murdered baby. The little body had been hidden in an attic and was mummified when they found it. He had seen a woman hit by a train, whose remains were in eight pieces. During his challenging career, he had also worked on the case of an old man who had been stabbed repeatedly in the neck, then cut into seventeen pieces, half of them stored in a freezer and the rest baked in an oven one by one to make him disappear. He had also solved the case of a millionaire burnt alive by his stepson, who had disguised the murder as a house fire. There were many troubling murders, sexual crimes and instances of sexual abuse. He had succeeded in solving all his cases. If there were an Oscar award for the best investigator, he surely deserved to win it.

The Seasoned Detective was due to retire in twelve days and on that hazy day when he received the call from the police station located two hours away from the city, he felt no desire to investigate the case.

'What race is the stiff?' the Seasoned Detective asked the sergeant on the other end of the line.

'Not one of ours,' the voice answered.

'So what? A ghost? A Javanese? An Arab?'

There was no answer other than a mumble.

'Well, let them go to hell then. Damn pig eaters!'

He did not feel like driving and, using the excuse of having to train a younger detective, he asked the Rookie to come with him to the crime scene.

He thought that the Rookie would be very helpful. He was hardworking, handsome, with big muscular arms. His butt was tight and sexy. He had joined the forensic police as a member of the Parasitology and Pharmaceutical Association of Hujung

Manani. He was the first medical forensic expert to be offered a post in the police force. Usually, forensic scientists preferred to work in the forensic department of hospitals.

It was because of these sorts of things that the Seasoned Detective felt that being the head of his team no longer made him happy. For him, a policeman should be trained to work as a policeman, not as a medical officer, a chemist or an entomologist.

A policeman should be allowed to accept occasional bribes because he was only human. He should also be able to beat up a suspect in custody, because that is what all policemen did (except in Australia and Scandinavia). It was what everybody did. Therefore, it was normal. And normal things should not change.

The trip was very unpleasant in the heat of the drought season. The Seasoned Detective was irritated because he had to solve the murder case of a victim who was not Malay.

'Some people should just croak and go to hell.'

The Rookie answered in a cheerless cynical tone of voice: 'We are all nutrients. When we die, we go back to the earth. It is the cycle of life . . . and race does not matter.'

These words shut the Seasoned Detective up for a moment. But he soon started to grumble again.

'Don't go thinking I'm choosy. I have had a brilliant career and I have solved many murder cases without discriminating against the race or religion of the victims.'

The Rookie laughed.

'Contradictions and ambiguities often occur in life if someone does not have clear values.'

The Seasoned Detective was angry but kept quiet at first. However, he could not remain silent for very long and spelled out the word 'croak': 'C . . . R . . . O . . . A . . . K . . .'

He had only a few days left to serve in the police force. He had no intention to discuss idealism with a rookie who was not even a real policeman but a forensic scientist. He preferred to keep his mouth shut and fell asleep a few minutes later.

The Rookie was not happy to serve as a driver. He disliked driving, actually. He had only got his driving license a few years ago, while he was studying at university. In fact, he had never liked cars. For him, people who felt superior because they owned an expensive car were superficial.

The Rookie was a village boy who had made it and become the pride of many. It was not the seventies but he did not waste any of his time at university studying regular courses such as engineering, information technology or the lamest one—business administration. He chose difficult classes. He took forensic science by accident, but became deeply interested during his final year at university.

He came from a tiny island off the coast of Hujung Manani. It was mostly ignored by city dwellers because it was not a touristy destination. In fact, not many people had heard of Jumpy Island, and those who had heard of it, made fun of its name, which they claimed was funny.

As an islander, he disliked driving land vehicles. He preferred travelling on the water—by motorboat, for instance. He used to help his mother, who had raised him and his siblings by herself, by bringing fish to the mainland by boat.

He felt at ease on the water.

On the mainland, all the nearby villages and their surroundings had been turned into plastic landfills. The area belonged to the Tycoon, who worked with a Chinese businessman under the One Belt One Road initiative.

This was all because of the Dictator who allowed irresponsible foreign investors to open plastic waste recycling factories on a large scale.

This was not investment. It was exploitation.

On Jumpy Island, which was not suited for building factories, the Chinese businessman had brought men from Xinjiang, Rohingyas from Myanmar and black people from Nigeria to make them work on pepper plantations.

Their living conditions were deplorable and it was no secret that they were actually slaves. The workers did not communicate with the islanders. Sometimes, one of them managed to escape and beg for help from the villagers. But often, these enslaved workers became handicapped. Some had their noses cut off. Others were missing one ear or several fingers, and they were all in a heartbreaking condition beyond description.

At the beginning, the villagers refused to help them as they were afraid. But one good action by his mother had shown the way to the other islanders. Of course, his mother was no Nelson Mandela, Abraham Lincoln or Martin Luther King, or even a politician. She was just a human being who took pity on another human being in need.

A man from Xinjiang had crawled under their hut and hid behind their old boat. He had helped his mother carry the man into the house, remove his muddy and soiled clothes, and clean his body. His penis had been cut off. His mother disinfected the wound and put ointment on it. The man passed out several times due to the pain. He stayed in their house for about four months.

During that time, the police searched the houses in the village. They searched their house as well, but each time there was a raid, he took the man to sea on his boat. Fortunately, the marine police never found them.

When the man was healthy enough to leave, he thanked his mother many times. He told her, 'Remember the man without a penis.'

His mother did not laugh but said, 'A man is not defined by his penis. I just want to be a good person. Out there, there are many men who are religious, but few who are good people. I prefer humanity to a penis.'

The man never forgot the words spoken by his mother.

Children playing by the jetty often found the swollen bodies of workers who had been tortured before they were killed, or who had drowned while trying to escape. The heroic story about his mother, who had saved the man with no penis, moved other islanders to help the slaves working for the Chinese businessman. After a while, the entire village became used to seeing mutilated men emerging from the bushes or shivering at their doorstep in the early hours of the day.

Therefore, corpses and disfigured bodies were nothing new for the Rookie.

The loud snores coming from the Seasoned Detective made him lose his concentration and he took the wrong road to the police station in the village. They had to identify themselves as members of the police forensic lab before the local policemen took them to the crime scene.

The body had been discovered deep in an oil palm plantation owned by Datin Lotis. Untas Andi, a foreign worker who shall be known as the Witness, told the police that he found the body when he was walking by and he smelled a horrible stench. He thought that it was perhaps the rotten carcass of a monkey, but when he came closer to the source of the stench, he was shocked to discover that it was a human body, decomposed beyond recognition, almost mummified.

Several cadaver dogs where still searching the area for fragments of flesh. A yellow police tape printed with the words POLICE LINE DO NOT CROSS surrounded the crime scene.

The corpse was naked and the parts of the body which still had some flesh on them looked wrinkled. Other parts showed the bones and the skull. The victim was sitting or had been propped up against the trunk of an oil palm. The sharp reek penetrated the nose and went straight to the stomach, and made everyone nauseous.

This was the Rookie's first case. For the first time, everything was laid out in front of his eyes and not in a textbook. The young man approached the corpse and inhaled deeply, once. He knew that after that, the stench would become familiar and would no longer bother him. This was a tip given by one of his lecturers when he was studying at the University Hospital of Hujung Manani.

The Rookie spoke to the dead body: 'Hello pretty, tell us what happened to you.'

The Seasoned Detective was surprised—the Rookie seemed quite competent. He was bending over all around the body, with his large sling bag containing who knows what, perhaps just all sorts of tools. He tiptoed on the soft soil. He even looked under the bean plants that covered the ground between the palm trees. This vegetation was planted in order to prevent soil erosion and to preserve the moisture of the earth, but now it might conceal a thousand secrets about the victim.

The Seasoned Detective preferred to spend his time questioning Untas Andi, while glancing once in a while at the Rookie hovering near the body. He seemed to be doing fine, staying near the corpse and taking notes. At one time, he picked something off the victim and put it in a jar of alcohol. Maggots were jumping from the fleshy parts of the corpse, signifying that the death had taken place quite some time ago.

The Rookie searched the crime scene with great attention to detail, even going as far as ten metres away from the body to pick up the roaming larvae that were crawling away.

The Seasoned Detective approached the corpse. Unfortunately, it was in a fragile condition and the various parts of the body seemed ready to fall off. Based on a gold chain which was still around the neck—which was black and covered with green flies—it seemed that the victim was female. Only her head and her torso, including both shoulders and her private parts, were still recognizable.

One of her hands, from the wrist to the fingers, was found on the ground. Perhaps the arm had been gnawed off by a wild animal. If they were lucky, they would be able to identify the victim from her fingerprints.

The stench penetrated the nose and was nauseating.

'Go to hell!' said the Seasoned Detective, before spitting on the ground. The stink permeated everything. For sure, he would have to soak his pants and his shirt in soap and water when he got home, later.

The Rookie shook his head. Could he not have some respect for another human being, who had been killed and dumped in an oil palm plantation in such an undignified manner? Why did insulting the victim satisfy a person like the Seasoned Detective?

The body of the woman was taken to the forensic unit of the nearest hospital.

The Rookie was excited to solve his first case, while the Seasoned Detective was just hoping that the identity of the woman could be found out quickly so that her relatives could be notified and the file could be closed before his retirement, which was only a few days away.

After decades of working with corpses, the Seasoned Detective was blasé and unconcerned.

They waited for two hours before the medico-legal autopsy could be carried out. In Hujung Manani, one could die of stress due to bureaucratic procedures!

A forensic pathologist and a forensic odontologist finally arrived; the Rookie knew them. Of course, they must have been friends at university. A policeman from the nearest police station filled in the Police Form 61 to authorize the autopsy.

So far, they did not know much. No identification documents had been found near the victim.

The autopsy started. *Let them handle the stiff,* the Seasoned Detective thought. He had been doing it for decades already. He had had enough of dead people.

So he sat down with a hot cup of newly discovered Cascara coffee and smoked Marlboros, letting the Rookie and the others examine the body inch by inch.

He could imagine them. First, they probably laid the decaying corpse down very carefully. The forensic odontologist must be looking at the teeth, while the Rookie was probably fascinated by the maggots and insects that would give him an approximate time of death. They would take samples of skin and fingerprints, if they could find any. Considering the condition of the corpse, they would not be able to gather much information. There was not much left to work with. In any case, the victim would talk. She would reveal something.

The Seasoned Detective sat in the waiting room, shivering from the cold air blowing from the air conditioning unit, which had just been serviced, while watching the latest season of *Game of Thrones*, which had just been released on Netflix.

However, he found the latest season boring. His mind started wandering, without purpose. What would he do at the end of the month?

He would be retiring after a brilliant career. He could not wait for retirement. He had no fixed plans yet, but he certainly did not want to keep working, even if he was offered to extend his service under contract.

The first thing he would do would be to fly to Bangkok, or perhaps to Amsterdam. He preferred Thailand, though. As an old, lonely gay man, he could only afford Thai boys. He would first have fun in the red-light district, then think of his next step.

One of his friends had suggested he go to Wuhan in China to find fresh young boys. But he was not attracted to Chinese gigolos. They did not wash with water, only wiping their genitals with toilet paper after pissing or shitting. They smelled bad. They were noisy. They were choosy. They were only interested in money. They did not know how to love. His friend had rebuffed him, 'Ah, you're just racist. Not many gays are racist, but you're one of them.'

Was he racist, really? He thought that was an exaggeration and he wanted to protest. Did they know what he had had to go through?

Damn stiff! She could go to hell.

When he was a child, his father worked on the wharves at Hujung Manani Harbour. The state leader, who was still young then, Datuk Priapus Mappadulung Daeng Mattimung Karaeng Sanrobone, had sold or leased the harbour to a Chinese company, which had developed it as a point of passage on the Silk Road by sea. The state leader had just succeeded the old Leader.

Working for a Chinese owner changed his father's life. His employer exploited his workers without mercy. His father worked more than sixteen hours a day. After five years, without ever expressing his love as a father, he died of tuberculosis.

His mother remarried soon afterwards, a Chinese man who also worked on the wharves. Why and how his mother could accept to marry a Chinese man was a mystery.

His stepfather was an animal who inspired hatred in him for any race other than his own. That man had no qualms about beating him. At school, many of his friends also said that they were suffering as a result of the economic takeover by China.

Moreover, his teacher, who was a member of the opposition party based on race and religion, which had been banned, also encouraged hatred for the Chinese.

That teacher explained that it was not racism, but nationalism. Slowly, his hatred for other races grew. Gradually, the desire to defend the rights of his own race bloomed.

One day, his stepfather left. He just disappeared. Perhaps he went back to his country. However, two weeks later, the police came to arrest his mother. Within a short time, only a few months after a quick trial, his mother was sentenced to death by hanging for killing her husband. In the cell, before being sentenced, his mother had told him: 'The Chinese are bad people.'

'The Chinese here or the Chinese in China?' the Seasoned Detective had asked.

His mother had only answered: 'They can all croak and go to hell.'

These words had left a deep impact on him.

After that fateful incident, he had decided to become a policeman. In a country where the leadership was greedy for power, being a policeman was the best protection against all kinds of oppression. Furthermore, who or what was more powerful than a policeman?

Throughout his teenage years, as an orphan, he had to work while he was still at school. One of his jobs that paid the most, was looking after the toilets on the wharves. There, he learned about the different sizes and shapes of penises, circumcised or not. There, his future took shape and became ingrained in him.

What did anyone know about racism? Those who condemned racism could go to hell. He laughed and then

hummed a few lines of the fourth couplet of the *Six Gurindam.*
What did the traditional poem say?

'But how can the Malays the chosen race be
When they trample others without mercy'

After joining the police force, he had been very cautious to
ensure that his sexual orientation and lifestyle were not known to
anyone. In Hujung Manani, minorities like him were considered
non-existent, despite the fact that they paid taxes, just like anyone
else. To that effect, he kept his distance from his colleagues. That
is why he never tried to flirt with the young men who joined
the force, even though their bodies were well-built and their
appearances pleased him. He would not jeopardize his career.

After about five hours, the Rookie, who had not yet had a
chance to shower, came out of the morgue to meet the Seasoned
Detective. The two policemen from the nearby police station
and the forensic experts took their leave.

It was night. See how much time is wasted by crime? Other
people have to make all kinds of efforts to find the person
responsible.

The Seasoned Detective had finished three jugs of Cascara
coffee, had gone seven times to the toilet to urinate, had slept
for a few minutes, and watched a movie on his handphone in
fast-forward mode. He yawned and without waiting for his
mouth to close, asked, 'What did the pathologists find on this
unidentified corpse?'

The Rookie, who had just looked at a decomposed female
body for the first time, took his time to answer. Perhaps he
was trying to figure out whether the question was sarcastic or
straightforward. He sat down, exhausted.

'That woman did not die in the oil palm plantation,' he stated with confidence.

'Hah, a young man's confidence has no equal!'

Behind the table where they both sat, the wall featured the portraits of Priapus Mappadulung Daeng Mattimung Karaeng Sanrobone, the leader of Hujung Manani, and his wife.

'I found larvae of the *Synthesiomyia nudiseta* fly. They were dead and dry, in the flesh near the waist.'

The Seasoned Detective answered by laughing.

Without paying attention to the forced laughter, the Rookie continued, 'This type of fly only lays eggs in dead bodies found indoors and scientists have not yet found any such eggs in dead bodies found outdoors. So, I assume this body has been moved by the killer from a house to the plantation.'

The Seasoned Detective stared at the Rookie. The young man was indeed attractive. Then, he sighed and said, 'This is the difference between us. I never got the chance to go to university. I am an old bachelor close to retirement. But at least I joined the police force as a detective with a good salary, and will retire with a good pension.'

The Rookie paid no attention to what he was saying and continued, 'Fortunately, the shoulder and arm were still intact. There was no BCG—or *Bacillus Calmette-Guerin*—vaccination mark, which shows that the victim was not a citizen of this country. We took hair samples for a DNA profile analysis.'

'Unfortunately, that means that we cannot make comparisons with the Registration Department records or police records. The file is going to be closed for now, but I can still retire with honours,' the Seasoned Detective boasted.

'There was no tattoo, but we found a necklace with a strange stone. Like a religious symbol.'

The Rookie took out a small camera and showed a picture of the locket that he found unusual. It looked like a coin from an ancient kingdom. The Seasoned Detective looked at it with interest. Suddenly, his investigative instinct was aroused.

'Mysterious,' the Seasoned Detective said jokingly. However, the young policeman refused to pay attention to the old man's behaviour.

The Rookie took a few sips of cold water and continued, 'There were also black soldier flies on the corpse. Usually, this species, *Hemertia illucens*, only lays eggs on bodies twenty days after death. I also found . . .' he said, while flipping the pages of his notebook to find the note, 'that most of the insect infestation was concentrated on the genital and anal areas. This shows that the victim was raped or sexually assaulted.'

The Rookie felt uncomfortable reading all his notes out loud. His voice trembled.

The Seasoned Detective sighed. 'So the flies came out of the pupae.'

The Rookie interrupted him. 'The corpse is starting to mummify.'

The Seasoned Detective was thinking. Flies lay their eggs on the body eighteen to thirty-six hours after death. After twenty-four hours, the eggs become larvae. Four to five days later, the larvae become pupae; and then it takes another four to five days for the adult flies to hatch. So the entire cycle takes about eleven days. He just muttered the word 'eleven'.

The Rookie corrected him. 'More than that. At least twenty days. The death or murder took place in a house and then the body was moved to the plantation. The victim may also have been partially eaten by wild animals that took away parts of the body.'

The Seasoned Detective clicked his tongue. 'So we are looking for a victim who disappeared about a month ago. If anybody reported her missing . . . If only it was that easy . . . Hah, I want to retire without any incidents. Unfortunately, people go missing all the time in Hujung Manani.'

The Rookie nodded. 'And I need to shower and get some sleep.'

'Yes, go ahead. That stiff is disgusting. Vile!'

'But she is still a human being and worthy of justice,' the Rookie insisted firmly.

There was something that the Rookie had not told his partner. He was hoping to get the lab results urgently. What was surprising was that the victim's private parts were still in good shape, although they had decayed a little. There were still traces of pubic hair and a viable pubic hair had been recovered from between the victim's teeth. This was exciting evidence. The DNA paternity test would take one to two weeks, and his friend at the forensic lab of the hospital had promised to give his personal attention to the matter.

For the time being, until the victim's identity was known or her relatives came to claim her, the body would be kept in the mortuary and identified in documents as 'Brought In Dead' (BID). For a while, the mystery would remain.

They drove back to the police headquarters in the city. The Rookie slept all through the way back. When they arrived, they had different plans. The young detective wanted to go home and sleep longer. But the Seasoned Detective, who had been resting all day, wanted to go to a restaurant. 'I'm hungry,' he grumbled.

The Rookie left and the Seasoned Detective went to a restaurant. He sat in a corner, with three chapatis on a plate in front of him, some curry and some dhal gravy, and watched television while he ate.

Let us turn our attention to the Seasoned Detective now.

On the news bulletin, one topic drew his attention.

'A famous religious preacher, who had been reported missing, has been found and was hospitalized today in Hujung Manani University Hospital with thirty other men, who all complained that their penis was missing.'

The Seasoned Detective looked left and right. That late at night, there were not many customers, and those who were there, consisted mainly of workers from a nearby plastic factory. None of them were paying attention to the television. They were either looking into their phones or chatting with their friends.

Had they not heard the word 'penis'? It had been said loud and clear, as if it had been the word 'sausage' or 'cookie' or 'banana'.

But the word he heard had nothing to do with food. He was absolutely certain that the newsreader had uttered the word 'penis'. Since when did people in Hujung Manani become so direct? The Seasoned Detective could not believe his ears. Did the pretty newsreader really use the word 'penis' on national television? What was so important about that strange news item that it was being reported in the news bulletin on national television?

While he was still sitting there with his mouth agape and wondering why nobody around him was paying any attention to the news bulletin which he thought was important, an old woman approached him.

The Seasoned Detective, who was sitting down, had to lift his face to look at the woman, whom he took for a beggar. She placed a photograph in front of him and asked, 'Have you ever seen this Ziji stone before?'

'What?' the Seasoned Detective shouted over the loud sound of the television.

'This. Look at this!' The old woman was holding his sleeve. She had deep-set eyes.

The Seasoned Detective glanced at the photograph. Where had he seen this type of necklace before? He groaned, uneasy. The woman did not want to leave him alone and she seemed to be whispering, or perhaps her voice was drowned by the sound of the television, which was showing an ad for mentholated oil. The Seasoned Detective pulled the edge of his sleeve out of the old woman's grip.

'This is a coin from the Shang Shung kingdom. It was found on the statue of Jowo Rinpoche, and it is plated in—'

'Eh, stupid old bitch, go to hell! Go to hell, go eat pork there!' the Seasoned Detective shouted at the woman in rags.

'This is a spell. You will need it. It doesn't matter if you're gay or not.' The raspy voice reached his ears. The old woman then touched the detective's palm. Their eyes met. There was a bright light in hers.

His heart started to beat faster immediately. 'Go to hell!'

'O karmmavasita. O datu. Drdhabhakti. Grant me Viryya.'

A few seconds later, the woman had disappeared.

The Seasoned Detective felt as if his hand had been bitten—there was an indescribable feeling of numbness. The feeling crept down, towards his leg, his thigh and then his genital area. He immediately wondered whether he had been poisoned. He felt that his penis was shrinking, retreating into his body. He could not breathe. He started sweating profusely. He was now in a state of panic as he had never been before.

Then he remembered. It was the Rookie who had showed him a photograph of the necklace. The Seasoned Detective stood up at once, looking for the old woman with the scary eyes, 'Hey you pig! Where are you, pig? You want to croak? You stole my dick! Are you Chinese? Give me back my dick! I am going to retire; I need my dick. Hey pig! Where's my dick? Go to hell!'

***

I am a psychiatrist working at Hujung Manani University Hospital. I am fifty-seven years old. This is the confidential report that I sent to the National Medical Council about the koro syndrome, after treating Datuk Priapus Mappadulung Daeng Mattimung Karaeng Sanrobone, the leader of the Republic of Hujung Manani.

This is my report:

Twenty-five days ago, I received a telephone call from the director of the University Hospital at about three o'clock in the morning, telling me that I had to attend to an emergency. I was informed that an ambulance had been sent to take me to the patient.

About half an hour after receiving the call—and although I had not had time to get ready—I was rushed into the ambulance by fifteen men in uniform, and taken away. During the drive to the patient's location, my eyes were blindfolded with a piece of black cloth and all the men who sat with me remained silent. They did not utter even a single word. The trip took about half an hour, or perhaps more, but definitely less than two hours.

The blindfold was removed after I was inside a building which seemed to be strictly guarded.

I was taken to a large waiting room. I still remember the room very well. There were rugs made of tiger skins. I saw three armchairs in a corner of the room. There was also a luxurious leather sofa long enough for a person to lie down on. On the main wall of the room, a painting attracted my attention. It was a work by Amedeo Modigliani, who painted many nude women. That painting from 1917 was the '*Nu couché (sur le côté gauche)*', which is worth more than 157.2 million dollars. If I remember correctly, the painting measured about fifty-eight inches by fifty-eight inches, and was the main focus wherever you stood in the room with white walls. It might have been a mere copy of the original work by the Italian artist, but it was fascinating regardless.

The white walls made the room feel airy. On another wall, there was a mirror that contributed to making the space look bigger, even though that wall was lit in a dramatic manner. The entire floor was covered with a thick carpet that reflected the owner's wealth.

It was obvious that my mysterious patient was not just anybody. Judging from the rich furnishings of the room, I was in a very luxurious residence. I was asked to sign a non-disclosure agreement, stating I could not disclose anything about the visit, the illness, or the patient I was about to see.

The man with a short moustache who made me sign the document, told me that there would be 'tragic consequences' if I did not comply and told anyone about this.

I agreed to this because for me, tragedy is only misunderstood comedy.

I waited for about half an hour before the patient, whom I recognized immediately, walked cautiously into the room. He was fidgety, extremely pale and his hands were shaking. His aide told me that he had a temperature of 39.5°C.

Although he was weak, he forced himself to tell me about what was ailing him. My very famous patient, whom I will refer to as the Leader, was a tubby man in his sixties with a fair pinkish complexion and greying hair. His lips were full and very pink. His aristocratic demeanour was evident.

Despite his weakness, he was still in full control of his style and appearance.

He was accompanied by a woman, whom I recognized immediately as well. Her facial expression was dismissive, with tight lips. She kept clearing her throat with an 'emmm' sound as if she was sucking a sweet under her tongue, and rubbing her nose, which seemed more crooked than usual. In this report, I will refer to her as the Leader's Wife.

The Leader took quite some time to tell me about his problem because he was very embarrassed, until his wife interrupted him, 'I believe his Johnson has been stolen. I think it's black magic, but his aide wants a full and detailed medical examination before we resort to traditional medicine . . . because this traditional medicine requires a lot of chicken blood . . . yes, blood.'

I must admit that I was shocked, excited, apprehensive and curious—all at once. I was experiencing a multitude of feelings. I cannot say precisely what I was thinking at that moment. I took a few seconds to calm down, took a deep breath, cleared my mind, and after I had managed to overcome the feelings of fear and pressure, I thought about my patient's situation.

I immediately understood why I was chosen and had been forcefully taken from my house like this. Cases of disappearing penises and their connection with witchcraft were ancient incidents which rarely happened in our modern times, where everything is based on science and technology, but it was not impossible, either. I had done extensive research on the subject, but the cases I had encountered were located very far from Hujung Manani.

In August 1590, two women, Jonett Grant and Jonett Clark, were tried and sentenced to death for witchcraft. They were executed in Edinburgh Hill Castle. One of the accusations against them stated that they had stolen the penis of a famous man in Edinburgh.

Of course, at the time, I had never heard of Sistine.

I must state in this report that the Leader's Wife was not interested in anything to do with modern medicine or science, and was trying to persuade me to testify that her husband's condition was the result of a very powerful black magic spell cast by his political enemies. She kept saying, 'Can I advise you something . . .' in her high-pitched voice.

As we all know, the political enemy of the Leader, his wife and his cabinet, is the Shahid.

However, as an expert psychiatrist, I told the Leader's Wife, in order to satisfy her curiosity and misplaced beliefs, that Western society also had such superstitions. If Hujung Manani had the *Tajul Muluk*, Western society was no less crazy, for they had the *Malleus Maleficarum* (1487), a shocking work of sexual fantasy.

The *Malleus* contains stories of witchcraft that I cannot certify to be true. There is a story about a witch who stole men's penises and kept them alive as pets. The penises were placed in bird nests. One victim, a local leader, requested that if she did not return his penis, she should at least give it a place of honour by placing it in the largest nest. However, the witch refused, telling him that she could not give his penis the largest nest because it was already occupied by that of a priest. A leader, a politician or a prince had no claim but to the smallest nest. However, she assured him that the nest was quite comfortable and warm, and his penis was well pleased with it.

At the time, I had neither heard of Serlingpa's name, nor of the spell he gave to Atisa.

In any case, the Leader's Wife was quite unhappy with my answer, but fortunately, the Dictator, who was not interested in stories of witchcraft, asked me to give my 'expert, reasonable, scientific, rational and plausible opinion'.

Therefore, I told him about cases that had happened in 1967 in Singapore and in 2003 in Senegal. I explained at length that in 1967, the news spread during several weeks in the months of October and November, that the illness may have come from people who had eaten pigs which had been vaccinated with the illness, which caused the patients' penises to suddenly shrink and withdraw inside their bodies, causing widespread panic and mass hysteria.

The Leader's Wife interrupted me, 'But my husband has never eaten pork. Even though sometimes, emmm emmm, he would like to.'

Without paying attention to his wife, who was straying away from the conversation, the Leader asked in an increasingly weak voice, 'Who got that disease, Doctor?'

Since I still clearly remembered all the details of the case, having written my doctoral thesis on the subject, I told him that the twelve cases reported in full detail in 1967 involved Chinese patients, the youngest one being four months old, while the oldest was forty years old.

'Chinese . . .' the Leader's Wife sighed. 'What do they want now?'

The Leader spoke up: 'But I am not Chinese. I am a true son of this land. I have Bugis blood. I am not Chinese.' He turned his head to look at his wife and as if in silent agreement, he added, 'What do the Chinese want now . . . What do the Chinese want?!'

I cleared my throat to indicate that I did not want to be interrupted.

However, I had to add an important fact. In Southeast Asia, medical textbooks about tropical diseases mentioned that many men of Makassar and Bugis descent in Celebes and West Borneo had also been found to suffer from this strange disease. There were also men from Pagoh in Malaysia. I noticed that the Leader was shocked by my explanation and was at a loss for words.

Perhaps, in his mind, he was thinking about his title, Mappadulung Daeng Mattimung Karaeng Sanrobone. As for me, an old Bugis proverb was foremost in my thoughts—you can rule 'something' in three ways: by the tip of the tongue, the tip of the penis, or the tip of the *keris*.

The Leader's Wife grumbled: 'First the Chinese, now the Bugis? Don't play with us, Doctor. Anyway, what is your race?'

I swallowed hard and tried to remain courteous. Fear came back to haunt me. If I were to be killed in this house, I would just disappear. I would be gone. Nobody knew that I had been kidnapped by the Leader.

The Leader's Wife relaxed and said in a soft voice, 'We are just trying to practise *tabayyun*. Nobody is angry.'

When the time came to examine the Leader, I politely asked his wife to leave the room. However, she insisted on staying and said these very romantic words: 'I will be with him through thick and thin. We have been emmm emmm facing all our problems together.'

Since she stubbornly refused to leave, the Leader reluctantly removed his trousers and his underwear and lay down half-naked on the leather sofa set in the middle of the room. I am sure that the nude lady in the '*Nu couché (sur le côté gauche)*' would have been laughing if she had been alive.

I observed the Leader's penis. I had never, in my wildest dreams, thought that I would one day not only look at the penis of the Leader of Hujung Manani, but hold it in my hand, press on his scrotum, and touch his glans. Since the pubic hair had been shaved, I immediately saw that the size, circumference and length of the penis were consistent with the international standard for Asian men.

First of all, I checked whether the ischio and bulbo-cavernosus muscles had contracted or were tense, which would have pulled on the other muscles.

'Good news, I believe that your penis is still functional. Perhaps it is just muscle contractions inside.'

The Leader's Wife frowned, rubbing her strangely crooked nose that resembled a beak. 'Uhhh, that must be painful, dear?'

I did not mention that sometimes muscles are pulled inward when a man is thinking about another woman when having sex with his partner, and as soon as he realizes that his fantasy does not match reality, he loses his erection and the penis retracts inside the body.

There was something on the Leader's penis. It looked like some sort of amulet, or a string, or perhaps a weight.

'I had to attach a lock at the tip of his penis to make sure it did not disappear.'

I drew a deep breath. I still could not believe that I was looking at the genitalia of the Dictator, who had been ruling the country with an iron fist for decades. The fixing of the weight must have been done in a state of panic. The Leader's Wife said that she had helped her husband by holding the shaft of his penis to prevent it from retracting into the body before attaching the weight on it.

'Actually, it's the lock from my travelling luggage.'

Oh God, was this a nightmare? If it was indeed an erotic dream, why did it have to involve the country's leader?

I really did not want to hear all the details because I was not interested and I was very embarrassed to think about the situation. I looked at the painting hanging on the wall of the room. This is what I had to face as a doctor. The naked woman in the Modigliani painting seemed to be looking at us, mocking us with her smile.

The woman stepped out of the painting and stood proudly naked in front of me. She laughed and said, 'Isn't the penis the most important thing for Malay people? The first Malay sultan who converted to Islam did it because he was fascinated that his penis had been circumcised while he was dreaming of meeting the Prophet.'

I chased the woman away. 'Shoo! Shoo!'

When I was doing my doctorate on the subject, I had found a thousand and one myths to cure the disease. Tying a weight was one of them; another one used in India was to rub a lime on the ear and forehead of the patient. I could not fathom what a lime had to do with a shrinking penis. But if we recall, when koro broke out in Hujung Manani, many men believed in this treatment.

The Leader told me that it hurt a lot when I pressed his pelvis and his lower abdomen. He complained that he had had trouble urinating since the problem had started, right after an important meeting with an anti-corruption officer, during which his head and body became very hot, he had trouble breathing and felt dizzy with vertigo. After taking a shower that night, he suddenly felt that his penis was being squeezed and he started to shiver, have a bad headache and feel heat below his waist. The feeling of his penis being choked lasted between ten to fifteen minutes, and the Dictator was terrified.

At the time, I did not know that the koro attack had happened while his mistress Sistine was sucking on his penis, and to prevent it from shrinking any further, Sistine had held onto the glans with her teeth.

I estimated that the size had decreased by 7.7 per cent. But without a penile plethysmograph to measure the penis accurately, I could not make a precise assessment.

I decided to give the Dictator a tablet of 10 mg of chlordiazepoxide, which happened to be in the medical bag that I had had time to grab before leaving my house.

'I need to place you under observation for forty-eight hours.'

I told the Leader's Wife that I needed to ask his aide to get me several things, including the measuring tool that I mentioned before, as well as a supply of calcium gluconate to be injected if a shrinking attack occurred again suddenly.

'So emmm emmm, is it witchcraft?' the Leader's Wife asked while glancing at her husband's penis from the corner of her eyes. At the moment, it looked like a wrinkled raisin, or a dried banana with a lock at the end.

The Dictator pulled his trousers back on and sat in front of me, self-conscious.

'Based on my examination and your explanation that you experienced shortness of breath, heart palpitations, pressure in the chest, nausea, pain in the body, chills, sweat, and that these symptoms all disappeared within one hour but your penis kept shrinking, I diagnose your condition as the koro syndrome. Yes, indeed, I believe that you *are* suffering from koro.'

'Koro?' the Leader's wife asked.

'Yes, the name comes from the word *kura-kura*, or turtle, as the head of the turtle can withdraw into its shell. This illness has been known for a long time, since the Srivijaya Era. But it is only a feeling, a mental illness. Not a real disease!'

'Ancient witchcraft!' the Leader's Wife shouted, as if she was excited, or perhaps surprised.

The Leader stood up and shook hands with me. 'I will give you a decoration and a title after all this is over.'

I simply nodded. What could I say? If I ever got a title for holding and treating the Dictator's penis, I hoped to God nobody ever found out the reason for the distinction!

I was then allowed to rest and I tried to sleep, but to no avail. I was now officially being held hostage by the Dictator. Nobody knew where I was. At lunchtime, I asked the Dictator's aide, the man with the short moustache, to bring me several medical journals from my office at the university.

I had to be ready, in case the Dictator suffered another koro attack.

I had no appetite. I only ordered some black coffee without sugar.

Two hours later, the academic journals I had requested were handed to me. I was absorbed in the reading of the newest discoveries about the koro syndrome when the Leader's Wife suddenly entered my room and shouted, 'It's shrinking, it's shrinking, emmm emmm, it's almost gone! My husband's penis is almost gone!'

I rushed to the Leader's bedroom. It was absolutely splendid. The walls were painted in a light brown colour. The rugs, just like in the other room, were made of tiger skins. Outside the window, the panorama of Hujung Manani's capital city was lit with a thousand lights. The city was beautiful, as seen through the sliding door of the Dictator's bedroom. Suddenly, the view reminded me that I was being held captive in this house, after having been kidnapped against my will to treat the Dictator.

His bed was in the centre of the room and my eyes were drawn to a painting by Claude Monet, placed near the dressing table, which was almost entirely covered with bottles of perfume. The painting could have been authentic. It was the *Portrait of Père Paul*, also known as *Monsieur Paul* or *The Chef*, painted in 1882. Categorized as an *'esquisse curieuse'* or a curious sketch, the man in the painting seemed to be observing the drama taking place in front of his eyes.

To me, this painting was another strange choice. Especially for a bedroom. Who would want to sleep while being watched by an old man wearing a chef's hat and jacket? The old man looked sad. His dark eyes were not focused on anything. He sported a grey and black scruffy beard around his tightly closed mouth.

While I stood fascinated by the French painting, the Leader's Wife said, 'This painting was expensive, you know, Doctor. We had to go through several agents and companies to get it.'

'My balls are gone . . . My balls are gone! I'm gonna die! I know I'm gonna die!'

The Leader was thrashing about on the large bed.

He was evidently experiencing the prodromal phase of an attack. He had just vomited before I had entered the room and was now groaning in pain, complaining about his testicles hurting him (but I assumed they were only numb).

The Leader was on all fours, his head bent down to implore his testicles, and his buttocks up in the air. I felt pity for him. The skin of his buttocks was covered with fine hairs. I saw that he had traces of diarrhoea around his anus, and there were some traces of diarrhoea on the sheet as well. This was normal. What was not normal, though, and was even surreal, was to witness the man known as the Dictator with only half his clothes on.

Within the next five minutes, the shrinking phase started, which was fascinating for me as a medical observer. The Leader complained that his nipples hurt and I could see that they were hard and swollen. The Leader was rolling around in pain on the bed.

I had to rub the Dictator's nipples to relieve the pain. His stomach was rippling with waves. I decided not to use the penile plethysmograph to do a phallometric test. I quickly gave him an injection of calcium gluconate and shouted for someone to bring ice. His wife quickly got some ice in a container. I wrapped a few ice cubes in a towel and applied it to the Dictator's penis.

He started sobbing and babbling, 'I'm gonna die, I'm gonna die . . . my balls are gone, I don't have any balls. You had that woman killed. She stole my balls.'

The wife kept trying to interrupt him, 'Can I advise you something . . . Shut up! Don't say anything! Shut up! Nobody died.'

In the midst of all this chaos, I repeated several times that he should not worry, that I would treat his penis very gently and carefully.

I must report that the situation was very tense and dramatic, with the Dictator sobbing, feeling depressed and mortified; while his wife, who would not calm down, screamed and yelled and created chaos in the lavish bedroom. Several servants walked in but they left almost immediately, embarrassed, when they saw the Leader naked and writhing in pain on the bed.

Fifteen minutes after the beginning of the shrinking phase, the Dictator told me that he felt impotent, and I realized that the penis had shrunk even further.

During all this, Datin Lotis, the Dictator's wife, was trying to persuade me that what her husband was suffering from was not koro but a magic spell—a ridiculous hypothesis, according to which the penis was stolen and caused to fly away.

'This is witchcraft. In the name of Birkin, in the name of Prada, in the name of my pink diamond from 2001, emmm

emmm, ten men had their penises stolen in Benin, in Africa,' she said while sniffling because her nose had become runny due to her constant crying.

She added, 'I know a shaman who can cure this type of magic spell by putting shredded holy verses on the glans of the penis. Maybe I should call the Tycoon to ask for his help.'

I breathed deeply as my heart was beating fast with anger upon hearing her suggestion.

When the situation calmed down, after the Dictator had stopped sobbing, I pleaded with him to let me observe him in a more intimate environment, without his wife being present.

It took me a long time to convince the Leader's Wife that her presence was not needed and actually did not help at all. The Dictator also asked her weakly to leave, and told her to go shopping in order to distract her mind from all this. After she left for a shopping trip, I gave the Dictator my professional opinion about his ailment.

'Sir, I have to speak to you frankly. What you have is called koro. In some medical journals, it is referred to as SPS or shrinking penis syndrome. Cases of SPS were reported in the 1880s in America, Russia and England. There is a report from a French doctor working in China of SPS or koro cases in China in 1908. Koro or SPS was only mentioned in clinical textbooks after 1936, and . . . errr . . . I am sorry to say, it was classified as a mental illness in the 1950s. In this context, SPS corresponds to a failure of the nervous system.'

The Leader looked absolutely shocked and answered, 'A mental illness? What's the use of all these details? Can I be cured?'

'I am telling you everything about koro or SPS so that you will give me straightforward answers, without hiding anything.'

'What do you mean? Err, I'm not the one who gave the order to have the woman k—'

'Well, if you are experiencing acute depression due to the pressures of your political career, which is often marred by scandals or due to pressure from political enemies, that can also cause koro. If this is the case, then I can give you the relevant medication. Fever, nausea and the other symptoms can also be factors of comorbidity, which is the occurrence of two chronic diseases at the same time. In India, cultural syndromes such as koro are caused by comorbidity. A very high fever cannot be examined in a lab and there is no clinical evidence of it. For a case like this, I might treat you with pharmacological therapy, or talking therapy. In Thailand in 1976, 2,000 people were affected by a koro epidemic and the doctor in-charge treated it as a psychosexual syndrome.'

The Leader was sitting still, staring into space. 'If it was up to me, I would have retired a long time ago. Long ago . . . but she won't let me. When all this is over, I want to go to Saudi Arabia to perform the small pilgrimage.'

'I just want you to be honest with me, so that I can treat you properly.'

I was taken by surprise when the Leader suddenly burst into tears.

'It's my aide who introduced me to the woman from Tibet.'

I swallowed hard. What Tibetan woman was he talking about?

The Leader started sobbing again. In between sobs, he spoke in a trembling voice, 'I was on the phone with the Tycoon. She was giving me a blowjob at the same time, when my wife walked in and caught us in the act. That's the first time I felt my dick shrinking. I screamed for help. My wife was shouting like she was possessed. But the Tibetan woman was trying to help me . . .

she wanted to help me. She had to hold the glans of my penis with her teeth to prevent it from disappearing altogether. My wife thought that she was trying to continue to suck my dick, in front of her, to challenge her authority. I was under terrible pressure. My wife ordered her bodyguard to come and drag the woman out of the room. I knew she would never forgive her. I heard her yelling, "Get rid of her! In the name of Birkin, blow her to pieces, kill her! In the name of Clinton, I will never forgive you!" Then I heard the woman cursing, "Don't play that game with me. I'll take his balls with me. In the name of Lama, of Atisa, of Serlingpa." When my dick was still in her mouth, she mumbled something in Tibetan or whatever language, I don't know. I only clearly heard the word "Drdhabhakti" before she was dragged away by force.'

Now all I could hear was the Leader's weeping. I kept quiet. I did not even dare to breathe. It was deadly silent. The Leader was still lying down and he looked exhausted. I imagined the naked woman from the 'Nu couché (sur le côté gauche)' stepping out of the painting and bending her head over the Dictator's crotch. I saw her starting to lick his penis.

The constant sobbing from the Dictator made the illusion vanish. There was no naked woman. Neither the one from the painting, nor the one from Tibet, who had come between the Leader and his wife.

As a medical practitioner, my focus was the Leader as a patient. I turned my eyes back to his genital area. The small lock was still tightly attached to the glans, which had begun to turn a darker colour. I was worried.

Without paying too much heed to the weird story that I had heard, I made a decision. 'I believe that this is going to happen again, and you are going to feel a lot of pain. Let me think first before I determine what type of treatment is most suitable for you.'

'Doctor, this is not witchcraft, is it? Tibetan black magic?' the Leader stuttered. 'I know that I am going to die, Doctor . . . If I have no balls, how can I continue to rule Hujung Manani? People already call me a traitor. This is so sad. This country needs me . . .'

'How about we first remove the lock that you have been using as a weight? The blood cannot circulate and the tip of your penis already looks black. We don't want to call the emergency services to remove it, right?'

The Leader nodded in agreement. He was frail and subdued. This was the Dictator who ruled Hujung Manani with an iron fist, and he was now lying down robbed of strength in front of me, as one of my patients. He was very weak. He was crying and babbling nonsense. He needed help. He believed he was going to die. And if I told anyone, who would believe that I had held the Dictator's phallus in my hand and that it was nothing to be proud of.

'Magic only works on those who believe in it.' That was all I could say. What else could I tell the Leader? I hoped he would listen to me.

The thought crossed my mind to frighten the Dictator and make him go mad. His fate was in my hands. He trusted me as an expert in my field of medicine.

But the chef from 'Portrait of Père Paul' talked to me, 'I have the choice to cut that penis off, cook it in a soup and serve it with mashed potatoes. But you don't have that choice. A doctor has only one choice: to cure his patients.'

'You are right,' I answered.

So at that time, I knew that my duty as a doctor was to cure the Dictator, even though bringing him back to health may lead him to become an even more ruthless ruler, after recovering all his strength and striking back from Riyadh . . . but with a low level of emotional intelligence. For my part, I never thought of letting the Leader suffer from the koro syndrome forever in order to make him weak, torturing and forcing him to resign or lose his authority. Letting a patient suffer without treatment was against medical ethics. He was, first and foremost, my patient.

Therefore, I should not bear any blame. I humbly believe that the mind controls the penis, and not the other way round. The chef in the Monet painting would agree with me. So would the naked woman in the Modigliani painting.

In this report, I wish to emphasize that the decision by the National Medical Council to blame me for treating the Leader is unwarranted and absurd. Their threat to revoke my medical licence is totally unfair. I will appeal to the Leader, the scientist, because as he said it himself, 'it is not about a penis, it is about the people'.

A doctor's duty and responsibility is to cure his patients, whatever their race, and even if they are half-demons. It is a fact that a dictator will remain a dictator until death. Believe me, I am not a follower or supporter of the Dictator because my duty—based only on my expertise—was to restore his physical health at a time when he was suffering from koro. A doctor is neither a minion nor, in familiar terms, a toady.

It is my hope that this report will clear false perceptions and contribute to reaching a just and fair evaluation of my services. I wish to be regarded as a modern scientist.

This is not fiction. This is a medical report. I am a psychiatric expert of Thai descent, fifty-seven years old, working in a professional and dedicated manner.

Adele

Okarmmavasita. O datu. Drdhabhakti. Grant me Viryya. The incantation was ringing in your ears, buzzing against your eardrums and implanting itself in your brain.

'It will enable you to see ghosts and ask for their help,' the shaman had said while nodding, trying to persuade you.

'Ghosts?'

For the past two days, you had been feeling like you were being followed and the 'thing' that was following you was just outside the window, looking at you while you were working. Ever since then, you had been shivering. Perhaps it was all related. Your thoughts recalled the shaman. And the incantation reappeared in your mind: 'O karmmavasita. O datu. Drdhabhakti. Grant me Viryya'.

Your office was square, measuring 3.7 metres per side. It featured a desk facing the window, from which you could see the elite neighbourhood of Hujung Manani's capital city. There were fires and thick columns of smoke in several areas. You wanted to know what was happening out there. There were many rumours. But since yesterday, the window was stuck shut. Perhaps the 'thing' had been holding onto it for the past two days.

The other furniture in the room consisted of a bookshelf, a computer desk, a console and a Cleopatra chaise lounge, on which you rested when you needed to take a nap. Perhaps the 'thing' was lying down on it right now in a voluptuous position. On the desk, there was a green desklamp, which gave a bright white light but did not hurt your eyes. There were scattered books and papers which you had not looked at for a while, and an opened bottle of sanitizer, which was empty.

For several days now, you had been going from your desk to the kitchen, coffee–bread–salad and back to the computer without blinking your eyes. If the rumours of the riots were true, then you were trapped in your office.

If the rampage went on for a long time, you might run out of food. Perhaps it might be better for you to pack your stuff, leave and stay in the True Patriot's luxurious residence.

You stared blankly at your laptop. You were holding a lit cigarette between your index and middle fingers, but you were not smoking it. The tip of the cigarette turned to ash and fell beside your notebook.

The built-in television in the Montgomery cabinet made of solid wood was on, showing a documentary on koro.

The True Patriot had contacted you four days ago to give you alarming news. Perhaps it would help. There were five police reports which looked unrelated, but the True Patriot believed that they were connected and that they all pointed in the same direction: the Dictator, or perhaps his wicked wife.

There was a report about religious school teachers suffering a koro attack and the explanation of the owner of a pig farm.

A messenger had arrived with a bunch of files for you to read. 'The True Patriot is inviting you to work at her house.'

'I prefer to stay here; I am not allowed to smoke over there. Anyway, I don't feel comfortable when I have to interpret her fantasies,' I told the messenger.

That was why you preferred to remain cooped up in your house, cut off momentarily from the outside world, with only the television as your link to the world.

The files contained various documents.

The first report was about a psychiatric expert of Thai ancestry from Hujung Manani University Hospital, who had disappeared without a trace. One of his neighbours claimed that he had been abducted by a man with a short moustache, while another neighbour saw the doctor surrounded by a group of men who were in plain clothes but looked like members of the Special Branch Police of Hujung Manani, which was infamously brutal. They were members of the Cobra Squad—a squad of assassins and kidnappers who answered directly to the Leader.

According to the information gathered by the True Patriot's office, a colleague of the psychiatrist's reported that a man with a short moustache had showed up with several other men to search his office. The hospital guards had been too afraid to stop them or to ask them why they were searching the office of a psychiatrist who specialized in stress, amok, hysteria and koro.

The guards did nothing to stop them. They did not dare enforce their authority. Perhaps, these were debt collectors . . .

The two reports regarding the psychiatric expert showed that something strange was happening, and based on most previous cases of abductions, this must have been arranged by the Leader.

You stood up, stretched and scratched your crotch, which was covered with thick black hair. The hair on the back of your neck stood up suddenly. You looked around you. You did not see anything.

But Sistine was there. She flew down from the ceiling, swaying her buttocks. She perched on the wooden buffet and hutch placed against the living-room wall, looking at the Portmeirion plates collected by your ex-wife. She swayed her butt there for a while. Then she flew to the wooden chest of drawers and landed beside the statue of an African woman. In the blink of an eye, Sistine was beside the computer desk, whispering, 'O karmmavasita. O datu. Drdhabhakti. Grant me Viryya'.

Sistine was rubbing against you, 'Hey hey EC, hey hey mamak, hey hey Enlarged Cock!'

No response.

You were in a different world, a different dimension.

You drew a deep breath, sat down again, and lit another cigarette. The second case was about a rookie detective, who had just graduated and joined the forensic police department. The young man was also reported missing. There were no witnesses to say whether he had been kidnapped or taken by force. However, one of his colleagues, a detective who had just retired, had made a police report about the disappearance of the young policeman. In the report, the retired detective claimed that they had been working together on a mysterious murder case involving a victim (who was not a citizen of Hujung Manani) who had been killed viciously, and the corpse had disappeared from the morgue of the hospital located upcountry (but not far from the capital city), after the autopsy.

You lifted your head and looked at the television screen. There seemed to be some kind of agitation or undefined panic. The emergency news report failed to keep your attention.

Koro?

Why should anyone worry about koro? Anyway, as far as you were concerned, your penis was long enough—even if it retracted a little inside your body, it would still be quite long.

This kind of stupid panic had become normal in Hujung Manani. For instance, there were often cases of schools (usually religious ones) where pupils became hysterical and injured themselves—they screamed as they scratched their cheeks, pulled their hair or hit their head on the wall until they bled. The television news or, to be more exact, the media in Hujung Manani, loved this type of stories.

You returned to your files. The newly retired detective mentioned several other strange things in his report, which had caused him to be held for several nights with a group of religious teachers, who claimed that they were suffering from repeated bouts of a type of illness—the report referred to it as a magic spell—which had made their penises shrink. All the men who complained of a shrinking penis had been quarantined in hospital before being moved to a hall where they were examined and treated together, before most of them were released.

The hair stood up on the back of your neck again.

Sistine was talking to you. 'Hey hey EC, hey hey Enlarged Cock. I am calling you, hey, are you deaf?'

You took a puff of your cigarette, then blew the smoke out. Outside, from your office window, you could see thick clouds of smoke from burning tires. You did not pay it much attention.

The third interesting case concerned a famous historian who taught at Hujung Manani University and had disappeared without a trace. He specialized in the history of Hujung Manani before the French colonization, when the small country still had a king.

The last time his wife had talked to him was over the telephone. She could hear that her husband's voice was trembling and that something was not right. The Famous Historian sounded hasty, passive and only answered 'okay' when she asked him to buy two packets of spices, a dozen eggs, a bottle of sanitizer and hygiene towels on his way back home.

The historian's wife had reported his disappearance to the police forty-eight hours later.

The True Patriot believed that this third case was also related to the others, although there was no evidence.

You had heard about the Famous Historian. There were two historians in Hujung Manani. One was Melah, who, according to the True Patriot, was a minion, an arse-licker who twisted the truth; while the other, Mat Adam, was astute, sincere, truthful and on the side of the people.

Sistine tried to interrupt you. 'Hey EC, I know what happened to them. Do you want me to tell you?'

On the television screen, you saw a group of religious men with a sort of yellow mark on their foreheads, which they claimed was for protection against the koro disease.

The fourth case, which puzzled you even more, concerned a monk from a temple in another country. That temple had been built on land near a plastic recycling site. The monk, a Tibetan man in his fifties, was employed by a Buddhist foundation to lead the religious ceremonies at the temple. Not much was known about the monk's disappearance. The temple people made a police report because they feared that the monk, who rarely went out, could have got lost, or worse, might have been hit by a car and his body kept in a morgue without identification.

The only reason that the True Patriot's political team believed that the monk's disappearance was connected to the Leader, was because the Dalai Lama's office had contacted the True Patriot's office and informed them that the missing monk was not just anybody but a 'Lama', an important leader, who held the key to many ancient treasures. All these disappearances had occurred almost at the same time as the emergence of the koro epidemic.

The fifth report concerned a famous Hujung Manani religious preacher. The *ustaz* was the darling of women, for not only was he young, he also knew how to preach and his physical appearance was very attractive. His three wives had made separate police reports in which they all claimed that a neighbour had seen a woman wearing a sexy robe leaving the house on the day of their husband's disappearance. The preacher's followers had started spreading the rumour that their idol had been kidnapped and was being held by members of the LGBT movement because of their leader's harsh stand against them. Several transgender women who were uneasy with the accusations and threats proffered by the religious group, also made police reports stating that they were feeling threatened and were afraid to be attacked without reason. They strongly refuted the claims made by the wives and followers of the ustaz that he was being held and tortured by the LGBT people, although they did admit that he was indeed very handsome, and that they sometimes used his photos when they masturbated.

You felt irritated; annoyed by all these cases of abductions.

That Thursday evening, you were analysing the five unrelated cases. You were trying to find the connection between the five individuals concerned and you were wondering why the True Patriot believed that they were all related to one person, namely the Leader.

You grumbled because the True Patriot had asked you to solve the mystery of the five cases.

And what was their connection with the koro epidemic, which was rumoured to be striking so many people at the same time?

What was the connection between the Dictator and a young detective investigating a gruesome murder, or with a psychiatrist whose office had been raided by the secret police? And what did this have to do with the Famous Historian who studied civilization during the rule of King Sod, or with a Lama who was learned but did not know much about Hujung Manani? Why would the Dictator kidnap a religious preacher who, according to you, was a useful asset for him in the country? These religious men supported kleptocrats and criminals like the Dictator, since the fall of the Dictator would pave the way for liberals (including the LGBT minority) to rise again.

Sistine shouted at you again. You did not hear anything at all. You yawned. She moved her hand in front of your face. You did not notice anything. You rubbed your eyes. Sistine shook her bum next to you, almost rubbing her tight buttocks on your sleeve. You did not feel anything. Sistine threw herself on the floor, frustrated that she could not manage to get your attention.

Because of these disappearances, you were sitting in front of your computer, clueless, feeling stupid and lighting cigarette after cigarette, even though you did not even smoke them. The True Patriot did not tell you why she thought that the five cases were connected with the Dictator or his shopaholic wife.

The shaman's voice whispered, 'O karmmavasita. O datu. Drdhabhakti. Grant me Viryya'. His face appeared before your eyes.

The newsreader on the television screen which was still turned on, announced that a koro epidemic was creating panic in the capital.

You scratched the tip of your penis and grinned. Sistine was actually playing with it in order to draw your attention. It felt ticklish, itchy.

You realized that the cigarette you were holding between your fingers was still lit, but was almost burned down to the filter. You stubbed it out and looked around you at the messy office. You looked at the photograph in which you stood next to the True Patriot.

Three years before, you had retired as the Editor-in-Chief of the *Hujung Manani Tribune* and joined the True Patriot's team as a media adviser. The opposition team, led by the True Patriot, had but one clear purpose: to overthrow the Leader.

But how? How were they to overthrow him?

They were not sure.

Before the Dictator came to power in Hujung Manani, the True Patriot had been regarded as his political mentor. As one of the members of the team that had negotiated the independence of Hujung Manani from French colonial rule, she was regarded as the mother of Independence and an important political leader. After Hujung Manani became independent, the Dictator's father, who was the True Patriot's friend, became the country's first leader.

His short term, which lasted merely five years, ended in tragedy. He was killed in a car accident which many believed had been engineered. The True Patriot replaced the Dictator's father and served as the second leader of the country for about ten years before handing over power to the Dictator. Honestly, Hujung Manani was fortunate to have had a woman as Leader. For these three elections, including the first time the Dictator was elected as the third leader, Hujung Manani witnessed democracy and free elections. That is when you were appointed as Editor-in-Chief of the *Hujung Manani Tribune*, the only newspaper in the small country. Little by little, it became the official newspaper of the government and you accidentally became an important figure in Hujung Manani's political landscape.

Then, little by little, the government of Hujung Manani became increasingly autocratic. You were swept up by that unhealthy development too.

As a result, the world of journalism—from editors to journalists and even writers—started to hate you, because you were considered as being part of the ruler's team of supporters.

Sistine poked her finger in your eye. You felt an itch and rubbed your eyes. Perhaps it was getting late at night. Or was 'something' bothering you? Sistine flicked the tip of your long penis. It hardened instantly.

People started making fun of your name, out of spite. Kadir Mohamed became Kadir the Mamak Dick. Some people used the initials EC for 'Editor-in-Chief', but it also stood for Enlarged Cock, like your ex-wife liked to tease you.

You were very enthusiastic about your job as the director of communications in Hujung Manani. Your stupidity enabled the Leader (who was not yet called the Dictator) to do anything. he wanted, until the day your wife, a scientist, could not stand it any longer and asked you for a divorce. She merely said, 'The Leader's wife is mad. Stay away from her. As for the True Patriot, she is a dreamer. Talking to her is like talking with a female version of Albert Camus.'

So you willingly divorced her. You could not suffer the True Patriot being criticized. She was like a mother to you.

'She uses fiction to fight religious edicts, to fight decrees. She turns religious edicts into fiction. She does that to decrees as well. Don't you understand?'

According to you, your wife, as a scientist, did not understand you, a journalist. How could she, when she was busy studying insects while you were reporting on the important events that shaped the society of Hujung Manani?

You knew that you would end up with a divorce when your wife discovered a type of flea or bug named *Microneta scholtzi*. It only measured 2 millimetres, and possessed genital organs that could be rubbed against a sort of comb on its body to produce a mating sound of 100 dB, known as the 'singing genitalia'.

How could you stay together as a couple? Divorce was inevitable. Perhaps you were also too proud of your heritage as a mamak, who had contributed a lot to Malay civilization.

For centuries, ever since the arrival of Islam in Hujung Manani, the mamak community had played an important part in shaping the country. Being part of that ethnic group explained the Tamil expletives that you liked to use, especially when you were angry with your employees.

For example, you called the sports sub-editor who liked to use sensational titles to put down the Chelsea football team, '*anaathai kaluthai*'; or the photographer who failed to bring you an interesting angle when tasked with covering the charity work done by the Leader's wife outside the orchid garden, '*yethava*'. Your favourite expression was '*ennoda poola oombuda*', reserved for the economics editor who tried to report the money-laundering activities of the country's Chief of Police.

As a result, you were disliked and called Kadir the Mamak Dick behind your back. At first, it made you angry but when a friend brought you a basket of *Cassia grandis* pods, which the locals call Mamak's Penis, you were amused and arrogantly turned the insult into a form of recognition.

You became proud of being called a Mamak Dick, claiming that it was a 'big' achievement. You liked the *Cassia grandis* fruits. They look like flower pistils that grow from a thin green stem hidden behind a leaf. When the fruit is ripe, it turns a dark brown colour and becomes dry as wood. It has a long shape, and inside there are flat seeds in small compartments that have a strong smell.

You knew how to enjoy these fruits. You could just suck them raw. Or you could eat them with grated coconut, and some people had told you that the thick juice could be mixed with milk and honey to make a sweet drink. However, your son, who was also well-endowed, was not comfortable with the nickname Mamak Dick.

You both possessed nine inch long penises. This explained why your son, your only child, was unlucky in your opinion, because he had been smothered by his mother; in the end, his ambition was to be successful as a scientist. He was even obsessed with becoming the first astronaut to land on Mars (but unfortunately, as usual, your son was not a citizen of Hujung Manani, and if one day he did succeed in his ambition, Hujung Manani would only be proud of the fact that he was your son).

Your son had moved to Malaysia with his mother. Of course, Malaysia was better than Hujung Manani in all regards. They had signed the Rome Statute, unlike Hujung Manani, which had signed many international conventions during the True Patriot's term in office, but had withdrawn its commitments due to many human rights agreements during the Dictator's rule.

As a divorced man who rarely had the chance to act as a father, and who had once been in cahoots with the Leader, you developed an inflexible personality and as a tough media analyst, you became very useful to the movement led by the True Patriot.

Your hard-on came back. Shit!

When you stopped working at the *Hujung Manani Tribune*, you felt lonely and immediately accepted the True Patriot's offer to be part of the opposition team working to overthrow the Leader.

After receiving the files regarding the abductions, you had been invited to meet a shaman who sold spells and charms. That woman claimed that she had provided magic services to the Leader's wife and that the latter trusted her. You were hoping that the shaman would tell you about the koro epidemic and the abductions. First, she had told a private investigator who worked for the True Patriot, that the Leader's wife was looking for the Ziji stone to strengthen her spirit.

That was the first time you had ever heard of the Ziji stone. The True Patriot asked everyone in her team to watch every move made by the Dictator and his wife. You were aware, based on the file regarding the disappearance of the young detective, that the stone had been worn by the famous murder victim from Tibet. Perhaps that was the connection with the Tibetan monk?

Sistine attacked you again. 'That's true,' she said. 'The Ziji stone is mine.'

She immediately started crying. But you were not aware of her presence beside you.

The voice from the television was hypnotic and made you sleepy.

According to the private investigator working for the True Patriot, they had got information from the shaman that the Dictator's wife had taken a supply of yellow-footed polypore (*Microporus xanthopus*). This type of fungus is used to treat irregular menstruation, tighten the vagina, get rid of body odour and increase fertility.

This was enough to make the Dictator's wife seem very bizarre. Reading all this information was like trying to solve a giant and complex jigsaw puzzle.

You liked challenges, even though you complained about it. Everything that the True Patriot had given you, all the bits and pieces of the puzzle, must be put together. Although you were baffled and anticipated that you might only end up facing even more difficulties, you were also excited and eager to fight against the Dictator's regime.

Sistine spoke up: 'Hey Enlarged Cock, let me help you fight the Dictator's wife. I was killed when her husband's dick was in my mouth. He suffered from koro and I was trying to prevent his penis from retracting completely into his body. That's why I tightened my mouth around it so it would not disappear completely.'

The hair stood up on the back of your neck. Your penis stiffened again, pushing against the loose boxers you were wearing.

Once, your son had expressed his worries about your association with the True Patriot to depose the Dictator. After ten years in office, the Dictator had become violent and vindictive, manipulating racial and religious sentiments in order to remain in power. 'Papa, you might end up killed and dismembered like Khashoggi. Or abducted like Amri Che Mat and Pastor Koh.'

You refused to entertain your son's concern and tried to calm him by changing the subject.

'Do you know that the journey to Mars takes seven months, as it is 227.9 million kilometres from Earth? To land on the planet, a six-man mission must carry a load of 40,000 kilograms.'

'Ah, you're too much, papa!' Your son was uneasy because he was not able to express his opinion. 'Mama is right, you don't care about our well-being.'

Your mind floated back to the shaman. Her face made you feel very uncomfortable.

'O karmmavasita. O datu. Drdhabhakti. Grant me Viryya.'

Since returning from your visit to the female shaman, you had been feeling as if you were being followed. You knew that the secret police of the Special Branch, spies and the Leader's men were watching you. But you could feel that now you were being followed by something which was not human, an entity from another dimension.

You were certain that something was constantly watching you.

Sistine wiped her tears and pressed her cold cheek against yours. 'It's true, I can see you, Kadir the Mamak Dick. I really enjoy seeing you . . . sometimes naked, sometimes dressed . . . looking out of the window, reading, but . . . I need to talk to you. I need to tell you something!'

You lit your third cigarette but you did not really smoke that either. Your head was spinning, trying to figure out the connection between the four or five cases in front of you and the Leader, as well as considering the possibility that the shaman had been telling the truth.

According to the woman, there were witchcraft sellers in Africa. They had shops in which one could find all sorts of spells, preparations, amulets and incantations to cast a spell on someone.

The Leader's wife was a strong believer in magic and witchcraft. She had ordered several spells that could be read in order to ensure that her husband's power would never decrease.

Did such sellers really exist? You listened to all these stories of sorcery without really believing them. You did not think that the shaman was giving you much useful information, or perhaps she was afraid to tell the truth. Actually, it had been quite difficult to convince her to talk to you and disclose secrets about the Leader's wife.

The woman kept saying that if the Leader came to know about it, she would be killed.

You tried to calm her fears. If her magic really worked, what was she afraid of?

'Don't be afraid, the Dictator's wife will not kill people who are useful to her. And you are a shaman with knowledge of many spells and charms—they need you. And anyway, if you help the True Patriot now, when we manage to overthrow the Dictator, you will be rewarded.'

Before you left, the woman had handed you a piece of paper with an ancient spell written on it.

'This will enable you to see ghosts and ask for their help,' she had said.

'Ghosts? Why would I need ghosts?'

'Yes, it's me . . .' Sistine said, flying to your left side and caressing your sideburn. 'I will help you, Kadir the Mamak Dick.'

The shaman had looked all around, without noticing Sistine who was standing on the right. The hair rose on the back of her neck when Sistine moved to the left.

'Yes, ghosts. Souls who are trapped in this world because they have unfinished business. They can help you in your work.'

O karmmavasita. O datu. Drdhabhakti. Grant me Viryya.

'Isn't this wrong?' you asked.

The shaman laughed. 'Wrong? In what way? Is it wrong for a farmer to use a cow or a tractor to work in a rice field?'

You scratched your head. The True Patriot's spy who had gone with you to meet secretly with the shaman chuckled and added, 'So using a ghost in order to work is the same as a farmer using a cow or a tractor to plant rice?'

The woman merely smiled. Beside you, Sistine was nodding, before bending her head and flying in front of you.

The shaman instructed you to burn incense when you read the spell written in Sanskrit. So far, you had not yet found the strength to call on a ghost. If one really appeared in front of you, what would you say to it?

Could ghosts really help you?

The shaman smiled. Then with a sharp look, she asked, 'Do you know Badang? The man who catches ghosts and eats their vomit? He has extraordinary powers and strength.'

'Hey, I'm not gonna eat ghost barf!'

The woman giggled. Sistine's laughter echoed hers.

She held your sleeve and said earnestly, 'It doesn't matter. But you should know that some ghosts eat the sperm of certain men and never let them go. Other ghosts steal their penis and keep it far out of their reach. There are ghosts who live for thousands of years and take the form of tigers and sometimes, they appear as human beings. You could call on a ghost. You should try it.'

What could be the connection between the koro epidemic, the latest abductions and the Leader and his wife? If you could really meet a ghost, you would not ask for anything special. You would only hope for one thing—to solve this enigma.

Sistine was still trying to talk to you. 'Hey, hey, *assalamualaikum*, hello brother . . .'

You went to the kitchen to get a drink, Sistine right behind you. You returned to your desk and Sistine continued to try to make contact with you.

The phone rang and you were startled out of your thoughts. You crushed your cigarette butt. On the other end of the line, one of the True Patriot's assistants spoke.

'KM, there are troubles in several locations in the capital. Have you been watching the news?'

The television was on. It showed a group of men wearing skull caps dragging the body of a dead woman, or was it a man dressed as a woman?

'The news has been on for a while. Isn't it something which is already mentioned in the abduction reports that I've been given? Religious groups accusing transgender women of causing the koro epidemic?' You added jokingly, 'If only the riots were about protesting against the dumping of plastic waste in Hujung Manani! Or the Dictator's financial scandals and abuse of power—'

The voice at the other end of the line shouted: 'Koro! It's koro riots! The koro epidemic! Many people have been infected and the situation is becoming violent. As you said, in some places, they are blaming the LGBT minorities and religious groups are out to get them. In other places, it has become a racial issue.'

You swore under your breath. 'Racial? Racist?'

You did not know what to do. Now what, how would Hujung Manani face this bizarre issue?

'Or perhaps it was engineered by the Dictator to distract the opposition and drown out their anger? The media narrative, the historical narrative—they can be modified at will,' you said.

The True Patriot's assistant continued, 'This is no laughing matter. A famous ustaz lost his penis, he was raped and later, his penis suddenly came back, and now his followers claim that the transgender community has put a spell on their idol.'

An ustaz, a victim of witchcraft?! You were shocked.

'His supporters went crazy. One mob killed a group of *mat rempits* and another group stormed a venue where a dinner was being organized by transgender women, killing many of them with keris. A large crowd of religious men then marched out onto the streets.'

You were speechless, thinking about the file regarding the famous religious preacher who had disappeared without a trace. Had he been found by now?

You suddenly thought of asking: 'So, what's racial or racist about this?'

With a grunt, the True Patriot's assistant answered, 'There have been koro attacks in several other places in Hujung Manani. People believe that koro was caused by Chinese people who have eaten unvaccinated pigs from Tibet.'

One word caught your attention: 'Tibet?'

The koro epidemic was causing a lot of confusion. Everywhere, people were looking for shamans and buying protection charms.

You got off the phone. You just realized that the news had spread to the entire world, while national television stations in Hujung Manani were still taking a cautious approach. The latest news bulletin stated that over a thousand religious men from a national association, who were attending a political meeting, had been hospitalized after complaining that their penises had disappeared.

What was their problem? For a short while, you were completely engrossed in the images shown on the screen. In your mind, a few verses of the third paragraph of the *Six Gurindam* emerged:

'When religious men behave like dogs
Along with the king they rob

When pious men a good example do not show
They do no good despite what they know

When pious men become pig-headed
They must be stopped or disaster will succeed

When behaviour is dictated by greed
The mouth opens to ask while the stomach is replete'

The report about what happened to the religious men made you realize how clever and accurate the writer of the *Gurindam* had been.

You laughed. You put your hand on your penis, rubbed it and laughed out loud.

So what should the True Patriot do now? The opposition could seize this opportunity to intensify hatred towards the Dictator and his wife. If successful, Priapus's regime would collapse and a phallus revolution, or a penis revolution, would erupt. Didn't all big empires fall because of trivial causes such as this one? Who knew, perhaps the revolution in Hujung Manani might succeed as a result of a fantasy about penises and koro? What was so strange about this? Didn't Malay people in Malacca, once upon a time, convert to Islam because their king had claimed that the 'royal penis' with its stinky foreskin had been circumcised in a dream?

Wait. The spell seller. The shaman.

If you followed the shaman's advice, what would the ghost do in this situation?

The television screen showed religious men marching in the streets of a filthy neighbourhood outside the capital city. They were cheering and shouting earnestly: 'Chinamen! Return our penises! Return our dicks! Return our pricks!' In the background, you could see a Quranic school.

You laughed until tears rolled down your cheeks. You had no idea how to react to this type of slogan. If you were still the Editor-in-Chief of the *Hujung Manani Tribune*, you would make sure that the next day's headline would read 'Religious men claim their dicks are gone' or 'Religious men have lost their balls'.

However, you immediately asked yourself: if this was indeed an epidemic, what would stop you from being affected? Who could be affected? The regime had not yet released any medical information to the public. The current health minister was useless, anyway.

You thought about the report from the psychiatric expert from Hujung Manani University Hospital. You pulled the file out of the heap of documents and papers that covered your desk. You eagerly read several explanations about psychiatry:

Dr Cakravantin specialized in studying diseases related to culture, such as *latah*, amok, hysteria and koro.

KORO.

'*That's* the connection!' You shouted.

You had found the connection, even though it was still not very clear and did not explain everything. The file gave the psychiatrist's background in great detail.

Dr Cakravantin was fifty-seven years old and from the photo attached to the file, he was wearing braces. He looked like a K-Pop artist.

His father was a cleaner in a Buddhist temple. You skipped several paragraphs, your eyes moving rapidly over the parts that you felt had no relevant information. You stopped suddenly and thought about the Lama who had disappeared. Perhaps there was another connection there.

The temple where Dr Cakravantin's father worked belonged to the Mahayana school of thought. The psychiatrist had obtained his medical diplomas in Bangkok before continuing his studies in Madras and then in Kuala Lumpur. In Malaysia, he studied with a scientist who later migrated to Israel. So, technically speaking, the psychiatrist had been a student of the scientist's and had started studying the risks associated with plastic waste. He finished his specialization in psychiatry in Kuala Lumpur and moved to Hujung Manani to teach at university. When he was still in Malaysia, he treated a member of the royalty from the South; the patient was not very intelligent and had become depressed after separating—or being forced by his family to separate—from a model.

The psychiatrist had also worked in Laos and Cambodia. The report mentioned the fact that while he was in Kuala

Lumpur, his family history had given him cause to feel uneasy, as if he was under surveillance. The information stated that his ancestor was a Thai soldier who had participated in the attack on Kedah (Saiburi) in 1879, captured Sultan Jaafar Muadzam Syah in Merbok, held him in Yan and then killed him in Gurun. Siam occupied Saiburi from 1879 until 1881, and Dr Cakravantin's ancestor had not returned to Thailand afterwards. The doctor's father had been offered work in a Buddhist temple in Hujung Manani when he was young. After marrying a Tibetan woman, he had chosen to settle down in Hujung Manani and change his citizenship.

Tibet again!

If Dr Cakravantin had really been abducted by the Special Branch working for the Dictator, was his disappearance related to the koro epidemic? If so, the Leader must have been informed about the illness spreading in the country, and the psychiatrist's disappearance was perhaps not a criminal act, but a measure taken to fight against the epidemic.

But then, why was the doctor abducted against his will? Was his disappearance connected to the disappearance of the young detective? And what about the historian who studied Malay civilization before the French occupation? Or the Buddhist Lama?

This was all very exciting, at first. But after the first moments of excitement passed, you were very worried. You felt tired. You were not an investigator, even though your journalistic training had been helping you study and piece together many stories.

But this was not a story. It was not fiction, but fact. About penises. Oh God, about penises!

The koro riots out there were real. You glanced at the television. Why would the transgender community be accused of having the power to make a man's penis disappear? That was bizarre. Before this, the LGBT community had been accused of causing natural catastrophes. Every time an earthquake struck or a volcano erupted in Hujung Manani, religious groups would claim that it was the consequence of social and moral diseases such as the existence of the LGBT people. As if transgender women were strange mutants. If the transgender community had such a power, why didn't they steal their enemies' genitals much earlier, before hatred towards them became violent as it had become now?

You knew that the religious community was turning its anger towards people who had nothing to do with the problem.

You scratched your cheek. Actually, Sistine was blowing air softly on your right cheek, stretching her neck, flying to your right, to your left, in front of you, calling your name.

You thought that the True Patriot could and should seize the opportunity of the unrest to create anger against the Leader and with luck, he can then be overthrown. Every crisis offered an opportunity. You really believed it. Your thoughts returned to the shaman and her spell. Could it all be true? Who could deny the existence and results of witchcraft?

You stood up, stretched and walked to the window from which you could see the whole city. There were firemen and a group of people burning tyres. Why wasn't the police doing something? Wasn't this an emergency?

But of course they were afraid to become infected and the Dictator himself was afraid that he had already been infected.

O karmmavasita. O datu. Drdhabhakti. Grant me Viryya.

If you recited the spell while burning some incense, would a ghost really appear and help you solve all the mysteries that were spread out on your desk? If Badang himself consulted spirits, why couldn't you do the same?

What did the shaman say?

Couldn't you try? Why be afraid of the unknown? That's what she had said.

You drew a deep breath in and picked up the piece of paper on which the spell was written in Sanskrit: 'O karmmavasita. O datu. Drdhabhakti. Grant me Viryya'.

Nothing happened. You stood up and went to the bookshelves. If your memory served you right, in a drawer, there was a stick of incense that had been left by your ex-wife, the scientist. Perhaps it could still be used?

She liked to burn incense before making love. She claimed that the smell excited her.

You rummaged in the drawer. You found five sticks. Hopefully they were not too old.

You lit a stick and inhaled deeply. Then you shouted very loudly: 'O karmmavasita. O datu. Drdhabhakti. Grant me Viryya!'

Nothing happened.

The voices from the television went up and down. The smoke from the incense pervaded the entire space. It smelled like tea, strawberries and roses. Perhaps the shaman had forgotten to tell you how to burn the incense while reciting the spell. Perhaps you had to shake it like Buddhists at the temple. Or perhaps you had to bend forward, prostrate, or some other ritual which you had not observed.

The voice on the television was asking people to calm down and stay indoors because the koro epidemic was spreading.

You brought the incense to the living room. You sat for a short while on the Westwood leather sofa and put your feet up on the Hanford ottoman from Chicago. You were restless and got up, bringing the incense to the kitchen this time.

Grumbling, you stuck the stick of incense in a pot containing a short cactus, on the dining table. You decided to relax by taking a warm bath before napping for an hour or two. At dawn, you would meet the True Patriot and suggest to her that the opposition camp should seize the opportunity offered by the koro riots, which were becoming increasingly serious. You were not sure how tense the situation was out there. But your penis had become tense—very stiff, really—several times during the past two hours.

You took off your clothes and turned on the faucets to fill the bathtub with warm water. While waiting, you brushed your teeth, urinated and rubbed the tip of your penis to get rid of the last drops of urine. You cleaned it and since the tub was now half-full, you stepped slowly into the bath. Part of your body felt cold, while the rest was embraced by the wonderful warmth.

You closed your eyes. In your mind, you thought about Mars and insects which could make sounds with their genitalia, while the fragrance of the incense pervaded the entire house.

You decided that what the True Patriot needed to do now to beat the Dictator was to convince the tyrant that he had caught koro. But how to convince all the men of Hujung Manani that the True Patriot, an old woman, held the solution to their problem—namely, the disease that threatened their manhood? You laughed, answering your own question. No problem if a man doesn't have balls, the solution of the problem lies with a woman. And that woman was the True Patriot.

Or the True Patriot could ask the scientist to come back. The old professor was highly respected in the whole world, and all the more so in Hujung Manani. After all, he had been awarded a Nobel Prize—the second Nobel Prize in the country, after the True Patriot.

Your penis hardened for no reason and you felt an extraordinary sensation of pleasure, as if your cock was being sucked. You fidgeted and as you opened your eyes, you saw a red-eyed woman with long hair kneeling in the tub, half her body in the water, her mouth around your rigid penis.

She lifted her ghostly face, smiled and said: 'Hello brother.'

You jerked and almost jumped out of the tub. The pressure on your penis was getting stronger. Your testicles were being squeezed. Then your chest heaved, your nipples hardened and your sperm shot out. Your head became heavy, you felt dizzy and you blacked out.

Your body slid down into the tub. Your head went under the water. Gulp gulp gulp.

GULP. Blub.

You drowned.

A cloud of sperm floated in the bath water.

***

So the story goes like this:

On a very hot day, in the intense heat, Wahidi, a famous preacher in Hujung Manani, woke up from a deep slumber. When he looked in his trousers, his bent penis, which was his three wives' delight, had disappeared. It was nowhere to be found. He realized that his phallus had been replaced by a vagina covered with very fine pubic hair.

Only the night before, Wahidi had criticized transgender women in his monthly *maghrib* sermon. In his religious lecture, he had said, 'If somebody chooses to become a transvestite, he is insulting Allah the Most Wise, Who has created them as man or woman. Each individual has their own role to play, and this is very clearly defined in Islam. But the emergence of a confused sexual identity, which is neither male nor female, is a Western agenda which is constantly trying to destroy Islam.'

After his very lucrative lecture (600 Ringgits for one hour and fifteen minutes), Wahidi had invited a few of the mosque people to a nearby coffee shop, not far from the city. One of these men was Nik Kamal bin Nik Makjuni, who praised Wahidi for his courage in denouncing the threat posed by the LGBT community in front of the audience that had listened to his lecture.

While sipping his warm white coffee, Wahidi said, 'We really don't understand these people's behaviour. They are just trying to tarnish our faith. The women have nice full tits and they want to hide them, wrap them under bandages and wear shirts like men. And the men, they have a hairy dick, and they want to get rid of it to get a pussy without a clitoris.'

At first, Nik Kamal bin Nik Makjuni, Syed Za'im bin Syed Najib al-Yahya, Wan Ahmad Tariq bin Wan Ahmad Busu and Badrullah Marwan bin Osama were shocked by Wahidi's crude and vulgar language. But after a while, they started giggling and everybody guffawed together. Wahidi's words were the hard-hitting lesson that they all needed. It was usual in the country for preachers to use that type of humour.

They also mocked and slandered the True Patriot and her opposition party. Wahidi said, 'That old bitch has lost her mind. She's talking shit and she should not be allowed to come back to power. If she does, all the liberals will be encouraged.'

Wahidi's followers nodded in agreement.

They left the coffee shop at about a quarter to one in the morning. Wahidi had to go to the house of his third wife, Hindun Nurul Wati Binti Haji Galak. They had only been married for four months and Hindun was worried because she was not yet pregnant. The other wives had started mocking her in their WhatsApp group.

Wahidi had promised to have sex with Hindun, and she was waiting for him in a flimsy and very revealing negligee. She had shaved her entire body in preparation.

After sex, Wahidi washed his penis and went to sleep, reminding Hindun to wake him up before dawn. Perhaps they could have another go or two before performing the Subuh prayer together. Hindun, an obedient, religious and faithful wife, set the alarm. She liked making love.

When the alarm clock went off at five the next morning, Wahidi had the energy to make love twice to his wife. While they were praying together, Hindun silently implored God to let her get pregnant, so that she could compete with her husband's other wives and they would stop making fun of her, calling her a barren woman. If possible, she would like to have twins.

After praying, Wahidi went back to sleep. He intended to get up around nine and go play golf with the Minister, whom some people nicknamed the 'Minister who came in through the ceiling', and others, the 'Minister who came in through the back door'. At night, he was supposed to preach in front of businessmen and factory owners about the use of plastic. In the kitchen, Hindun was preparing carbonara pasta with meatballs for breakfast, following Jamie Oliver's recipe. The man was an infidel, but his recipes were out of this world. Wahidi always advised his wives that in this regard, they had to be progressive, by taking good things from the West and rejecting the rest. Always use tabayyun. After kissing Wahidi's cheek and affectionately rubbing his penis (which was still rigid, for some reason), Hindun left her sleeping husband to go to Fazeeda Boutique, downtown. She wanted to buy five of their latest-model veils. If she had to scramble with other customers, she would do it with steadfastness. Her sister who was studying in Malaysia, at the Malaysian University in Perlis, had asked her to buy the controversial Sweet Love veil. Indeed, they should always endeavour to look as pretty as possible.

At about eleven, two hours after he had intended to get up, Wahidi stretched as he opened his eyes. The next thing he did was rub his dick. He was extremely proud of his majestic cock due to its impressive size. Startled, he looked inside his pants— the bent cock which was the object of desire of his three wives had disappeared! It was no longer there! In its place, there was a vagina with very fine pubic hair. Wahidi thought he was having a nightmare. He pinched the lip of the vagina and felt pain, proving to himself that he was really awake.

God is most powerful. *Kun faya kun.*

How could he explain that he was Wahidi, when there were two boobs on his chest? He could not stay around his family because he could not explain this miraculous transformation. How could he tell his children that their father had become a woman, from top to bottom? They would not know whether to call him Dad or Mom. He wanted to ask Syed Za'im bin Syed Najib al-Yahya for help, but could his friend, who led the Islamic movement called the Muslim Community is Utterly Superior (MUCUS), understand that such mysterious things could happen in this modern world? How could he tell anybody at all, that there were many types of fish; but that there were also starfish, which were not fish, and flowerhorns, which were. And so there were human beings, men like him, whom Allah's great power transformed into women, and it could not be explained by science, and even less by religion.

He could not explain the fact that he, Wahidi, a man with three wives, a long beard and a wide chest, had suddenly become a woman with a curvaceous bottom and voluptuous breasts.

This was a total shock. It would definitely stun his wives, his friends and all his followers.

And so this is what happened. Wahidi remembers that it was a very hot day, when he ran out under the blazing sun from his third wife's house. He grabbed one of Hindun's lycra gowns and wrapped his head in an ND Owl Shawl before driving his Alphard to a mosque.

He did not know where to go. He was completely numb. He kept touching his genital area, still not believing what had happened. In the parking lot of the mosque, he burst into tears. He implored God to have mercy on him. While he was feeling so distressed, Hindun returned home and did not suspect anything. It was only after Wahidi had disappeared for several days that Hindun's neighbour told the police investigator that on the last day Wahidi had been seen, a woman wearing a tight Lycra gown and a veil that looked like a Lavish Love Square hijab had rushed out of the house in a frenzy and driven away very fast in an Alphard.

Hindun Nurul Wati Binti Haji Galak had then contacted the first and second wives, Bahiah Burduri Binti Satdin and Bibiana Layolet Binti Abdullah, to talk about it. They quickly came to the conclusion that Ustaz Wahidi was involved with another woman (who was wearing a Lycra gown and an ND veil). They had many theories—perhaps that woman had cast a spell on their husband, or she was a Shiah woman who had gone astray; she was a follower of the ludicrous and absurd Millah Ibrahim cult; she was a liberal who went undercover to seduce their husband. Then other stories developed—she was a spell and amulet seller whose aim was to steal the penis of religious men. Even worse, she was a follower of the True Patriot, who was trying to overthrow the Leader, who was Allah's representative on earth. The aim was to destroy religious men allied to the Leader.

In the parking lot of the mosque, Wahidi, completely devastated and mystified, kept sobbing. A man who had just finished the Zohor prayer knocked on the glass of the Alphard window. At first, Wahidi hesitated to roll down the window. But almost as if it were moving on its own, his right hand pressed down the switch that opened the car window. It was as if his brain was no longer working.

'Why are you crying, *ukhti*?' The young man with a stubble asked in a gentle voice. He sounded sweet, comforting and kind. 'Can I help you?' he added in a soothing voice.

How could Wahidi answer him? Would the young man believe, for example, that he was Wahidi, even though he did not look like him at all? The man would just laugh at him. Perhaps that man had prayed behind him and was part of his community? Even worse, he could be a student in one of his religious lectures. What kind of answer could he give him?

Deep down in his heart, Wahidi knew that he would never return to his original condition, and he also honestly believed that he would never find out the truth. Would the young man believe that he was once a man whose penis made all the other students jealous at University Kubra in Medina, Saudi Arabia? He was not a woman and this was a nightmare, like the one experienced by Alice of *Alice in Wonderland*. The only difference was, there was no Humpty Dumpty. The young man would think that he was crazy. And then what would he do?

Wahidi only had a few seconds to answer those two questions: 'Why are you crying, ukhti?' and 'Can I help you?' His answer could save his life if he knew how to seize the opportunity, or it could destroy him. He answered, 'I just converted to Islam and my parents kicked me out of the house. I don't know where to go.'

As soon as he answered, he burst into tears.

'What's your name, ukhti?'

Wahidi glanced at the collection of CDs placed in the car by
Hindun, his third wife. There was a CD cover with the number
twenty-five on it. His wife always sang along with the songs on
that CD by Adele, if she was not listening to a lecture on the
Quran by Ustaz Zahazan.

So Wahidi answered in a sad voice, 'My name is Adele.'

This is what happened next. Wahidi was brought to the
house of the singer of religious songs, Zikir Baik, whose stage
name was Z Good. Wahidi, who was now calling himself Adele,
was still in disarray. For one week, he became Z Good's sex
slave. Ladies and gentlemen, in order to avoid any confusion, we
shall from now on call him Adele.

O dear God, what was happening?

Well, after Z Good had found her in the parking lot of the
mosque, Adele, not knowing what to do, had agreed to go to his
house in his car. Of course, we cannot blame Adele, who was
still numb and could not think straight. Her mind and reasoning
were still like those of a man. Only her physical appearance had
become like that of a woman. In other words, she was a man
trapped in a woman's body. Masha'Allah, perhaps that was what
happened to Ellen DeGeneres and Irshad Manji. Adele knew
she could not go anywhere. How could she go back to her three
wives' houses? How could she ask her religious friends for help?
Therefore, Z Good's offer to take her back to his house was the
most logical solution to her problem. Anyway, where was the
logic in all this?

Kun faya kun.

Adele had to change to a new narrative from now on. Her
new story was the following:

She was a *mualaf*, a new convert to Islam, and her parents, who were of Chinese and Kadazan descent, had kicked her out of their house for converting and for being active in the Warisan Party in Tenom, Malaysia. She had nowhere to go, so she packed her bags and flew to Hujung Manani. She did not know anyone here. Perhaps after things cooled down, she would look for a job at the plastic factory. She wanted to ask for help from the MWAH office (the Muslim Welfare Association of Hujung Manani) but she was aware that her breasts were too large and the staff would look down on her. Out of options, she had rented a large car and driven on without any specific destination in mind, lost in the capital of Hujung Manani while crying her heart out.

'Don't worry, ukhti, I am a Salafi,' Z Good whispered to Adele as soon as she agreed to follow him. They were in his car, on the way to his house outside the city.

'Do you know what a Salafi is? What about the Salafist Movement?'

Adele wanted to answer because her first instinct was to lecture him to show her knowledge. After all, she had graduated from Kubra University in Medina. But she was no longer Ustaz Wahidi. She was just Adele. Therefore, she answered his question by shaking her head slowly. She was still trying to imagine what was going to happen. She felt dirty, weak, exhausted. She needed protection. She needed the kindness and attention of a man. Perhaps that was what it felt like to be a woman. She understood what it was like to have been created from a man's rib. She needed Z Good's help and compassion.

'The Salafist Movement is a movement that fights against anything which is bad for Islam. In your country, Malaysia, there are many of those; for example, the Shiah, the liberals, the LGBT, the atheists, the infidels, the Pakatan Harapan supporters, and in particular, the DAP members. They want democracy. We reject that kind of democracy. We are lucky here, in Hujung Manani, to have a Leader and his wife who are wise and put Islam first.'

Adele was shocked to hear this erroneous explanation.

'But . . .' she said, wanting to correct him.

'I know that you voted for the Warisan Party in Malaysia before. But don't worry. Allah forgives those who repent,' Z Good answered while staring at her voluptuous breasts which could not be hidden. Z Good's penis hardened when he thought of her tits which looked firm and heavy. He could see her nipples through the fabric. He adjusted his position and pretended to look at the traffic in front of him.

'Are you thirsty?'

Adele nodded.

'There is some cordial over which the "Surah an-Nisa" has been read. I bought it at the mosque. Help yourself,' said Z Good while offering her a drink.

Adele, who was thirsty, drank from the bottle.

'It's delicious.'

'It has been blessed,' Z Good answered with a satisfied smile. In his pants, his boner did not go away. He could imagine his hands rubbing Adele's pinkish nipples. She probably wore a pink bra. He did not know why the colour pink really excited him. He could feel a drop of semen coming out of his dick.

As soon as they arrived at his house, the man, who was a singer of religious songs, showed Adele to a room where she could rest. The room was tidy, with a large clean bed. There was a guitar on a guitar stand in a corner, and a shelf full of CDs of religious songs. On the wall near the window, a clean white Haramain robe was hanging, together with a red and white turban. On the wall near the door, there was a neatly framed poster.

'These are my idols,' Z Good said eagerly.

Adele drew a deep breath and swallowed hard. The poster featured the portraits of Abu Bakar Baghdadi and the Mufti of Hujung Manani, whose followers had nicknamed him the Liverpool Mufti.

'Please take off your clothes.'

Adele was shocked by Z Good's suggestion.

'What I meant to say was that you can change your clothes here.'

Adele suddenly felt disrespected. She started to panic. All of a sudden, she realized that she was in danger, even though she was wearing a veil. The portrait of Abu Bakar Baghdadi kept overlapping that of the Liverpool Mufti; they were waltzing in front of her eyes, making her dizzy. Then she remembered the drink that Z Good had given her in the car. Adele was now very scared. What if Z Good suddenly wanted to have sex with her?

'What have you done to me?' Adele asked weakly. Suddenly, she could no longer feel the floor. It was like drowning to the bottom of the sea.

In a daze, she saw that Z Good was removing his traditional Malay tunic, displaying his muscular and hairy body. Until now, he had only been able to masturbate until the skin of his penis became sore while thinking of veiled models, but this time, his fantasy had suddenly appeared in the flesh, like a dream come true.

'Please don't do anything. I just want to . . .'

Adele could no longer see clearly. She could only hear, from very far away, Anuar Zain singing an old song from 2007, entitled 'Lelaki ini'. The singer's voice was melodious, clear, with a nice vibrato.

One day and one night later, Adele regained consciousness. Her head was heavy. She felt weak, disoriented and stupid, and her temples were throbbing. Her hands were tied to the metal bed and her feet were also handcuffed to the bed frame, so that her legs were wide open. She wanted to vomit. The smell of sperm made her nauseous. Her private parts were in pain. She realized that she had been raped.

Perhaps that was how Reynhard Sinaga's victims felt.

O Allah, so this is what it feels like to be a helpless woman! Adele was ashamed. Her body was totally exposed. She tried in vain to unfasten the ties around her wrists. She saw bruises and bite marks on her chest. Certainly, Z Good had licked, fondled, bit and squeezed her breasts as he liked. She was sore inside her newly acquired vagina. He must have penetrated her countless times, even though she was not wet and ready. Fortunately, she could not remember anything. Being a woman was agony. She wanted to scream for help, but she was unable to make a sound. She looked left and right. The bedroom had not changed. She could see the poster of Abu Bakar Baghdadi and the Liverpool Mufti. *Astaghfirullah!* She had been raped repeatedly in front of them. And she was still naked as a worm.

Adele remembered the religious lectures she had given when she was still Wahidi. She often talked about a husband's rights over his wife. The wife was required to submit to her husband's sexual desires, even if she was riding a camel or frying fritters in the kitchen.

Adele started crying. Truly, she was in agony.

She had never thought about all this before, when she was a man. She kept sobbing, naked and she remembered how she had once violently criticized the rape awareness campaign organized by the liberals in Hujung Manani. Their slogan was 'Rape is rape, no excuses'. She had ridiculed the campaign and dismissed it, arguing that a Muslim man did not need his wife's consent to have sex with her. Of course, he was a man with several wives and he had very strong sexual needs. He believed that once a woman was married and had received her dowry, she could not refuse her husband's demands, unless she was menstruating. He thought that sexual intercourse was an obligation, and that it was sinful for a wife to refuse her husband's requests for sex; as far as he was concerned, rape within marriage was a concept created by the West. Therefore, sex on a camel's back, on a bread oven or in a car were not only permitted but must be granted immediately.

Poor Adele was lying spread-eagle naked on the bed and she felt smelly and mortified. She was nothing more than a weak female—an instantly created woman—who had been duped by a man pretending to be a Salafist and raped countless times after drinking a supposedly blessed beverage which had made her unconscious.

Adele stayed like that, outstretched naked on the bed, for several hours before Z Good came back. She implored him, 'Let me go. You say that you are a Salafist. People like you do not do these things to women. You have used me as a sex slave . . .'

Z Good merely answered, 'I do not think that you are a good woman. Only pure devout women can be taken as wives. Do you remember which party you voted for in the last elections?'

Adele started crying. 'How do you know that I am not a good pious person? You don't know me.'

Z Good laughed as he took off his trousers. 'I know that you are not a chaste woman because you told me that you voted for the Warisan Party. That means that you are a liberal and so I can do whatever I want to you.'

Z Good then removed all his clothes. His penis was erect and stiff. Stretched and tied to the bed as she was, Adele could not do anything, despite trying to wriggle and struggle—the raffia ropes and the handcuffs that restrained her hands and her feet were too tight. Z Good rubbed the tip of his penis against Adele's swollen vulva. She screamed in a hoarse voice. Then her eyes opened wide as Z Good inserted his long and strong penis into her vagina. He thrust several times, before coming all over her stomach.

Adele knew that he would never let her go free. So after being raped once again, she pleaded with him to let her be his sex slave. She accepted her situation and decided she would let him have sex with her any time—even on a camel, or a donkey, a cow, a tractor, anything—just as long as she was not tied up to the bed like that. He could lock the door and the iron grille of the house every time he went out. She just wanted to be untied from the bed. In return, she would be a good housekeeper for him—she would clean, cook, iron his clothes, cut his toenails, sweep the floor, brush the mouldy bathroom tiles, clean the windowpanes, do his laundry and wash his car, wipe the ceiling, and get ready for when he came back home. She knew that Z Good was often thinking about her large and supple breasts. She pretended to be horny, and that having sex with Z Good was so pleasurable, so much better than eating original handmade noodles. She imitated her wives' moans when they were having sex, 'Oh yes, oh yes, oh I like it, I like it so much, oh yes, from behind, please don't stop honey . . .'

At first, Z Good was not convinced, but Adele did not give up. She was patient. Finally, Z Good agreed. She cooperated well with him. For the first time in her life—or rather, in Wahidi's life—she voluntarily sucked a man's dick. The first time she performed oral sex, she remembered her criticisms of 'perverted homosexuals'. Z Good forced Adele to swallow his sperm and she slowly gained his trust. Once, while she was kneeling down in prayer with her forehead to the floor, Z Good suddenly got excited, lifted her praying clothes and sodomized her. She was raped on the prayer mat. Her tears rolled down her cheeks, slowly falling on the mat, exactly on the embroidery of the dome of a mosque. That is how horrible it is to be a woman, Adele thought. There is more pain than pleasure.

Z Good also showed her various illustrations from a sex manual for Malay Muslims entitled *The Lost Traitor*. Adele knew all the positions and techniques from the *Kamasutra*. She was forced to comply. But deep in her heart, she was hoping to be able to escape one day.

Once, while Z Good was not in the house, Adele found something strange in the kitchen. She did not know that the strange substance covered with a batik cloth was triacetone triperoxide.

Adele was a sex slave to the handsome religious singer for an entire week before she was let go.

***

The entire story is about penises and related matters. So it goes like this:

Adele had just finished performing her prayers and she was imploring God to free her from this agony. She felt the pain and anguish of Yazidi women from the Sinjar mountains, who were enslaved by ISIS extremists. For a moment, she thought that the True Patriot should be allowed to return to power. She ought to support the opposition.

But let us go back to Adele's, or Wahidi's, story:

Z Good came back exhausted from recording a programme at LaLa Hijrah TV, where he was interviewed by Aman Idriz, who had asked him to sing his song entitled 'Chah the Pure Woman' live. Afterwards, he had rushed to the Maestro Nonasis television station to attend the programme *Popular Ummah (PU)*.

The previous evening, he had spent the whole night in the studio practising a new song written by Yasin Thuulaiman, entitled 'The Most Beautiful Forgiveness of the Jihad'. In other words, he was not in a very good mood. When he reached home, he found out that Adele had only cooked plain banana fritters. He was hoping to find the 'viral kuih keria', a fritter made from sweet potatoes, under the food cover. He was disappointed with the food. In addition to that, he thought that Adele was taking her sweet time to pray, as if she was avoiding him.

To relieve his frustration, he wanted to have sex. But she refused politely, saying, 'Darling, may I remind you that we are not married?'

'Eh! I thought we had a temporary marriage agreement.'

'But, you're a Salafist. Not a Shiah.'

Adele's sharp retort irked him. He felt insulted to be called Shiah. That was the worst insult for him. He became furious. He removed his belt and whipped Adele with it. Then he jumped on her and stripped her of her white silk praying outfit of the Siti Khadijah brand. Without thinking, he removed Adele's G-string and opened her thighs as wide as he could.

He had the shock of his life and screamed: 'Oh my God! WHAT IS THIS? I am speechless!'

Between the pink labia of Adele's vagina, a tiny penis had appeared. There seemed to be two genital organs, male and female. Perhaps that was what the Islamic Genital Department was looking for when they insisted on checking the genitals of transgender people.

Z Good was shocked. He could not believe his eyes.

'Astagfirullah! I fucked a stinking trans! You're one of those LGBTs, right?'

Z Good clenched his fist and punched Adele on the mouth, splitting the corner of her lips. Her head was throbbing with pain and everything started spinning around her.

Suddenly, she was in his car. He dumped her by the side of the road, near a street that led to the city. She was left alone in the middle of the night, in the pouring rain. She started walking, with nothing more than the clothes that she was wearing.

She was drenched in the downpour. She was wearing a white T-shirt without a bra and a batik sarong, which she had not changed for several days. In her wet clothes that clung to her body, Adele looked very sexy. Don't forget that she had a bruise at the corner of her mouth.

She walked for several kilometres towards the city. She stopped for shelter under a highway overpass. There were several men with their motorbikes, probably workers from a plastic factory, who were also sheltering there from the pouring rain. They stared at Adele. It was difficult to ignore their puzzlement at what a pretty and dishevelled (but still attractive) girl was doing under an overpass like this. Was she human, or a ghost?

Adele was shivering from the cold. Flashes of lightning kept lighting up the sky, followed by thunder. The men sheltering under the overpass were part of a group of mat rempit who were racing on the highway before they had to stop to seek shelter from the rain. They were not factory workers, as she had thought.

Adele realized that she was being touched on her back. She remembered a religious lecture she had given at a mosque, where she had said that women are raped because they do not dress properly; they like to look sexy and men cannot be blamed. Tears rolled down her cheeks. She felt her heart thumping in her chest. *Dub dab dub dab*. Her bum looked round and sexy, with the wet batik material moulding her hips, her buttocks, her thighs and her calves. She covered her breasts with her hands. She was aware that without a bra, her breasts were sticking out and attracting attention. She knew that they could see her nipples.

She started sobbing. She realized that if nobody came to save her, she was going to be raped by the group of men.

At the time, the koro epidemic was spreading. But Adele did not know it.

Now, let us turn our attention to the group of mat rempit that threatened Adele.

The young men had been horny and thinking of sex since the night before. Adele's unexpected arrival was like a dream come true. So they surrounded her and one of them—Mat Yi— pulled her behind a pillar which was a little away from the group. When Mat Yi (who originally came from Pasir Mas) was about to penetrate her, he realized that she had a short penis. Mat Yi became furious because he felt that he had been duped and he started to beat her.

Suddenly, Mat Yi's thighs became stiff, and a strange numbness spread from his stomach to his pubic area. His penis which was engorged a few seconds earlier, was now suddenly very painful. He screamed in pain and held the glans of his penis. But the organ kept shaking and was slowly shrinking and retracting into his body.

One of his friends, concerned, held him to try to calm him down. But he felt the same numbness and they all started to feel the same. One by one, all of Mat Yi's friends experienced the same sensation.

At the same time, two police cars patrolling the area for signs of the koro epidemic arrived on the scene. The rain had stopped.

A miracle, a divine kun faya kun event, had happened. Adele touched her chest. It was suddenly flat. The two fleshy mounds which had caused her so much stress for the past seven days were no longer there. She looked down. She was no longer wrapped in her sarong, which must have been pulled during the struggle. The first thing she saw was a penis.

Her hand wrapped around the shaft of her penis. It is safe now to start using the name Wahidi again. Seeing that his bent penis was back, Wahidi started laughing hysterically. His face was red with joy despite being covered in bruises. God, the vagina was gone and his penis was back! Wahidi laughed like a mad man.

When the police arrived, they were shocked to witness Wahidi, the famous religious preacher, naked and proud of his nakedness, laughing uncontrollably. They had no idea what to do about the group of bikers writhing on the ground and shouting for help, either, claiming that their penises had been stolen by a transgender woman.

So this is how Adele, or rather Wahidi now, was brought to University Hospital and transferred to a quarantine centre, where he was found by his wives. His religious followers, who wanted to prevent their idol from being publicly shamed, fought with the group of mat rempit, who were detained at the same quarantine centre.

That was how the fight happened. But many rumours spread, one among others that Ustaz Wahidi was a victim of koro, that his penis had been stolen by a gang of bikers, and that a shaman had cast a spell on him to make him lose his memory. In short, religious leaders had been shamed by people who used witchcraft. Wahidi had been kidnapped, bewitched and tortured by a group of transgender women in order to spread their liberal agenda.

Wahidi's followers went on a rampage, fuelled by rumours which were all false and fabricated. This is how followers of Ustaz Wahidi ended up attacking transgender women, accusing them of being the source of the koro epidemic.

As for Wahidi, he was detained in the psychiatric ward of Hujung Manani University Hospital because he kept ranting and accusing Z Good, the singer, of raping him and using him as a sex slave. Wahidi's wives were disappointed because after deep reflection, he told them that he would, from now on, support the opposition led by the True Patriot.

Psychiatrists did not believe that for one week, Wahidi's penis had disappeared and was replaced by a vagina. There was no way that they could believe the tale of a penis and a pair of testicles disappearing like that.

They told Wahidi's three wives that their husband was probably suffering from a stress-induced mental illness.

'A man has two testicles, or gonads, each weighing an average of thirty grams, and oval in shape. They contain a thousand fine-coiled tubes called seminiferous tubules, each measuring between two to three feet in length,' the medical expert explained.

Wahidi's wives looked at one another with wide-opened eyes. They thought that they knew all about penises and testicles.

'Those seminiferous tubules produce fifty million spermatozoa in a day. The testicles also secrete the male hormone, namely testosterone, in the Leydig cells. If it was true that Wahidi had lost his testicles, he definitely would not be the man that we can see today.'

The psychiatrist's conclusive report made Wahidi's wives cry. It was true then—their husband had gone mad. He used to be very conservative and now he suddenly believed that the True Patriot was 'the mother of Hujung Manani'.

Wahidi's case was only one of the many cases reported in Hujung Manani.

It had occurred at the beginning of the koro epidemic, which turned into mass hysteria and in turn, caused the koro riots, one of the most frightening events in modern history.

The Tiger

In Hujung Manani, the True Patriot was untouchable. Despite openly criticizing the Dictator, no action was ever taken against her. As the 'Mother of the country's Independence', the ninety-seven-year-old woman represented the power of matriarchy, the only one who could oppose the Leader and his wife. It would have been excessive to send the police to arrest the fragile old lady, however powerful she was, and throw her in jail. Her ancestors were also warriors. The Dictator would never do that to her, as he needed to preserve his image in the eyes of the world.

In an interview for *The New York Times*, the True Patriot was once asked why she had fought for the country's independence and why, after having retired, she had returned to politics to launch an opposition campaign against the Leader, whom she labelled a Dictator. Her answer was very poetic: 'Not all places have a sky like the sky in Hujung Manani. Our sky is a wide-open space, where the moon shines bright and thousands of stars glitter in the night. Here, in Hujung Manani, we are surrounded by mountains that protect us with their thousand mysteries. The voices of the crickets, the owls, the wild dogs and the wolves are scarier than our reality. Hujung Manani is a fantasy land, but also a haunted place, where dragons roam free.

The arena where all the evil gods fought. The first place where the Beatles' song 'Revolution' made it to the top of the charts. Hujung Manani is a mystical country whose magical qualities cannot be denied. Here, mattresses, pillows, blankets, sheets, traces of sperm, underwear and pubic hair can tell tales. Body parts such as penises and anuses can tell stories, and they can even be called to testify in court. In Hujung Manani, the official drink of the opponents of the colonial regime is liquid arsenic. Here, batons, truncheons, water cannons, tear gas and bullets can walk, fly, work and act by themselves to look for people who are praying, children holding a balloon, pregnant women and doctors having sex in their car. One must be wary of animals such as pigs, goats, cows and especially snails, for they can spy on you and report you.'

This type of answer by the True Patriot was freely interpreted and she was immediately considered to be a wise woman full of sage advice. Some even called her a female saint. It created a sensation.

The True Patriot's appearance was also iconic. She always wore a *baju kurung* of a dark shade of yellow. She once joked that she was a queen without a crown. We will discuss later why she described herself as a queen without a crown.

Her hair was white as snow and she did not wear a veil. Her pointy nose made her appear very attractive. She always wore a pearl necklace. In fact, she was willing to compromise just about anything, except her pearls. It was a symbol of beauty for her. She had several pairs of glasses which she changed every day, all in cat-eye style and flirty colours, like Marilyn Monroe.

The True Patriot had been married three times. Her first two husbands had died while they were still young. She divorced the third one. She had a son from her second husband, but he was assassinated. History textbooks mention that her son,

Haji Ben Adik, died heroically while fighting against the French colonialists. But she knew that her son had been murdered by her third husband. The French had lost most of their power at the time. We will talk about this later.

She had married her first husband when she was sixteen. He was a Hazara man from Quetta in the Pakistani province of Balochistan. This was not a coincidence, since the True Patriot herself was the daughter of a Hazara man named Haidar. Her mother, Qurratulain, was a Malay woman from Hujung Manani, related to Piah Berkah. She was an English teacher, while her father sold fabric. The True Patriot did not talk much about her parents, because she had been raised by her maternal grandmother. In fact, she did not remember her father very well since he had died when she was still very young.

Her first husband had had a lot of influence over her. Although it was an arranged marriage, she had truly loved Hassan. One of the most valuable items he had given her was a book entitled *Nahjul Balaghah*, which was one of his wedding gifts. On the first page, Hassan had written: 'Pertiwi, forgive me for marrying you at such a young age, but I am confident that you will accomplish many great things in this life and that I am but one of many stops along your journey.' The marriage did not last long, as Hassan died of illness soon after.

Now the True Patriot no longer had any relatives, apart from her political team, which functioned as a family.

In an interview with *Times* magazine, the True Patriot was asked what her most valuable contribution to the country was. The journalist had expected her to mention the death of her son, which could be construed as her sacrifice to the nation. However, she once again left her political opponents speechless and her supporters in awe, when she answered: 'When I was fighting for the independence of Hujung Manani, the country was only painted white. Even the rainbows that appeared in the sky after a noon shower had seven shades of white, ranging from cream, ivory, baby powder, eggshell, seashell and bone white, to snow white. It was a colourless world. France had deprived Hujung Manani of all beauty. But when my friend became the First Ruler, we started to discover colours. We painted our houses and everything around us became red. There were many shades of red. Then our first leader was killed and I had to replace him. I told the people to paint their houses in more peaceful colours such as green, so that our eyes would not hurt. Slowly, we began to learn about colours. The trees became green again, the houses were painted blue, and all types of purple, orange and indigo flowers grew. Everything became peaceful again. But all this is meaningless if all this beauty is replaced by black. I am not against black. One of my husbands was a black man. But the black that confronts us today is of only one tone, when there are so many shades of black: onyx, ebony, obsidian, raven or jet black.'

The True Patriot's answer raised a thousand questions. However, it also created a fascination which earned her extraordinary attention and people started looking forward to her comments.

Her second husband was named Jesus. They met when they were studying at the Sorbonne University in Paris. Jesus was from the Ivory Coast, another French colony, which was also a cocoa producer. That was long before Hujung Manani became a landfill receiving plastic waste from all over the world.

Their union was blessed with a son whom they named Benedict. Later, he became known as Haji Ben Adik in Hujung Manani. Jesus was a rising author who had moved in the same literary circles as Jean-Paul Sartre. It had started in 1929 when Jesus was studying with Simone de Beauvoir at the Sorbonne. It is no secret that the True Patriot was deeply influenced by *The Second Sex*. She mingled with Roland Barthes, Michel Foucault and Jacques Derrida in the 1970s. Those literary giants often had dinner at her house. She was also a close friend of Ali Shariati's when she was in France.

As a result, the True Patriot's philosophy of life was a fusion of the existential belief that life is meaningless and even absurd, together with the opinion that one must champion social justice, like Shariati. These two principles were intimately bound together, although it was hard for people to understand. However, the mixture of various ideas and ambitions shaped the True Patriot into a good civil leader in later years.

The Dictator had derided the True Patriot's marriage to Dr Jesus, calling it a union between two indigenous peoples. Meanwhile, Malay Islamists and religious figures liked to mock the late Jesus, persistently questioning the religious status of the True Patriot and of her son Haji Ben Adik, 'Are they Christian?'

The True Patriot would answer this type of question by saying, 'My religion is struggle. Religion has never been about roots, or cocoa, rubber, tin; religion has never been about the office or the republic; religion has never ever been ruled by a king; religion has never been about muftis and fatwas, either; religion is about morals and the road to perfection. For this reason, religion is about opposition and the fight for justice. Human life is about *telos* and *logos*.'

The True Patriot was in Hujung Manani, visiting her grandmother—who was a descendant of Piah Berkah, the female leader who had defeated the Malay Sultanate of Hujung Manani—when the French colonial authorities seized her passport to prevent her from moving and placed her under house arrest. Jean-Paul Sartre, Simone de Beauvoir, Roland Barthes, Michel Foucault and Jacques Derrida signed a petition to ask France to release Pertiwi. She became an international figure and received the Nobel Prize for Peace in 1995, sharing the award with Joseph Rotblat.

Her imprisonment separated her from her husband and their son. She became depressed, but the harsh treatment at the hands of the French turned her into a poet. Pertiwi started expressing all her repressed thoughts on paper. She wrote three books of poems which were full of fire and a theatre play entitled *The Grandmother's Comb* which contributed to bringing about Hujung Manani's independence from the French rule.

This was when she met the First Leader, the Dictator's father. To be more exact, the First Leader was the one who got in touch with her, enticed by her extraordinary influence. Rejecting their differences in approaches, they agreed to work together to oppose the French colonial power and fight for Independence.

The French authorities, who were under increasing pressure, had exiled Jesus from France and forced him to return to Abidjan in the Ivory Coast. When he landed at the Félix-Houphouët-Boigny airport, a sharpshooter fired four bullets which struck his eyes, his forehead and his legs, killing him instantly. The assassination once again brought the True Patriot's name to the attention of the world. Her face appeared in many international newspapers.

The True Patriot only met her son again ten years later. Then, for the fifteen years that followed, Benedict became his mother's spokesperson and the unique face of Hujung Manani's independence movement. A black man was fighting colonialism in Southeast Asia. Benedict, or Haji Ben Adik, was a handsome man admired by everyone, his Hazara-Malay-African blood sculpting the beautiful features of his face.

In the course of the fight for independence, the First Leader suggested a strategy that hurt the True Patriot's heart and soul. Since they were but a small country in the Malaysian peninsula, Hujung Manani needed the help of its neighbour, the Federation of Malaysia, which had already gained its independence from the British. Malaysia comprised several states in the peninsula, as well as Sabah and Sarawak in Borneo. It was no secret that Malaysia wanted Hujung Manani to join the federation because of its abundant resources of palm oil, cocoa and tin.

However, the True Patriot wanted their small country to emulate Singapore or, like Brunei, to respectfully reject the offer to join the Malaysian Federation. She believed that stuck between Malaysia, a former British colony, and Indonesia, which was under Dutch colonial rule, Hujung Manani should create its own history. As a French colony, Hujung Manani was different and unique in a variety of ways.

The True Patriot was of the opinion that Hujung Manani should stand on its own because of its difference, without refusing to cooperate with other countries in the region as a newly independent nation. However, the First Leader thought that Hujung Manani should quickly become independent and join the Federation. If it did not work out, the country could emulate Singapore and leave the federation later.

The difference in opinions between the First Leader and the True Patriot was due to the fact that the former, who was the Dictator's father, was a Malay nationalist who wanted to associate himself with religious leaders and garnered the ambition to re-establish a feudalistic government. The First Leader regretted the fact that Hujung Manani was not ruled by a king and his heart bled when the country became a republic after gaining its independence from France. Thus, the First Leader proposed that the descendants of Emperor Sod (the last king of Hujung Manani) should return to sit on the throne. The First Leader was a graduate from a university in England. On the other hand, the True Patriot, with her French education, her friendship with socialist and anti-colonialist figures and her two marriages with men from minority groups, belonged to the Left.

In the end, the True Patriot was tricked by the First Leader into asking for Malaysia's help when communist guerrilla groups appeared in Hujung Manani. For the record, this small country was not conquered by Japan during World War II because of its close ties with Thailand. The Malaysian communist movement was not relevant to Hujung Manani because the movement had appeared in Malaysia with the purpose of mobilizing an armed conflict against the Japanese invasion, and later, against the British.

The First Leader suggested that Hujung Manani should benefit from the rise of the Malay race and the rise of Islam in the world, considering the fact that Hujung Manani was a Malay nation, despite the existence of a large Chinese and Indian population.

For Benedict, this approach to race and religion was unacceptable. The Malays did not have to be automatically Muslim, just like Filipino Malays, and Islam should not be the automatic religion of Malays as it was in Malaysia. He disagreed with the association of race with religion. The First Leader, who believed that the True Patriot's son was an outsider because of his black skin, was looking for a way to eliminate his influence.

The opportunity presented itself when the First Leader used the same magic spell as the one Hang Tuah had used on Tun Tijah to force the True Patriot to marry a member of a Malaysian royal family. The man held the royal title of Ungku. The union between the True Patriot and the Ungku erased the 'black stain' of her marriage to Jesus and made Malay people in Hujung Manani stand behind the independence team led by the First Leader and the True Patriot, despite the enormous differences that separated them.

In order to trick the True Patriot into going through with the strategic wedding, a movie star from the Jalan Ampas studio was invited to deceive her. The First Leader had promised him that he would revive the popularity he had lost after moving from Singapore to Malaysia. He promised to build him a movie studio in Hujung Manani that would be as magnificent as the studios in Hollywood.

The indigenous shaman who prepared the same spell as the one used by Hang Tuah on Tun Tijah warned them that the spell would be broken if the Ungku behaved stupidly in public. What did the shaman mean? Needless to say, the shaman did not indicate what kind of action could be described as stupid.

The marriage to a man who was a thug, a party animal and a hypocrite pretending to be pious and ceremonious in the palace, made the True Patriot uneasy. Yet, for some reason, she found it difficult to get away from him.

The love spell broke and the True Patriot realized that she had been deceived when the Ungku showed his true self. He wanted to impress his wife and so went to a shopping centre owned by the Japanese. There, he told all the shoppers to get 30,000 dollars' worth of groceries from the supermarket. He wanted to show his wife what a generous man he was. He told the shoppers, 'We shall pay for all this. We are blessed to have married a socialist. Therefore, this is our wedding gift to the people who are suffering as a result of inflation and the rising cost of living. We give you forty-five minutes from . . . now!'

That was definitely a moment of stupidity. Shoppers scrambled to grab items from the shop. They went mad, grabbing, pulling, hitting, shoving and racing to fill their carts with as many items as possible. Within forty-five minutes, the supermarket was turned upside down, as if it had been attacked by rioters or zombies. The stupid lure of 30,000 dollars had turned the crowd insane. Chaos magnified when customers rushed to the cash counters. They were pushing and shoving one another; some people fell down and the consequent stampede required thirteen ambulances to ferry the injured people to hospital. To this day, 13 May is remembered as a dark day in the country's history.

The magic spell cast on the True Patriot was instantly broken. All because of that stupid action.

Regretting her carelessness and blaming herself for letting herself be fooled in such a way, the True Patriot asked her son for help to get out of the marriage. Benedict, who had been refusing to talk to his mother because he did not approve of the marriage, made plans to neutralize the First Leader's influence by inviting the nearly extinct Malaysian Left-wing parties to open branches in Hujung Manani. Benedict believed that the global rise of Islam in the 1970s could be rivalled by the rise of Leftist movements based on social justice.

Haji Ben Adik contacted Dr Badang, a friend from their student days in France. Dr Badang was a scientist who received funds to study the cause of male infertility in the South. Unfortunately, Haji Ben Adik was killed before he could put his plan into action. The First Leader jumped on the opportunity to blame France for the assassination. The True Patriot was too grief-stricken to protest, despite knowing that this was all her third husband's doing.

The True Patriot eventually succeeded in freeing herself from the grip of the palace with the help of Dr Badang, who will hereafter be known as the Scientist. Her escape from Malaysia was also facilitated by sympathizers of Gus Dur. Pertiwi hid in an Islamic school in Indonesia before returning to Hujung Manani when the situation had calmed down. Gus Dur healed the True Patriot by reciting many prayers. Upon landing in the capital of Hujung Manani, Pertiwi held a press conference to announce that she was free and would not return to Malaysia. As a sign of protest, she wore men's clothes: a tunic called baju Melayu Telok Belanga with black pants and a golden *samping* around her hips, paired with high-heeled shoes.

At the historical press conference, the True Patriot declared, 'I did not fight for Hujung Manani's independence from French colonialization merely to become a slave to the palace. We are not living in the era of Demang Lebar Daun. From this day forward, I am free like Tijah and I will fight Hang Tuah until the end of days.'

She continued by reciting a passage from the *Six Gurindam*:

'If a king is dishonest
The past is erased

Do not abandon the country
This is the reason kings go unruly'

After only eight months, the brief marriage filled with lies came to an end. Pertiwi became known as 'the queen without a crown'. As a response to this sobriquet, she started to wear yellow.

Afterwards, she remained silent and seven months later, Hujung Manani gained its independence. Elections were held and the First Leader was elected president. During the elections, a referendum was carried out to find out whether the people of Hujung Manani wanted to join Malaysia or become an independent nation. Although she did not run a campaign, the True Patriot's beliefs—and namely, her rejection of feudalism and racial and religious politics as practised in Malaysia—benefited the cause of Leftist parties in Hujung Manani. Moreover, Pertiwi was a fifth-generation descendant of Piah Berkah and Nyemah, who had succeeded in overthrowing the monarchy in the country. Leftist parties grew into a powerful opposition. By supporting the True Patriot and calling her the 'queen without a crown', they had created the myth of an invincible leader and placed the First Leader in an uncomfortable position, in which he could no longer harm her.

The True Patriot chose to stay away from politics and started to write literary works again. She held a strong position and was regarded as one of the leading figures of Hujung Manani's independence movement, together with the First Leader and Benedict.

A short time later, the First Leader died in a mysterious accident. Rumour has it that his car had crashed while trying to avoid a tiger that was crossing the road. General elections were held to elect a second leader, and the Leftist coalition convinced the True Patriot to become a candidate. She won the elections and became the Second Leader.

However, Pertiwi's political enemies did not let her rule peacefully from the very beginning. Lotis, with the Tycoon's help, designed a plan to destroy the True Patriot by releasing a video recording of Pertiwi having sex with a girl during a visit to Sandakan. The girl had pert tits and light chestnut hair. The video clip revealed Pertiwi's lesbian affinities. Later on, the girl appeared in another video with the following statement: 'I am the woman in the sex video, which was recorded without my knowledge. I request the United Nations to investigate the matter.'

The video caused a ruckus. Yet, people did not believe that the woman in the recording was Pertiwi. She was considered too old to sit on an unknown girl's face.

Slowly, Priapus' political influence weakened. Despite being bombarded with all kinds of wild accusations, for instance that she was a scientologist (based on a photo taken when she was having dinner with Tom Cruise), the people regarded Pertiwi as an exemplary woman leader. Pertiwi's authority was so strongly established that it withstood all the slanderous accusations and could not be challenged by Priapus, the Dictator, who merely relied on his father's legacy.

Thus, when the koro crisis broke out, the international media rushed to hear the True Patriot's opinion. Moreover, the Dictator seemed to have disappeared, keeping silent and refusing to issue any statement. When the people needed direction from a leader who chose to remain absent, they listened instead to the voice of a loving mother.

The True Patriot's only answer to the flood of questions from the media about the epidemic which had stolen, cursed or shrunk some men's penises, was the following: 'Ammore Mio L'ammore esiste quanno nuje stamme vicino a Dio.' which means, 'My love, love only exists when we are close to God.'

Her singular statement raised even more questions. What did penises have to do with God? Perhaps it was an example of how absurd Islam could be?

The True Patriot sent a long memo, together with several files containing reports of people who had been missing and were believed to have been kidnapped, to Kadir Mohamed. If that memo were to be published, it would have caused another wave of panic. It read:

There was a mega earthquake ranking 8.9 on the Richter scale, as registered by seismographs. However, in Hujung Manani, we know that the quake was caused by a giant.

The giant lived in the sky among the nimbi and cumuli. In the middle of the city grew a giant bean. The giant bean reached the sky and the giant lived at the top. He came down every six months to steal cows, sheep and sometimes people.

The country was corrupt. One characteristic of a corrupt country is that it spreads fear among the population, so that everyone lives in such terror that they dare not resist.

The giant roamed around for a while and we could hear cows and buffaloes mooing, sheep bleating in their pens, chicken clucking, ducks quacking and geese honking in alarm as they were chased by the giant. Then the giant went back to the giant bean and climbed up to the sky.

How do we fight the giant?

We must chop off the beanstalk before he reaches the top, and he will fall to the ground and die.

There is no harm in trying. I will chop the beanstalk off. The giant will not see me and before he reaches the top, he will realize that a mere woman, just like everyone else, is ready to risk her life.

If I can call on all the people of Hujung Manani to grab anything they can—an axe, a knife, a *parang*, a saw—to chop the beanstalk down, I will.

The giant, realizing the danger he is in, will climb faster, but the top of the beanstalk will fall to the ground at the same time as he reaches the sky.

The beanstalk will be destroyed and the giant will be trapped in the sky, unable to come down. Then we can all rejoice.

How was KM to interpret that long memo? It was no surprise when he locked himself up in his room for several days, smoking cigarette after cigarette, haunted by a ghost, reading the True Patriot's memo repeatedly, which was replete with hidden meanings.

A woman leads by example.

Once, the True Patriot was asked about feminism and she replied: 'Have I ever told you a short story that I wrote a long time ago? It is about our struggles against the French; how difficult it was for me to cross a particular lake. The story goes like this:

Once upon a time, my grandmother gave me a comb. It was the only thing I had to fight for independence. In truth, the comb was quite large. It was no ordinary comb. It was magic and could be used only once before its magic disappeared and it became ordinary.

'What should I do with it?' I asked.

My grandmother said, 'Pertiwi, you are our saviour. It is written in our ancient family book that a saviour will come to free us all from French tyranny and other forms of injustice. You have inherited Nyemah's and Piah's strength, and they were the ones who wrote the book.'

'How do you know?' I asked. I still remember how I swallowed, overwhelmed by hope and the heavy duty that was waiting for me.

'I know because of the red birthmark on your breast, which is mentioned in Piah's book. It is the sign of a True Patriot.'

According to my grandmother, I had to cross a lake—the Hujung Manani lake—in order to gather strength. There, at the other side of lake, a challenge would be waiting for me. If I needed to, I was to use the magic comb. But how, I did not know.

After my grandmother's death, I went on a journey that required me to cross a lake of fire nestled in a crater where a three-headed dragon lived.

He was a Draconian dragon.

I remember how I faced the challenge. I walked for days to reach the shore of the lake. After a long time, I arrived at the top of a cliff, and the lava that filled the lake was glowing in front of my eyes. I went down the stiff slope as if I was an experienced mountain-climber. The legend said that a three-headed dragon lived at the bottom of the lake (a real dragon, mind you, not the one in Chinese calendars that brings *ong*). It rarely showed itself, but every few years, when the colonial powers felt threatened, they would order the dragon to show its heads, or its tail, or its wings, or its legs, or its penis, or any part of its body, in order to scare the population of Hujung Manani. The terrified people would beg the colonizers for mercy, imploring them not to let the dragon eat them.

I built a raft to cross the lake. I cut down several types of trees—teak, maple, cengal, bamboo and rubber—I tied them together with cow skins, wool from sheep, and ropes, and I covered it with zinc, fabric, canvas and several types of skins. I had to wait for the full moon to rise before attempting to cross the lake because the lava only changed into water during the few days when the moon was full. However, the threat posed by the Draconian dragon remained the same at all times. It could be watching me and could strike at any time. Draconian dragons only existed in Hujung Manani and Brunei; they were extinct everywhere else. There were, of course, other smaller types of dragons kept in other places, with different names and characteristics, but for the same purpose.

In Hujung Manani's history books, this particular dragon was originally used to keep peace at the border, but when power fell into the wrong hands, it was used to terrorize the ruler's opponents.

I did not know what the Draconian dragon at the lake looked like, but I had been told that one single flick of its tongue could kill between two, thirty or several hundred people, depending on how angry it was. The dragon stuck its three heads out at once. The first head would strike first, killing a few people, usually poets and artists. The second head would then strike and kill hundreds of innocent victims from among teachers, politicians, religious scholars and students. The third head struck silently.

I still remember the long and stressful night.

The full moon rose and shone beautifully over the landscape. I rowed the raft to the centre of the lake. The water was cool, no longer boiling hot. Do you find it strange? Well, I already told you, Hujung Manani is a strange place. It is a world that does not exist although it is real, and exists although it is imaginary.

I only had thirty-five hours to cross the wide expanse of the lake, with the added condition that I must never stop rowing or the water would turn back into lava. The water was cool and crystal-clear under the raft and it was hard to believe that fire could cover the surface of the lake—that lava normally filled the crater. It was incredible because I could see what was at the bottom of the lake with my own eyes.

I could see soft corals undulating in the water—green, yellow, blue, red, orange, brown and white. I saw a school of small fish swimming peacefully, rays dancing together, and I even glimpsed a *pla phayoon* (in Thai; we call them *dugong* in

Malay, and the English call them 'sea cows'), big-eyed tuna fish, barracudas, as well as many different types of seaweeds swaying stunningly in front of my very eyes. I felt as if I was in Trang in Southern Thailand. I kept rowing. The surface of the lake was calm, as if the horrible dragon did not exist.

After rowing for more than thirty hours, I could see the other shore of the lake in front of me. Amazingly, I was not very tired although I had been rowing for hours. I am a woman with the strength of a man.

The lake was calm and the moon was full. The ripples I created with my oars made a beautiful sound. I was sure that I would reach the shore without any problems.

I was so sure of it . . .

All of a sudden, the water started churning slowly, and at first I thought that it was only the sound of my hurried rowing. However, I started to suspect that something was wrong.

I did not know what to do.

I saw the Draconian dragon raise its first head. It had eyes as red as balls of fire. With its flat nose and scarred face, it looked ugly and repulsive. There was pus flowing from the wounds on its head and its saliva was hot and putrid. I had never seen a more frightening, filthy, disgusting and menacing face before. The heat of its breath was searing the nape of my neck.

I froze, not knowing what to do. I was petrified and confused. Lucky for me, I did not suffer a bout of hysteria. I felt like a child in Steven Spielberg's *Jurassic Park*, coming face to face with a T-Rex. If I moved even a little bit, or if I exhaled, I would be in danger.

Splasshhhh

The dragon's tail flipped the raft over. I was thrown into the water and gulp, gulp, gulp . . . I thought I would drown at the bottom of the lake. I only realized what had happened when I saw the huge tail striking the water again. The swirling and churning of the water was about to swallow me.

A gigantic wave pushed me and carried me as if I weighed nothing. White foam formed on the splashing water. Suddenly, the whirling water became stronger. My body was pulled downwards but I struggled, kicking my feet in protest. I refused to be dragged to the bottom of the lake. I could hear the dragon's terrifying hiss. *Hhhhisssss . . .*

I gathered all my strength and swam, swam, swam as strongly as I could. My instinct told me that I would not die that day. Not at the bottom of that lake. I would not let an evil smelly dragon whip me with its tail or lick me. I struggled against death and refused to give up, and I swam.

Without a thought for anything else, I focused my sight on a goal: the shore of the lake. I refused to give up. The dragon was still twirling in anger in the middle of the lake because I had dared to cross the lake where it lived, without asking for its permission.

The Draconian dragon flapped its wings and whipped its tail in the lake. It was a formidable and frightening sight. *Hissssss . . .* It was moving aimlessly in the water. I suddenly realized that the Draconian dragon was blind, and if I could swim to the shore faster, I would be able to escape.

The dragon was indeed blind. However, blindness is not always a good thing. In this case, I needed all my intelligence and cleverness in order to escape. The dragon's blindness was an advantage but on the other hand, the monster could just strike anything and anyone without any remorse.

I managed to reach the shore safely and after a few steps, I was exhausted. I collapsed on the beach and fell asleep. I only woke up on the following day when the rising sun shone its bright rays on my face.

And this is how I fought against French colonial power. And I will do it again if I have to. I still have the magic comb given to me by my grandmother. As a result, I am very confident.

It was very confusing to wonder what the connection between that long answer, full of fantasy and imagination, and feminism was. However, everyone was used to this type of answer from her.

To answer another question, namely, what was required of a leader to manage the country properly, the True Patriot answered by making statements that would be hated by people such as Kadir Mohamed's ex-wife, the scientist who had discovered the insect with genital combs that sang. The True Patriot said:

'My grandmother taught me worldly knowledge, such as literature. I memorized thousands of verses by Shakespeare and Walt Whitman, as well as all the poems by Arthur Rimbaud, from "Première Soirée" to "Les Illuminations", which I know by heart. My absolute favourites are the poems from the collection entitled *Une Saison en Enfer*, (*A Season in Hell*) in English, as well as Les Remembrances du Vieillard Idiot.

'This does not mean that I ignore our poetry. I know the *Six Gurindam* by heart. I particularly like the verses which are political in nature:

"If merchants are ruled by cupidity
They will ruin the country

If on the throne an earnest king sits
Treacherous traders want to take what's his

If traders obey commands
They bend to a hidden government

If traders have money aplenty
They care not for the country

If they are allowed their treachery
Evil merchants will sell out the country"

'I also acquired scientific knowledge, such as mathematics. Every day, I learned the discipline of trigonometry, which was introduced by Muhammad Ibnu Musa al Khwarizmi (750–850 AD). I also learned the discipline introduced by Thabit Ibn Qurrah (835–900 AD), in particular how to solve cubic equations such as $x^3 + a^2b + cx^2$ through geometry, by finding the intersection point between the parabola and the hyperbola, while knowledge of the Pythagoras Theorem gave me headaches.

'I then studied physics. My grandmother insisted on teaching me that movement is a vector, for instance, or the question of reflection of aplanatic surfaces, and she told me that this science had been introduced by Ibn al-Haytham (965–1039 AD), but that later, a man named Snell van Royen claimed that he had demonstrated the Law of Refraction. I also studied astronomy and I really like the knowledge introduced by Abu al-Abbas Ibn Muhammad Ibn Kathir. I was fascinated to learn how to calculate the volume of the moon in reference to the volume of the earth, as well as other bits of knowledge that made me want to faint every time I heard such terms as terrestrial distance, apsides of the Sun, and eclipse ecliptic. I was excited to know that Al-Biruni had claimed that the earth revolved on its axis 600 years before Galileo.

'I also learned another discipline that introduced me to sulphuric acid, nitric acid, hydrochloric acid, aqua regia, sulphates, nitrates and of course, arsenic.

'I learned that 900 years before Lavoisier established the Law of Conservation of Mass, Abu al-Qasim Salamah Ibn Ahmad al Majriti had already written about it in *Rutbah al-Hakim*. This does not even include the medical knowledge that made me feel overwhelmed when I read such books as *Al-Hawi, Sirr al-Asrar*, and the thirty volumes of *Al-Tasrif li man 'Ajaza 'an al-Ta'lif*, which made me an expert in pharmacology.

'After studying literature and science for two years, I was taught economics. In other words, under my grandmother's tutelage, I was immersed in knowledge. I was saturated with it.

'After I studied economics, I had gained a better understanding of the main principles of capitalism such as the freedom to own property, economic freedom and competition, including believing that unbridled competition creates a divide between workers and employers. I was also interested in the main principles of socialist economics, namely collective ownership of the means of production, economic equality and how labour laws are oppressive. I realized how the plastic waste industry had been exploited by the Tycoon.

'Finally, my favourite subject of all was politics. I learned the meaning of democracy and the difference between direct and indirect democracy. I preferred direct democracy and became wary of dictators like Sulla, and I observed how totalitarian regimes use laws to justify all their evil deeds. I also read books about imperialism, how a certain group could be dominated by other people or other groups of people. I studied the ideas of many important figures, from Immanuel Kant to Martin Luther, Karl Marx or Charles Louis de Montesquieu. There were also strange new -isms, such as nimbyism, derived from the expression 'not in my backyard', an ideology that opposes development because of the environment, injustice, etc. In Hujung Manani, nimbyism is beginning to take root, in the form of opposition to an economy based on plastic instead of cocoa. I was also interested in political studies, especially when we started learning about Trotskyism. Eventually, it became clear to me how corrupt Hujung Manani's political system had become under foreign powers. I understood how corrupt the French system in Hujung Manani was, and why bribery could grow, or why money politics could develop.'

This is how the True Patriot's character made her immune.

But how would Hujung Manani face the koro crisis?

The magic comb. Perhaps Hujung Manani needed the True Patriot's magic comb.

The unrest due to the koro epidemic became worse. The True Patriot received exclusive information from insiders that some cabinet ministers had been infected by the disease. She believed, indeed, that the mufti of Hujung Manani, otherwise known as the 'Liverpool Mufti', was suffering from koro and that he was infected after he gave a sermon commanding the population of Hujung Manani to keep supporting the Leader, as he was God's representative on earth.

According to the True Patriot's secret informants, all the cabinet ministers who had been infected by koro had the same predilection—sex!

Like many other people, the True Patriot wondered what caused the victims of koro to be affected by this strange affliction, and what made those who were not affected, immune to the evil curse.

Was it really a curse or witchcraft? Could the magic comb defeat this type of evil spell?

While the entire population of Hujung Manani was panicking, bewildered and confused, and wild rumours were spreading in the rest of the world, bringing disgrace upon the country, the True Patriot believed that they had to find the cause—or causes—of koro.

It was not that the True Patriot did not have the same idea as Kadir Mohamed, namely to seize the opportunity created by the unrest to overthrow the Dictator. Of course, the True Patriot agreed with him that Hujung Manani should be improved as soon as possible, but the main issue that her team was facing was how to convince the population of Hujung Manani—and in particular, the men—that the opposition block and herself had sufficient knowledge about koro as well as its cure.

The problem was that before preparing the cure, they needed to identify the source of the problem. But what was the source of koro?

Perhaps she had to consult the Scientist.

The True Patriot knew that one of the men suffering from koro was a religious celebrity who had three wives. The fact of having three wives could be equated with sex addiction. Why were men who were very active sexually more susceptible to suffer from koro?

Was sex itself the problem? Or was the issue something else?

In order to answer this question, the True Patriot wished to gather as many narratives, cases and incidents as possible, of men who believed that their penises had been stolen. Although experts claimed that women could also suffer from koro, resulting from the feeling that their breasts had shrunk or disappeared, cases involving women had not yet been reported in Hujung Manani. Therefore, only men were involved at the moment.

One of the reports that caught the True Patriot's attention concerned a group of religious teachers who had caused a panic because they had been infected by koro. The report stated that eleven pupils from a madrasa located in the interior of Hujung Manani, near the Malaysian border, had left the school to go to a nearby town. Every two weeks, the boys had permission to go to the town to buy necessary items such as laundry detergent, shampoo, pencils or anything else they needed.

They were accompanied by three teachers, who were to ensure that they did not waste any time or loiter unnecessarily. Discipline in this type of religious school is quite tight. They had taken a public bus to go into town. At a stop along the way, a middle-aged Chinese man had boarded the bus. Another person on the bus had talked to the Chinese man in the Hokkien language, apparently asking him why he was taking the bus and why he was troubling other people. The two men seemed to know each other and they spoke loudly, like people from mainland China. Uncomfortable with the situation, the bus driver had asked them to calm down and stop arguing, or they would be thrown out of the bus if they continued fighting. The Chinese man became furious and they both started arguing, causing everyone on the bus to become alarmed.

Then the man who had confronted him started shouting in Malay so that everyone could understand him: 'He is the owner of the pig farm that was closed down. He should be in quarantine! He should not be going around infecting other people with pig flu. His wife is from Wuhan!'

The Chinese man immediately started to defend himself, saying, 'I don't have pig flu. I don't have any disease. I don't eat snakes or any other exotic animals.'

'No pig, no pig,' he kept repeating. 'Not Wuhan,' he also said.

Caught in the midst of the commotion, the madrasa pupils only stared at the exchange without intervening. The man who had threatened the pig farmer punched him without warning. The farmer fell on his face and started sobbing, while mumbling a sort of spell.

When he stopped mumbling, his aggressor began to panic while holding his crotch. He shouted that the other man had done something to him because his penis was gone.

The bus driver immediately stopped the vehicle and lost his patience. The three religious teachers consulted one another before one of them said: 'This is why we do not have any contact with Chinese people. They are najis, they eat essential najis, and they like to soil public places with their najis.'

The ustaz started shivering as soon as he finished talking. A strange feeling spread upwards from his toes to his groin, gripping his testicles before greedily biting the glans of his phallus, and he felt a mixture of pain and numbness in his groin.

He started to panic, screamed, and without warning, the other two teachers were also infected with koro.

Because somebody had to act rationally in that situation, the bus driver, who had not been affected by koro, made a decision. He started the engine and drove to the hospital located in the nearby town. He stopped the bus directly in front of the emergency department.

The five men were still screaming and crying incessantly when the paramedics put them on wheelchairs and pushed them into the examination rooms.

Something very interesting happened then, according to the True Patriot's observation. The bus driver and the eleven pupils were not infected. Just in case, paramedics examined their genitals and their anuses to make sure that they were perfectly healthy and free of koro.

One of the doctors in attendance, who was a forensic expert, correctly identified that one of the pupils had abnormal lesions in his anal area, and after being coaxed to tell the truth, the boy admitted that he was 'sodomized often'.

'By whom?'

The boy answered, 'by the ustaz', and therefore all eleven boys were examined, which led to the conclusion that they were indeed free of koro, but that they had been victims of sodomy for quite a long period of time.

The three religious teachers, who were numb and dejected, were immediately examined by medical officers. There were blisters underneath the shaft of their penis (which kept shrinking), and it clearly showed that they had been having anal sex.

The doctors in the emergency department were certain that they had uncovered a crime involving religious teachers.

They detained all of them, except the bus driver, who was allowed to leave to resume working. The authorities declared a curfew because riots caused by koro in many places were out of control. The koro riots became violent and in several places, in particular in urban areas, rioters were targeting transgender and liberal people.

The True Patriot believed that the report was an important clue. She did not know what it meant yet, but in her opinion, it was very significant in order to understand the koro epidemic.

She told her private secretary: 'This crisis is not about saving men's penises. These riots are about the people.'

The secretary scratched his head. How could dicks and people be related?

The True Patriot gathered all the members of her team at her residence. They all came, except KM, who could not be reached since the day before. Twenty-seven people belonging to the opposition—her family—met to hear her statement, which her private secretary titled 'Not penises but people'.

She hoped that the feminist and elegant title would encourage the population of Hujung Manani to rise against the Dictator, who, strangely enough, had not yet issued any statements either to calm the spreading unrest or to inform people about the koro epidemic.

In other words, the country was at a standstill and the True Patriot was expected to offer her opinion, which had always been highly regarded in the past.

When the members of her team met at her house, it became clear that the Dictator had lost his power and was not responding to the crisis caused by the koro epidemic. Everyone expected the True Patriot to come up with a solution or a remedy.

Her message was important.

The members of her team were asked to figure out how to send that message so that it would be understood by everybody.

Her press secretary proposed that a video recording be made and sent to international media, hoping that the local media would follow suit.

However, the True Patriot's message did not mention anything about penises, did not give any solutions, and did not make any promises. It contained one more fairy tale to calm the people.

A fairy tale that had just been written so that the population of Hujung Manani would stop and look at the past, which was full of values and teachings that could be used as a guide.

The True Patriot's strange message went like this:

Once upon a time, there was a poor man in China who was called Poor Chinaman. Poor Chinaman had two cute kids called Luk Sun and Hu Moh. Tragedy struck and the children's mother died after suffering from cancer and depression for years. The death caused great sorrow to the family, which was living in extreme poverty.

Poor Chinaman was sad and lonely, like other widowers, and he did what other widowers often do: he took another wife. The pretty bride, a spinster, was a retired Chinese opera performer. She had a stocky body and wore size fifteen shoes. She liked to hurl insults at people and when she was in a bad mood, she shouted obscenities at the people she disliked. She called them pigs, bastards and baboons. Because of her involvement in opera, she thought of herself as a star.

The woman had no love at all for her step-children. You would be right to think that she treated them like dogs, and their condition was like Cinderella—scolded all day long.

Luk Sun and Hu Moh were not given any food, while the evil woman's dog was treated like royalty. The Great Dane was white with a little bit of black fur on its ears and neck, and he was gentle with the children. They used to call the dog 'Pig'.

All the delicious food was reserved for Pig, who ate cakes, curry puffs, coconut pastries and tartlets, while the children starved.

The obnoxious woman abused the children but she was clever at hiding her despicable behaviour. Their house was hidden from view and far away from other neighbours', so the abuse was allowed to continue without anyone noticing. Poor Chinaman worked hard for a living and did not know that his children were being abused every time he was not at home.

One day, Luk Sun and Hu Moh were so hungry that they stole food from the woman's dog. They fought over the leftover biryani rice and honey chicken. They were rolling on the floor when suddenly, Poor Chinaman returned home and was shocked to see his children fighting. He was so shocked that it was only after he reached the market that he realized that he was not wearing any underwear. Upon seeing his children fighting with the dog over a piece of chicken, he had called his wife but the woman was clever. She blamed Luk Sun and Hu Moh for being slobs who liked to loaf around, rolling on the floor with animals. The wicked stepmother added, 'It is not that I don't feed them. But these kids don't know how to be grateful and they always misbehave like this. I don't know what to do with them anymore, darling.'

Poor Chinaman was shocked to hear his wife's words and without checking whether they were true or not, he hit the poor children with his belt, adding to their misery. Luk Sun and Hu Moh screamed and tried to tell him the truth, but their voices were muffled by their sobbing. The father was blind to their terrible condition as he was under his evil wife's spell. Luk Sun and Hu Moh started to hate him. What was the use of a father who not only did not protect them but added to their suffering?

Luk Sun and Hu Moh could no longer stand their father's refusal to see the truth and his unfair treatment of them. That same night, they ran away from home. They wore trackpants and each stole one of their pretty but evil stepmother's T-shirts: Luk Sun picked a Reebok T-shirt while Hu Moh took an Adidas T-shirt. Then they ran to the beach where a jong called *Equanimity* was anchored.

Aboard the jong, the two cute children hid in the cargo hold near the food provisions, without being noticed by the crew. Therefore, they had no problems finding food when they were hungry. They had easy access to Maggi instant noodles, sardines, jam, Gardenia bread and Peel Fresh orange juice. After sailing for months, the jong stopped in a country that looked beautiful. Luk Sun and Hu Moh left the ship and swam to the shore, and started walking in the direction of a mountain. It took them several days to reach the top of the mountain. There, they saw a brilliant light and they continued walking towards the source of the light, where they found a sleeping dragon, curled around a luminous green magic stone.

They planned to steal the magic stone, thinking it would make them rich. On their way down the mountain, they collected valuable plants, such as tongkat Ali, kacip Fatimah, knotgrass, pecah kelambu leaves, gadung and mengkunyit roots, and mengkula bark, and then sold them at the market located at the foot of the mountain—which was situated in Hujung Manani. They used the money to pay for their return fare to China. Back in their country, they both worked very hard, forging sharp metal and copper tools to kill the dragon. They gathered weapons for years until they reached adulthood and had both got married to women of their choosing. On the night of their wedding, the two couples sailed to the land of the mountain with a shiny top to steal the dragon's magic stone. They climbed the mountain eagerly, fought and killed the dragon, and stole the stone.

The fight with the dragon to seize the stone took quite a while, and if television had existed at the time, it would have been broadcast live as it was awesome. The magic stone would give its owner infinite wealth and both couples would be able to open many types of shops and settle down comfortably near the mountain.

They worked hard, gathering roots used in traditional medicine and selling them to scientists. Herbs such as rancang besi, derhaka mentua, tunjuk langit, jaga roots, kucing galak and temusu roots which are mixed with tongkat ali to make a strong concoction. Their trade developed quickly. The fact that they worked hard is one of the reasons why Chinese people in Hujung Manani are so successful, becoming millionaires and living far better lives than Malay people, who are clueless about living in a way other than hand-to-mouth.

As soon as the message was delivered, members of the opposition tried to interpret the whimsical abstract codes contained in the True Patriot's tale.

A policeman came and whispered something in her ear. Immediately, the Mother of Independence frowned. Tears appeared in her eyes, but she remained stoic and did not let them roll down her cheeks. She asked the man something in a low voice and he answered even more quietly. One could only see his lips moving as he was saying something extraordinarily important.

The frown on the True Patriot's face disappeared after only a few seconds. She quickly assumed her usual expression—the impervious face of a queen without a crown.

A few minutes later, the entire opposition camp heard the sad news that KM had died at his house. He had apparently fallen asleep in his bathtub and drowned. There was no trace of struggle. No evidence of murder. Perhaps KM had been tired. Indeed, his computer and his television were on when his son stopped by for his regular visit. The house even smelled of incense.

The questions that the True Patriot had whispered to the policeman were the following: 'How was KM's penis? Were there any traces of shrinking or disappearing? Did he die because of a panic attack caused by koro?'

The man answered: 'Madam, his penis was intact. Its size was the same. In fact, it was erect.'

'Help his wife and children to make proper funeral arrangements. If his penis was still intact, it means that he was a good man.'

The press secretary approached the True Patriot. 'Your message is going to reach the entire world in a few minutes. But we expect that Hujung Manani will not participate in the press conference. We were told by the General's daughter that there is a live Pak Lokan performance tonight.'

A large smile spread on the True Patriot's face. If Hujung Manani's official media could only broadcast a Pak Lokan performance in the middle of a crisis caused by an epidemic, she had good reason to smile. It meant that the Dictator's position was precarious.

'Where is the Tycoon, the plastic boss leading the cartel behind the Dictator and his wife?'

'Our information is that the financier is ill.'

***

The statement issued by the True Patriot made Datin Lotis very angry. How dare she?!

In the name of the Ziji stone, she had done everything she could to become the First Lady of Hujung Manani. She was not going to let that bitch stop her now. To fulfil her ambitions, she had even killed her own father-in-law, but the damn woman had taken away her chance at enjoying life as the Second Leader's wife.

Fortunately, the bitch had chosen to remain in power only briefly and her husband had succeeded in becoming the Third Leader after catering to the religious types, who were increasing in number in Hujung Manani as a result of the rise of religious and racial conservatism in neighbouring countries, namely Malaysia and Indonesia.

Sharing borders with Malaysia (in the South), Indonesia (near Riau) and Singapore (near Punggol), Hujung Manani could not avoid being impacted by the political, social and cultural trends affecting its neighbours. What differentiated

Hujung Manani from its neighbours, though, was the fact that it had been colonized by France, who had seized the opportunity created by the Malay sultanate's unjust rule to overthrow the monarchy.

Decades before, Datin Lotis had met Priapus for the first time at a fundraising dinner to save tigers. Lotis was in her second year of veterinary studies at the University of Hujung Manani. She never finished her studies to become a vet, because on that night, Priapus was attracted to her firm buttocks and somehow, he thought that her crossed eyes added to her beauty. It was no secret that Lotis had seduced the Leader's son on purpose.

Priapus had stared at Lotis' rear end and swallowed his saliva. 'Your butt is tight.' He had wanted to take her right there and then.

Lotis had giggled and replied: 'What? My butt is right?'

'I want you.'

'Eh, you're naughty, I'm not that kind of girl.'

As soon as Priapus had fallen in love with her, she was determined not to let him get away. Lotis' nails were long and sharp and she dug them into Priapus' flesh. The man was a womanizer.

Tigers. One of the questions asked by the *Washington Post* was why Lotis had chosen to become the patron for an organization protecting tigers. Weren't there many other animals that deserved protection? For example, why not work for the protection of the slow loris, or the pangolin, which was considered exotic food in Asia?

The Leader's Wife had laughed and answered with grace: 'Do you know the Malay proverb that says if a tiger is feared because of its teeth, what do people fear when it has lost its teeth?'

Of course, the journalist for the *Washington Post* did not have an answer. Lotis continued, 'It means that a man who is in power is feared, but when he loses his power, all those he had oppressed, rise and fight against him.'

True, for a few years at the beginning of the Leader's government's rule, he and his wife sold that they were 'in favour of oppressed groups'. Lotis had suggested to her husband that they should use the common people's rhetoric to compete against the True Patriot's popularity.

Lotis had also suggested that they should get closer to religious scholars, since Hujung Manani was experiencing an Islamic revival, a reflection of the global trend. Priapus agreed with his wife, because they both came from the same town in Hujung Manani, namely Tahir. People from that town are usually regarded as rebels and agitators.

The True Patriot, however, was in her own league. The blood of warriors flowed in her veins. Lotis remembered how the damn woman had reacted to their political package.

She had recited an old pantun:

'Since a mite married a tick
Many geese now carry spurs

Since tigers have become religious scholars
Many deer now come to recite the *Qur'an*.'

Priapus' first reaction had been anger, but Lotis had calmed him down. In politics, one must never rush in order to stay long. Lotis answered the slander with a question: 'How can there be a pantun poking ridicule at religious figures? Even worse, comparing religious scholars with tigers?'

The True Patriot would not let Priapus have fun with religious scholars, while at the same time partying with investors such as the Tycoon. So she fired another pantun:

'Men at war fall flat on their face
They build a fort on their left

In the jungle tigers roam free
Weeds extinguish fire.'

Lotis knew it was a direct provocation. She understood the meaning of the pantun perfectly—it compared her to a tiger who pounced on its prey at will.

When the True Patriot was asked to explain what she meant, she contented herself with answering: 'Ah, as a lover of tigers, I just recalled a movement in silat gayong which imitates a tiger jumping in order to avoid an enemy, for example by diving into water.'

Of the many political episodes that the Leader's Wife had to face with her husband, this was perhaps the most vexing. She could not let him be disparaged. Since his absence was sorely felt, she organized a Pak Lokan performance and ordered the official media to immediately stop reporting on the loss of control over the situation created by the koro epidemic. Unfortunately, she could not get in touch with the Tycoon and had no idea where he was.

The Dictator's wife thought of nothing but the Pak Lokan performance. She also had to control the police and the army, overcome the reluctance of the cabinet ministers, and control whoever tried to take advantage of the current chaotic situation.

It was not the first time that she was organizing such a performance. The art form, made famous by Long Senik Mulut Merah in the Kelantan Palace, had been on the verge of extinction when it was revived in Hujung Manani, despite having disappeared from Kelantan.

It was reported that Datin Lotis became very interested in Pak Lokan performances when a Russian beauty queen narrated her artistic experience of watching a dance inspired by the clapping of a Pak Lokan in Moscow. That performance had been staged for a royal wedding ceremony.

At first glance, a Pak Lokan performance is a type of dance inspired by various animals such as whistling cockles, clapping clams, quails splashed with rubber, and small pigeons caught on a hook. However, Datin Lotis fell in love with the art form for three reasons.

First, historically, the first performance had been held in front of King Mohong Dom Priya and witnessed in secret by the palace cook. While watching the strange dance, the cook had inadvertently cut his finger and blood had dripped into the vegetable dish he was preparing for the king. As the monarch watched the performance while eating the dish, he felt a surge of energy and power. Thereafter, every time he wanted to demonstrate his power, the king ordered a Pak Lokan performance to be held, which he watched while eating food that contained a few drops of blood. And every time, the people were easily fooled into believing everything they were told. Or perhaps they were frozen by fear. Throughout Hujung Manani's history, many people rejected the monarchy. They had even spoken against the king. But the idealization of feudalism by conservatives in Hujung Manani as a result of a romantic view of Malay history, was a growing trend, and Lotis wanted to capitalize on the art form performed for royalty.

Second, Pak Lokan performances were imbued with magic and witchcraft, and were often used as a medium of healing. In fact, the main performer or Pak Lokan, had to be a shaman. For this performance, they had invited Tok Daim Tempoyak, who was a powerful healer versed in the practice of bageh, which is the recitation of spells and incantations with background music to cure patients. Some time ago, Tok Daim Tempoyak had treated a minister who could not forget his Uzbek mistress. The minister's wife had complained to Datin Lotis. Despite seeing several shamans, the minister still could not see his wife—all he could think about was his mistress.

During the performance, Tok Daim Tempoyak, who was also known as the Tok Bageh, started to tremble uncontrollably; he shook his arms as if he was flapping his wings, shook his head forward and backward, left and right, and became possessed. He mumbled an incantation and with his eyes open wide, he exhaled. Suddenly, without warning, the minister who was obsessed with his Uzbek mistress walked up onto the stage and vomited.

Tok Daim Tempoyak asked in a deep voice, 'What do you want?'

'I want to be healed.' The minister's voice was shaky as he wiped vomit from the corners of his mouth. The Tok Bageh cursed him in an unknown language and the minister collapsed and passed out. When he came to a few minutes later, he looked better. The first word he uttered was 'Samarkand', proving that he no longer thought only about the sexy woman from Uzbekistan.

Third and last—the first time Datin Lotis watched a Pak Lokan performance, she felt attracted when the Tok Bageh imitated a tiger exhaling. According to her, it was special and funny at the same time. After the performance, she met Tok Daim Tempoyak and excitedly told him how she had really enjoyed his imitation of a tiger. As they were shaking hands, Tok Daim Tempoyak kept her hand in his and seizing the opportunity, quickly baited Datin Lotis to fulfil his material interest.

'Do you want to know how to control a tiger? A powerful person such as yourself might need this kind of knowledge . . .'

She was immediately fascinated. 'What do you mean?'

Tok Daim Tempoyak continued to tempt her. 'Isn't the tiger wild and powerful?'

The rumour among the people is that since then, the Leader's Wife has had the power of a tiger, which she uses to threaten and maul anyone she wants. It is not surprising, since Lotis attacked her own father-in-law.

For this reason, the relationship between Pak Lokan and Datin Lotis was not ordinary.

What is the power of the weretiger like?

John Turnbull Thomson, who served in Malaya between the years 1838 and 1841, describes in *Glimpses into Life in Malayan Lands* how he discovered tiger footprints when he was walking on the bank of the Juru river with his friend Oamut and a Malay man. John was afraid when he saw the footprints but his Malay companion reassured him, 'Don't worry Sir, this is dato, he will not do anything to us.'

The Malay man added, 'Dato is our ancestor and he does not interfere in human affairs.'

John was perplexed. This was a strange idea. After walking upstream for a while, they came up to an old blind man resting under a tree. The conversation between John, Oamut, the Malay guide and the old man was captivating. According to the old man, a long time ago, he was strong and brave. He went to the jungle every day to cut rattan, with which he wove mats. One day, he was attacked by a tiger. He fought back, unwilling to let the animal break his bones and tear his flesh. They fought and the man slashed the tiger on the head with his parang. When he opened his eyes, he had become blind and he heard his wife beside him telling him that they had found him lying in a pool of blood next to a dead tiger. They had carried him back home, cleaned and dressed his wounds, and removed the claw that was buried in his skull. The old man had gone on to live a long life, had many children and grandchildren, and he believed in the following: if you can defeat a tiger, its magic power will pass on to the man who had caught it, conquered it or killed it.

As soon as one obtains the power of the weretiger, he can defeat anyone he wants.

However, the situation was critical. The epidemic was spreading and the Leader himself was weak after being infected by the strange disease. Whether the illness was physical or only in his mind, Lotis knew that she could not use her weretiger power to distract the attention of the population and of her husband's political enemies. The magic power only worked to threaten and subjugate; not to heal.

Datin Lotis had to act quickly. For the time being, only people in their immediate circle knew that the Dictator had lost his mind because he was suffering from koro. Since the day before, he had been delirious, talking to his own cock. It was depressing to watch the most powerful man in Hujung Manani talking to his penis like a madman. At times, he cursed and gripped his testicles angrily, at other times, he laughed while stroking the length of his member, and often wept as he witnessed his phallus shrinking away. He kept repeating, 'I am not a traitor. I am not a traitor.'

What else could it be if not witchcraft?

While the country was in the grips of the koro epidemic, a live performance of Pak Lokan on television would distract people. If anyone was a victim of black magic, the healing provided by the performance would benefit them as well.

Therefore, it was announced that a Pak Lokan dance would be performed.

The press was summoned. Stop all the nonsense. Stop reporting news of an epidemic which 'does not exist'.

The General was summoned. Stop the chaos. If the army had to go out in the streets with tanks to stop the riots, she would give the order to do so.

The Director of the Special Branch was summoned. Make anyone resisting the orders disappear. Make members of the damn woman's team disappear.

The Tycoon was summoned. However, she was told that the old capitalist was resting due to a high level of sugar in his blood. He was diabetic, they said. He often passed out, they said. He had to rest, they said. Bad excuses. The coward bastard! If he was invited to play golf, he would turn his coat in a second.

They all had to listen to her. She was the wife of Datuk Priapus Mappadulung Daeng Mattimung Karaeng Sanrobone, the Leader of the Republic of Hujung Manani.

The Pak Lokan performance was organized upon Datin Lotis' initiative, because the Charm Seller, or the Shaman, whom she often visited, had volunteered to treat the Dictator.

The Dictator's Wife cursed the True Patriot, before, now and forever. When she watched the CNN report covering the campaign to save Hujung Manani from the koro epidemic, she felt threatened.

What koro? The Leader was not suffering from koro. If necessary, he would get naked and show everyone his genitals. There must be some jurisprudence that religious scholars could use to issue a fatwa allowing it. But for the time being, there was no need for all that. What was needed now was the rule of law. Where were the police and the army? Why were they letting the riots spread? What were they waiting for?

Since her husband was incapacitated, she felt compelled to step forward. Indeed, in reality, in many situations, it was often, if not always, she who stepped forward and her presence was overwhelming in the country's political management.

While waiting for the Dictator to recover or heal from that crazy disease, she had to do something. The General ought to be reminded of his loyalty. There would be no Arab Spring in Hujung Manani. Then, the Director of the Special Branch should be reminded to keep providing information from the field.

Where were the police? The people must not step on them.

Datin Lotis was counting on the treatment—injections of calcium gluconate, coupled with a daily dose of olanzapine and lorazepam to treat the psychotic symptoms—to heal the Leader.

However, that stupid Thai doctor had told her that it would take at least four weeks before Datuk Priapus was back to normal.

Four weeks was wayyyyyyyyy too long in politics. One day was already too long a time. So she had ordered the psychiatrist to be locked up with the Tibetan Monk. The Tibetan whore had said something about 'Lama, Atisa, Serlingpa' when she was caught being intimate with the Leader.

She hoped that the Director of the Special Branch had succeeded in forcing the Monk to reveal all his secrets, so that with any luck, they could find a cure for koro. The Director of the Special Branch had expressed his worries because the Dalai Lama had intervened and the disappearance of the Monk had become an international issue. However, Datin Lotis insisted that the holy man should not be released and that they continue torturing him until they could find out what he knew about a cure.

Let them call it a forced disappearance. After everything got back to normal, the kidnapped people would have to be silenced. Only this time, there must not be a trail, like the one left by the Tibetan prostitute. If they had to use C-4 to blow the corpse into fragments, she would make sure that the Special Branch was in charge of it. Otherwise, they could just be sent off to North Korea.

She had to get ready to face the damn woman as soon as possible. For that purpose, she had called the Charm Seller early in the morning. She had asked him what he could do to help the Dictator recover his penis. Recover his peace of mind and his mental health. The Thai psychiatrist's treatment was taking too long. She was in a hurry.

Datin Lotis had not expected the damn Tibetan female to have such strong magic. She thought that the witchcraft that she had learned from both Tok Daim Tempoyak and the Charm Seller was sufficient. But evidently, someone was stronger than her.

The Leader's Wife now focused her thoughts on the damn woman who was opposing her. The bitch was still powerful even though she was an old fart. She was still dangerous. What should she do about the ranting old fart? If only she could send someone to poison her . . . The old bag had been their main enemy from the start.

'Feminist, puh-leeze! I am a woman too. I fight to empower women. I also come from Tahir. See how powerful I am? Who says I do not use my power to outdo men? See how Priapus kneels in front of me? What kind of feminist does Hujung Manani want? What do feminists want?' she kept mumbling.

When the Shaman arrived at the residence early the next morning, they kissed on the cheeks, clapped their left hands together and screamed, 'Shahhhrukh Khan!' They were both hardcore fans of the Bollywood movie star. It was a small ritual that they had been observing for a while, ever since they had started confiding in each other.

The first thing the Leader's Wife did was to thank the Shaman.

Surprised, the man only chuckled, hoping that Datin Lotis would tell him more.

'You have sent an efficient spell to emmm emmm kill Enlarged Cock, the damn woman's right-hand man. It was very important as a reminder, a warning. I don't know how you did it, and ah, why you can't do the same thing to the old bag. Let her go to hell! Nobody would suspect anything. She's already got one foot in the grave. But she won't croak yet!'

The Shaman frowned, before his mouth stretched in a grin. The Leader's Wife did not know that he had not been honest and had not done any such thing. Kadir had died a natural death. She did not know that Kadir had been reciting a spell that he had obtained from the Shaman and that he had met a ghost. She did not know that the True Patriot's team had met the Shaman. Nor had she been told by the Special Branch who had found out about it, that the Shaman had met in secret with KM and the True Patriot's private investigators.

What Datin Lotis knew was that the Shaman was admitting failure and that he could not do anything. She could use the power of the tiger that she controlled, but she had to secure the Leader's position first.

The Shaman said, 'The only solution is for your husband to admit that he is a victim too. Who knows, perhaps people will feel pity for him? The Malay people in Hujung Manani are quite compassionate. They will feel sorry that something bad has happened to him (even though he is usually the one doing bad things to others); sorry that he has been hurt (although he is the biggest pain); sorry that his enemies have cast a spell on him (even though he not only casts spells on his own enemies, but does not even hesitate to have them kidnapped and killed). Malay people are quick to feel sorry. Don't worry. Malay people even feel sorry for thieves, burglars, traitors, corrupt people; well, they even feel sorry for crooks. Malay people like to keep up appearances. As a result of feudalism, Malay people have no values.'

Datin Lotis was speechless for a moment. The Shaman continued: 'This is just one solution, mind you. There are many other ways to solve this problem. But for me, the best solution is in the hands of the Tibetan Monk.'

Datin Lotis nodded in agreement. She was easily convinced that the Monk was the one with the solution. She wanted to go to the villa where he was being held and force him to reveal his secrets.

That same night, at the beginning of the Pak Lokan performance, Datin Lotis was seated next to the General. On her right was the Director of the Special Branch. She whispered to the General that she wanted him to read the ancient oath from the Srivijaya era; the Stone Well inscription—unique and full of magic.

'In addition to that, the army should make sure that the True Patriot is arrested for treason.'

The General raised one eyebrow. He was very careful, as if he was walking on a rotten wooden bridge over a river full of crocodiles.

The sixteen performers walked onto the open stage. They arranged their instruments carefully: flutes, big and small gongs, big and small drums, kesi. The performers were wearing special costumes for their television appearance. Their baju Melayu tops were black with short sleeves with a gold thread embroidery on the edges of the collar and sleeves. The men wore a tengkolok on their head and two pieces of fabric on their shoulders, which crossed over their chest. The two women who were to sing, wore a traditional baju Melayu with long sleeves over trousers. A piece of fabric was wrapped around their waist. Tok Daim Tempoyak's garments were similar to the other performers', but his tengkolok was pink.

Out of the sixteen performers on the stage, six were musicians. Four men, called tukang alak, would form the chorus. The two women would sing and dance. There was also a shepherd, or animal handler, and finally, the most important performer was Pak Lokan himself, who would determine the flow of the story.

Yellow glutinous rice, an egg white omelette, a regular omelette and fried rice grains were placed on the stage as protection against bad luck. They took up only a tiny portion of the large 40 feet square stage.

The press was ready. The camera was focused on the shepherd. Pak Lokan began the performance by making offerings. He stepped left and right, before tightening the strips of materials wrapped over the performers' shoulders.

Music started and the shepherd began singing to signal the beginning of the performance:

'The cockles can whistle
The clams can clap

The quails are stuck in rubber
The pigeons are caught on hooks'

A server went around offering the special guests drinks and pieces of fruit on a platter.

The chorus was very loud, repeating the verses while hopping in place as they sat cross-legged, clapping their hands. Their function was to make the performance cheerful so that everyone's spirits were high and Pak Lokan could find his groove once the frenzy reached its peak. The verses of the chorus were now being sung according to different rhythms.

For a short while, the special guests remained quiet. Datin Lotis had not invited cabinet ministers because in the middle of this crisis, she could not trust any politicians. The presence of the General and the Director of the Special Branch was enough to prove that the Dictator was still in power. It was also sufficient to warn anyone not to turn coats.

Datin Lotis turned to the General. 'Sir, in 683 AD, the ancient Malay king of Srivijaya named Sri Jayanasa, commanded that an inscription be carved on the Stone Well. Do you know what this inscription said?'

The General did not reply. The inscription was the most prestigious exhibit at the Hujung Manani Museum. In fact, the image of the ancient inscription appeared on the flag of Hujung Manani, on stamps, on banknotes, on mosque pulpits, in Christian churches, in temples and altars, and even on gates marking the country's borders. Her husband wanted it to appear on every single symbol of the nation. Like a reminder not to disobey or ignore the Stone Well. The Dictator had taken care of this as soon as he had taken control of the country.

The old soldier considered Datin Lotis' hesitant expression. She smacked her lips, rubbed her nose and spoke again. 'You do know, don't you? You do know?'

She cleared her throat 'emmm ... emmm ...' as if there was a sweet under her tongue.

Hiding his irritation, the General answered her question. 'Of course, it is in our children's textbooks. Sri Jayanasa put a curse on those who would disobey or betray him.'

Datin Lotis smiled. On the stage, Pak Lokan was imitating a bird, flying around the space like a pigeon. The shepherd was holding a stick with a hook on which a grasshopper served as bait. He was following Pak Lokan, trying to make him grab the bait.

The Dictator's wife continued with confidence. 'The inscription threatens to curse traitors, among which rajaputra (royal princes), kumaramatya (ministers), bhupati (local rulers), emmm emmm senapati (war leaders), nayaka (local leaders), pratyaya (aristocrats), haji pratyaya (lower royals), dandanayaka (judges), tuha an vatak (labour leaders), vuruh (labourers), addhyaksi nijavarna (lower supervisors), vasikarana (metalsmiths/weapon makers), catabhata (soldiers) like you and the army, emmm emmm adhikarana (officers), kayastha (people working in shops), sthapaka (artisans), puhavam (ship captains), vaniyaga (merchants), marsi haji (royal servants) and finally hulun haji (royal slaves).'

The stage shook under Pak Lokan's footsteps and the music was loud. A server refilled Datin Lotis' glass with water. The liquid gurgled as it filled up the glass.

The General cursed Datin Lotis silently. The 'female tiger' had managed to memorize that list! However, he was not a stupid soldier who obeyed orders blindly without thinking. Even tigers had weaknesses. A long time ago he might have obeyed any orders. But now, there was love in his heart. Love for a pure and sincere woman. Datin Lotis had forgotten that the General's daughter was the Director of Hujung Manani Museum. She did not know that his daughter supported the True Patriot, and had once told her father: 'There is a reason why the Stone Well inscription uses the symbols of a snake and a bowl, and not that of a tiger and a bowl.'

'What is the reason?' the General had asked his daughter. She was his only love. Since his wife had died of cancer many years ago, he had looked after their daughter with devotion. Even tough soldiers have a soft spot in their hearts.

Datin Lotis did not know that his beloved daughter had changed his way of looking at the world and that he always pictured her in his mind. She had said, 'Papa, the snake in the inscription represents the evil that must be avoided, while the bowl is the combined symbol for Buddhism, the religion of our ancestors at the time, together with the local culture. It represents "cleansing oneself". It is an oath for the leader in the political structure of Srivijaya to do his job properly. It is not an oath to obey at all costs. It is not a tool of feudalism. It is not a threat which shows that Sri Jayanasa was an unjust ruler. It was merely a ritual during which the ruler had to drink pure water from that bowl. It was an official ceremony when ascending to the throne. The current Leader has interpreted this ritual according to his own interest, so that it can be used to instil fear.'

'Are you lost in your thoughts?' Datin Lotis suddenly recalled him to the present. The server came to refill the glass of the Director of the Special Branch with ice-cold water.

The General imagined that he was drinking water from the antique bowl and that it was being broadcast live by the media. In the name of feudalism.

Long live feudalism! Royalty had been overthrown in Hujung Manani. But the Leader still had to be worshipped.

Pak Lokan was now imitating a sheep, butting his head against a coconut which was rolled on the stage by the singers and the chorus. For a little while, Pak Lokan danced like a supernatural sheep possessed by a spirit. Suddenly, he stopped and mumbled a spell. At the same time, the main singers stood up on the left and right sides of the stage, and exchanged verses with each other:

'Mak Bujang crows loudly
The frog can dance

Why do you sit brooding
Come and dance with me.'

'I have no problem drinking water from the sacred bowl of the Stone Well to prove that I am not a traitor,' the General said in a firm tone of voice.

The Leader's Wife smiled. She did not know that the General had risked making that statement because he believed what his daughter had told him. He just ignored Datin Lotis' interpretation. The truth was that the General knew that the Dictator was suffering from koro and was going mad at home. Datin Lotis did not know this either that the General only considered her the leader's wife, and not as Sri Jayanasa. He had heard that the Dictator spent his days sitting in a corner of his room, talking to his dick.

On her right, the Director of the Special Branch did not say a word. He seemed to be absorbed in the performance. However, he was listening intently to what was going on around him.

On the large stage, Pak Lokan stood up, then sat down, stood up again before sitting down again, before he finally stood up, clapped his hands on his thighs and his chest and lastly on his mouth. The four men forming the chorus cheered and sang loudly:

'Teka Tana Rek Tana
The dance of the Keling from the Red Land

Rek Tana Rek Tana
The dance of the Keling from the White Land.'

The Director of the Special Branch spoke in a low voice which was difficult to hear: 'Shouldn't he say mamak instead of keling? Since when do the songs in a Pak Lokan performance deal with racism?'

The Director of the Special Branch was thinking. Reports from the ground indicated that the Leader was being watched by the population. Or rather that the people were getting tired of him. The opposition movement led by the True Patriot was gaining influence. The people were abandoning religious leaders. In addition, these religious figures who were respected and should have been able to crush the koro epidemic, were not actually immune to the strange disease. What had happened to Ashraf Wahidi, the famous preacher, should have returned the public's support for religious scholars. There were still a few people who followed them fanatically. However, they regarded religious figures as the Leader's puppets, and as such, were easily manipulated by him.

Reports from the ground also confirmed that the tiger had lost its claws.

In fact, he knew that tigers were not intelligent animals. He remembered the short note written by Daniel Vaughn in 1857, describing how some Malays had trapped a tiger that was terrorizing a village. Once upon a time in Seberang Perai, a region of Malaysia, there was a wild tiger. It had tasted human flesh and become addicted to it, so it kept attacking villagers. The wild tiger had managed to enter into a house, attack a man and drag his body into the jungle. The tiger had left the half-eaten body on the grass while it went into the bushes to play. Fortunately, Eting was there. Eting was a man of mixed Malay and Thai parentage, known as samsam, and he was handy with a gun. Upon Eting's advice, the half-eaten man with his mouth wide open, his broken ribs and his flesh torn from his chest 'like a cow slaughtered for the Eid al-Adha celebration', was brought back to the house, leaving a fetid trail of blood behind. Eting sat on the roof, waiting for the tiger to return for its prey. As he had expected, the animal felt hungry and came back to finish eating the human whose head he had already torn apart. Eting shot the tiger in the head.

That was not the only account about tigers reported by European travellers. The Director of the Special Branch had found another story written by Carveth Wells in 1913, when he was in Malaya. The man had recorded his experience in a book entitled *Six Years in the Malay Jungle*, which told the story of a nurse who had just arrived in Malaya. She stayed in a bungalow at the edge of a thick jungle. One night, the air was so hot and humid that she pulled her mattress next to the window. She opened the window as wide as she could to let the cool night air refresh her body. She fell asleep, until she was woken up by a loud scratching sound outside the window. She noticed a head with shiny eyes and glistening teeth, and she realized that it was a tiger. She retained enough sense not to scream like a mad woman and instead, she threw a pillow at the tiger. Confused, the animal started tearing the pillow apart with its sharp claws, thinking that it was its prey. Impatiently, the tiger filled its mouth with down feathers and fibres. When it realized its mistake, it rolled around on the girl's bedroom floor as it tried to spit out the pieces of pillow that were lodged in its throat. The nurse ran to get her employer, who shot the tiger dead.

'Why are you telling me all this?' The Director of the Special Branch had asked his predecessor.

The man had looked him straight in the eyes as if he wanted to warn him. 'In your line of work, you will come face to face with tigers. When you do, remember my advice. Do not fight. You will never be able to defeat a tiger in a fight. You would get mauled to death. In order to defeat a tiger, you need to deceive it.'

The Director of the Special Branch listened carefully, thought about it and asked, 'With a pillow?'

The man who was about to retire and leave him to face danger in his place, nodded. 'You must know when to use a pillow. It is not a weapon, but it will save your life.'

Had the time come? Was it time to throw the pillow? Time to trick the tiger?

Datin Lotis seized a fork, stabbed a cube of white melon flesh and brought it to her mouth. The General pretended to be enjoying the Pak Lokan performance, so Datin Lotis turned her attention to the Director of the Special Branch. 'Did we get anything concrete from the Tibetan monk?'

The Director of the Special Branch cleared his throat. It was suddenly feeling sore. A pillow. He knew that the time had come to fool the tiger.

'You do know, right, that the Monk was kidnapped to help us solve the koro issue? Not to offer him a nice holiday in our

luxurious villa on the shore of Hujung Manani lake. That place
is where we detain our enemies. You know, my daily routine has
been disrupted. I should be in London, or Tokyo, or New York
emmm emmm shopping. Not dealing with all this useless stuff.'

The Director of the Special Branch cleared his throat again,
trying to dislodge the phlegm that was stuck. The General was
intently listening to their conversation. Would they have to listen
to Datin Lotis complain all night long?

Pak Lokan was running quickly around the stage, imitating
a monkey. He was making faces and screeching in an annoying
voice, showing his buttocks and lifting them in the air, under
the watchful eyes of the shepherd, who was trying to prevent
him from running away. The shepherd pretended to feed the
monkey some yellow glutinous rice.

'We are losing patience, you know. If you have to resort to
violence, just do it. The Chinese are not afraid to torture the
Dalai Lama, what do we care about a simple incense-burning
monk from a small temple!'

The Director of the Special Branch drank some water with
his straw. He was thinking about a pillow. And a tiger. After
clearing his throat several times, he spoke up, 'We don't need to
use force. It's not necessary. If it was any regular stubborn Shiite
or Christian, we would just capture them and torture them. We
would get rid of them. But this Monk is not just any monk,
Datin.'

Datin Lotis inhaled. She could feel a wave of anger rising in
her chest, wiping away any other emotions.

The shepherd was chasing after Pak Lokan. Loud music
filled the space.

'He's just a monk, right?'

'Monks are not like Muslim scholars. They have much more
integrity.'

The Dictator's wife wanted to tongue-lash him but she controlled her anger. They were surrounded by journalists reporting on the grand Pak Lokan performance. The event was even being broadcast live on television.

Pak Lokan was now imitating a bearded pig. The part when Tok Daim Tempoyak imitated a pig of the S. barbatus barbatus species, which was often found roaming in the Malay peninsula and Borneo, was always lively. This time, Pak Lokan wore a hairy mask curved at the top and in front, with its jaws drooping. He had made the mask specially for tonight's performance. Pak Lokan was dancing and undulating as if he was communicating with spirits. People in Kalimantan believe that the bearded pigs that live in the jungle link human beings with the spirits of dead people.

The shepherd chased after Pak Lokan, who was nodding his head and scratching the soil, getting ready to charge. The shepherd shouted:

'Eh louse, eh tick
Why have you come all the way here?
Don't bring your diseases to us
Who can offer us treatment?'

The chorus sang loudly 'eh pig eh pig eh pig, eh boar, eh pig eh pig!' while laughing, clapping their hands and cheering as if they were at a party.

'He's just a monk. What are you afraid of? Monks only eat vegetables,' Datin Lotis insisted, with a threatening tone in her voice.

'Eh pig eh pig eh pig, eh boar, eh pig eh pig!' the chorus sang loudly. The cameraman recording the live event had fallen asleep.

Tok Daim Tempoyak imitated a person suffering from koro. He collapsed on the stage, rolled over and kicked his legs. The chorus singers cheered and laughed at him.

'We have locked up the Monk with the Famous Historian. We have been able to record everything they said and did, Datin. Keeping them together in the same villa has given us results. They showed off their knowledge, revealed a lot about themselves and we have more or less obtained what we wanted.'

Datin Lotis took a deep breath. Why was everything so slow? The Thai doctor was taking too long to treat her husband, the information needed to cure the Dictator of koro was also taking too long to get. What was Tok Daim Tempoyak waiting for before healing people? Chanting spells? Reciting incantations? Had he already done the part where he imitates a tiger? Did she miss it?

Pak Lokan had his hands around his neck and his voice had become hoarse and very low. It looked as if he was being strangled. His hands reached out in the air. His performance looked very realistic tonight. Suddenly, one of the musicians stood up and screamed before he collapsed on the stage while grabbing his penis. It was extraordinary.

'Based on the conversations between the Famous Historian and the Monk that we have on tape, we know who can be infected by koro and who cannot.' The Director of the Special Branch replied to the Dictator's wife enquiry. His eyes never left the stage. But all he could see was a pillow, and a tiger.

'The Famous Historian used a keyword in his conversations with the Monk.'

Datin Lotis was impatient. 'What? What?'

'Racism.'

'In the name of Birkin, in the name of my pink diamond, in the name of plastic waste . . . Racism?' She was puzzled.

The General who had remained quiet until now, finally spoke up, 'Koro is caused by racism? Who said that?'

'A pantun indicates an old cure. It goes like this:

What to do with a rusty blade
It can be scrubbed with white vinegar;
What is the epitome of treason
It is putting one's race above all others.'

'In the name of my hubby! That's the source of koro? Don't treat me like an idiot! Don't you dare treat me like an idiot!'

The Director of the Special Branch confirmed the information that he had obtained. 'It's correct, the cure is even indicated in the army report about the American Marines who were infected by a form of koro during an expedition to Kuala Batu.'

'Hah?' Datin Lotis was furious. She could feel her canines elongating and her claws itching to come out and strike.

The Director of the Special Branch suddenly started to feel uneasy. He kept his eyes on the stage even though he was talking to the Leader's wife.

'Can you clarify that, please?' the General said in a barely audible voice.

Now, the Director of the Special Branch focused entirely on the stage. The shepherd was circling the musicians who had forgotten everything, and moved toward Pak Lokan, who was still thrashing about on the floor while holding his neck with both hands as if he was being strangled.

The cameraman was still fast asleep and snoring loudly. The performance was being broadcast live in the entire country.

'Yes, racism. Apparently, only racists are affected by koro. Perhaps, perhaps it would be good for the Leader to appear in public and prove that he is not suffering from the disease. That he is not racist. That would shut the people and the opposition up.' The Director of the Special Branch spoke honestly. Honesty is a pillow for a tiger. Despite his urgent tone of voice, his eyes did not turn away from the stage.

'What about the Ziji stone? Have you got it?'

The Director of the Special Branch nodded. The damn woman could have any necklace in the world but she still wanted the stone worn by the Tibetan prostitute around her neck. What kind of greed was that?

'We gave it to your assistant.'

There were unusual movements on the stage.

The Director of the Special Branch said, 'Tok Daim Tempoyak is no longer himself.'

The General added, 'Of course, it's because he is a Pak Lokan. He is channelling.'

Datin Lotis closed her mouth in a tight line. So, the Ziji stone was already at her official residence? She should not appear too happy. Instead, she wanted to ask, apart from appearing in public, what other tactic or trick could the Leader use? However, she was not sure that they were allies yet.

The shepherd sang in a loud voice:

'Hey clam,
I want to know where you came from
If you came from the forest edge, I want you to go back to the forest edge
If you came from a village, I want you to go back to the village
If you came from a hill, I want you to go back to the hill
If you came from a river, I want you to go back to the river

If you came from the sea, I want you to go back to the sea
Let everything go back as it was before
Let all my children be safe.'

As soon as he finished talking, Pak Lokan flapped his arms wildly. The shepherd walked around him while sprinkling glutinous rice. The musicians played the opening melody, although they were still in a trance in the centre of the stage. Pak Lokan was still rolling on the stage as if he was possessed. The shepherd recited some sort of spell and Pak Lokan suddenly shouted in a hoarse voice.

'Ghost . . . Ghost . . . Tibetan ghost. My name is Sistine. I was murdered. Murdered by Lotis. I was happily sucking Priapus's dick when it disappeared and Lotis ordered the Special Branch to kill me.'

The cameraman was startled from his micro-sleep and looked around, failing to grasp what was going on. His mouth was wide open while his camera was focused automatically on whatever drama was happening without a censor on the stage.

The Leader's Wife was speechless for a while, trying to understand what Tok Daim Tempoyak had said.

At the same time, the Director of the Special Branch felt something grabbing his toes and like a snake, the feeling crept up the soles of his feet to his calves, his thighs and his groin, slowly numbing them. He immediately realized that he was having a koro attack. Before he could even stand up and yell, his penis had retracted and disappeared into his crotch. He screamed in panic.

Datin Lotis was confused. 'In the name of Prada! In the name of Gucci! In the name of plastic waste! What is going on?'

The cameraman was still broadcasting the event live.

The General did not know what to do or what to think. The only thing he could think of was his penis. Why was his penis still there? Why wasn't he affected by koro? Masha'Allah, Masha'Allah, he still had a penis!

On stage, Pak Lokan was still shouting, 'Ghost! Ghost! Ghost . . .'

And the whole country was in shock as they watched the Pak Lokan performance.

The Play

The curtain opened. The venue was sold out for the opening night and sales for the following nights were promising. The play represented an important documentation of the history of Hujung Manani. Entitled *The Koro Riots*, it recorded the background story of how the Third Leader, the Dictator, and his wife were overthrown.

However, according to the Rookie Detective, who was the author and director, the play only focused on what happened in the villa located on the shore of Hujung Manani lake, and not so much on how the Dictator was overthrown by the True Patriot. Nor on the revolution led by a woman and supported by many women. Not really. In fact, the play would only show the most boring parts of the story.

The stage was still shrouded in darkness.

The Shaman was in the audience.

The Tycoon was sitting in the most strategic row, facing the stage, in the middle of the room, together with his son.

The Fourth Leader, the Scientist, and his wife were sitting in the balcony.

There were three distinct areas on the stage. First, there was a living room, furnished with a sofa with linen upholstery and leather armrests and a wooden coffee table covered with a thin layer of glass. Underneath, a carpet featuring blue, black and mustard yellow abstract motifs contributed to evoke a luxurious, comfortable and stylish residence.

The second area featured a BoConcept dining table and eight chairs. A buffet table made of Marquina black marble caught the eye. There was also a low book rack with two statues of the Fertility goddess.

The third space resembled the living room with a dense stage arrangement of vintage furniture. In the left corner, one could see an antique English Hexagon side table with open shelves. Next to it, there was an armchair with an ornate carved headrest. A tapestry-covered cushion was placed in the armchair. Finally, there was an antique French console cabinet.

The table was set with dinner plates and salad plates, and gold-plated cutlery. In the centre of the table, there were two porcelain chandeliers of different sizes, and a three-tiered stand displaying pastries.

The three spaces were meant to inspire a feeling of wonder among the audience, who were transported to an elegant villa. A villa where victims of kidnapping were locked up and held at the mercy of the Dictator and his wife.

The director wanted the audience to forget that they were watching a contemporary drama about the tragic moments experienced by the Famous Historian, the Psychiatrist and a Lama or Monk, who had been held captive for forty days. They would be tested by a 'pretty ghost'. The audience was told in a pamphlet that the drama would recount the last day of their captivity before they were eventually released.

Spotlights would focus on the actors as they appeared in each area of the stage.

The spectators were chatting, bursts of laughter could be heard and most conversations were carried out in whispers.

The lights came on, illuminating the stage. Two actors dressed in pig costumes appeared. The name Little Rose was embroidered on the First Pig's chest, while the Second Pig displayed the name Prince J, embroidered in the same fashion. Several spectators started laughing as they witnessed the absurdity of the situation: two pigs in the middle of a magnificent villa. Both pigs featured very long snouts.

The First Pig spoke up: 'I hope they can stand the pressure. Forty days is too long. Two weeks in quarantine already feels too long.'

The Second Pig grimaced. 'Today is the fortieth day. If they go mad, it will happen today.'

The First Pig disagreed. 'If they were to go mad, they would have done it during the first or second week. After forty days, they are emmm saner than ever. Moreover, you are talking about the Monk, who is used to practising meditation, and the Famous Historian, who spends a lot of time analysing historical events. As for the Psychiatrist, I am sure that he knows how to handle himself in any situation.'

The Second Pig grunted. 'This would not have happened if the Tibetan woman had not been cruelly murdered.'

The First Pig lowered his head, lifted his face and shook his head with regret. 'It's true. She was just a translator, not really a prostitute or a mistress. She should not have been condemned to death. I hope her soul finds peace in the afterlife.'

As it had been reported that the play entitled *The Koro Riots* had been based on a true story, it garnered a lot of attention, and artists, activists and art afficionados had described it as 'an absurd drama full of beauty'. The author of the play was new in the field and this was his first work. He worked as a forensic scientist and a detective for the Hujung Manani Police Force.

People were eager to watch the play because it was based on the experience of the author, who had been detained with three other victims. Too many rumours had circulated about the fall of Dictator Priapus and his wife during the koro riots. To this day, nobody knew the truth for certain. Two years after the riots, people celebrated the anniversary of the toppling of the tyrannic Third Leader. The staging of this play was part of the ceremonies in remembrance of the martyred True Patriot.

The First Pig shouted, grabbing the attention of the audience: 'If that Tibetan woman has become a ghost and is haunting Hujung Manani—which is actually happening—we cannot evade her.'

The Second Pig sighed. 'Her ghost has frightened many people. She flies here and there, and strikes as soon as night falls. Many people have died of fright. She will not leave as long as she has not obtained her revenge.'

The First Pig faced the audience and declared with gusto: 'Her vengeance will only be complete when the neck of the man who deceived her is broken.'

The Second Pig chuckled. 'But does the Tibetan ghost want to kill that man?'

'That man is none other than the Dictator!' the First Pig shouted.

'What she wants is the tiger!'

The light faded gradually and the stage became dark. When it became bright again, the stage showed the living room and its props. Two Chinese men were seated. The first man was middle-aged. He played the part of the Monk and was sitting cross-legged on the carpet, facing the audience. He was wearing the saffron robe of a monk. The contrast between his robe and the abstract pattern of the carpet was striking.

The second actor, who also looked Chinese, was playing the part of the Famous Historian. He was sitting in front of the glass-covered coffee table, also facing the audience.

The Famous Historian spoke first. 'Today is perhaps the thirty-ninth or fortieth day that I am here, and I am tired of eating pork.'

The Monk, apparently meditating, did not reply. His eyes remained closed and his bald shaved skull reflected the spotlight.

The First Pig, who was fat with a large stomach, crossed the living room as he said: 'Ah, you are lucky that you do not eat meat, only vegetables.' He then moved a few feet away.

Another Chinese man who played the part of the Psychiatrist entered from stage left and interrupted the conversation, 'It is not good to eat so much pork. A group of scientists have studied cellular activity in the brains of thirty-two slaughtered pigs. They found that the blood vessels started carrying blood again, and brain cells resumed their metabolic activity, including responding to drugs. When they analysed a slice of the pigs' brain tissue, they discovered electrical activity in the neurons. So, they concluded that part of the brain was still alive.'

The Famous Historian scratched his head and replied: 'In that case, we can treat strokes, brain injuries resulting from accidents and even Alzheimer's. Did you know that when people die in cold weather, their brain keeps functioning? Stroke patients with a clot preventing blood circulation to part of the brain for sixteen hours, can recover brain function as soon as the clot is removed.'

'This is unethical. Science without ethics,' the Monk interjected angrily.

Everybody was quiet for a few seconds.

The Famous Historian broke the silence by announcing: 'We can try to return to the proposition that we made in our second week here. We asked the Server to help us, to free us from here. If the guards at the gate are careless, we can sneak out without being seen.'

The Psychiatrist laughed with contempt. 'Don't forget, the Server is a policeman from the Special Branch. He might even be a soldier, judging by his haircut and muscles.'

'I am just tired of eating pork. We don't even know if the meat comes from vaccinated pigs or not.' The Psychiatrist spoke seriously as he sat in the armchair. 'As I said before, all this has to do with koro.'

The Famous Historian added immediately: 'I read something interesting the day before yesterday. It happened during the attack by the Americans in Kuala Batu in 1832 in Aceh.'

The Psychiatrist turned the head in his direction. 'Was it related to koro? Or to ghosts?'

'To koro,' the Famous Historian replied briefly as he stared at the Monk, who was not moving. He could not tell whether he was asleep or deep in meditation.

The Monk cleared his throat and said: 'Did you say that the Americans attacked the Malay world in 1832?'

'Oh, he's not dead yet!' The Famous Historian quipped after the Monk spoke up.

The Psychiatrist looked at the Famous Historian with a surprised expression: 'Really, Americans came to Southeast Asia? I thought it was only the English, the Dutch, the Spanish, the Portuguese—'

'Don't forget the French,' the Monk added. 'Ermmm, perhaps America was looking for a place to dispose of their plastic waste. This is where the West sends its rubbish. And our future generations are at risk.'

There was laughter in the audience. The Scientist and his wife were among those who laughed the loudest.

The Famous Historian chuckled. 'Hear, hear . . .'

The Monk's voice could be heard, 'Huh, postcolonialism.'

Some spectators laughed, showing that they had understood the dig.

'This is all about black pepper,' the Famous Historian started to explain.

'Black pepper or koro?' the Psychiatrist interrupted.

'Or plastic? Canada, Australia . . . They send their plastic waste to our country. They are so self-important over there, but they send us their shit here. What do they think we are? A dumpster? A toilet? Plastic can cause infertility in men, you know!' the Monk exclaimed playfully.

Sitting in the audience, the Fourth Leader, namely Professor Badang, and his Jewish wife smiled.

'Both. May I explain? It is my turn to speak,' the Famous Historian replied with a touch of anger in his voice. 'In February 1831, an American ship sailed to the Kuala Batu harbour in the province of Aceh. The ship called *Friendship* was under the command of Captain Charles Endicott. When the captain went ashore with a crew of his men to secure a cargo of pepper, a band of pirates boarded the *Friendship* and killed the first officer and two other crew members. Then they stole all the valuable cargo. Four sailors managed to escape by diving into the water and hiding in the jungle.'

The Psychiatrist walked closer to the Famous Historian. The Monk remained sitting cross-legged on the carpet.

'Captain Endicott sought help from a village head called Po Adam. They received help from three other American ships that were sailing not far off the coast. They all contributed to recovering the *Friendship*, which was badly damaged. After making basic repairs, Captain Endicott sailed back to Salem and asked for help from the American President at the time, President Andrew Jackson, who had slaughtered many native Americans during the Creek Indian war. In his third State of the Nation Address in December that year, President Andrew Jackson told the Senate and the House of Representatives that he had ordered to 'inflict chastizement' on the pirates. He said that 'the usual course of diplomatic proceedings between civilized nations could not be pursued' as the perpetrators were pirates and he informed Congress that he had dispatched 'a frigate with orders to require immediate satisfaction for the injury and indemnity to the sufferers'.

President Jackson dispatched the frigate *USS Potomac* under Commodore John Downes. The Potomac set sail on 28 August 1831, several months before the State of the Nation Address. When Downes reached Kuala Batu on 5 February 1832, he disguised his warship as a Danish commercial ship. He found three proas guarding the harbour, which was protected by five forts along the coastline.'

'They used a warship to attack a state?' the Psychiatrist asked with impatience. 'That is not fair!'

'Shush! Be quiet!' the Monk stopped him angrily.

'Well, the *Potomac* was not just any warship. It was a first-class frigate carrying forty-two 32-pound short-range cannons and eight 8-inch Paixhans guns equal to seventy-two cannons. There were 300 men on board.'

'So, 300 men fought against an entire town?' The Psychiatrist was purposely trying to irritate the Famous Historian.

'Let him talk!' the Monk answered in an angry tone of voice.

The Famous Historian continued, 'On 6 February, Downes divided 282 marines into three groups and ordered them into the ship's boats which carried cannons. They burned down the wooden fort in Kuala Batu and sank the three proas in the harbour.

The Psychiatrist was not satisfied. 'What really happened? Tell us, what happened?'

'Each boat fought against one fort. The natives fought fiercely. The *Potomac* fired her cannons. After an intense battle that lasted five hours, four of the forts were burnt down and the three proas were sunk. The survivors sought refuge in the last fort.'

The Psychiatrist wanted to know more. 'Did they keep fighting?'

'The problem was that the Americans did not attack the last fort,' the Famous Historian replied angrily.

'So?'

The Monk interrupted the dialogue. 'For three days, the Americans attacked buildings and houses in the town of Kuala Batu and killed more than 100 women and children. Finally, Commodore Downes burnt down the last fort after the Malay chief surrendered.'

The Psychiatrist was speechless for a while. Then he asked, 'So America didn't just do it in Okinawa, Afghanistan, Iraq and Pakistan, but also in Kuala Batu in the Aceh province?'

'In all of Asia!' the Monk exclaimed. 'That was just the very first example of American interference in foreign countries' affairs under the guise of protecting commercial interests and the safety of their people.' The Monk was extremely aggravated and his words expressed his anger. '150 civilians were slaughtered with cannonballs and bullets, including women and children. In the last fort, 300 warriors were killed. And the Americans only lost two men and counted eleven casualties. One of them was seriously injured and died later.'

'Really?' the Psychiatrist, unable to hide his emotions, asked.

'America . . .' the Monk sighed woefully.

The Famous Historian retook possession of the stage, as the other actors looked at him in silence. 'But there are three things that I wish to discuss now. First, who was the Malay man called Po Adam, who conspired with the Americans? He claimed that Muhammad, the chief of the pirates in Kuala Batu, refused to negotiate—but was it true? Second, was what happened on the *Friendship* really an act of piracy? Or was it just an excuse fabricated by colonialists? Perhaps Holland, France and England purposely wanted to scare America to prevent it from doing commerce in a region under their control? And third, on the way back to America, the *Potomac* stopped in Hawaii and 200 marines complained that they were suffering from the Kuala Batu curse.'

The Monk chuckled softly at first, but then his shoulders started shaking as he tried to control his bursts of laughter.

'The Kuala Batu curse?' the Psychiatrist repeated.

'This is why the actions of the *Potomac* in Sumatra were heavily criticized when it returned to America, forcing President Jackson to give an explanation in the fourth State of the Nation Address,' the Famous Historian continued.

'The Kuala Batu curse?' the Psychiatrist muttered to himself, while the Monk was still shaking with laughter.

'Lieutenants Alvin Edson and George Terrett complained that when they were fighting on land, in Tuko de Lima village, they started feeling that their penis was shrinking significantly. This was reported in the official frigate's log, which is kept in the Library of Congress,' the Famous Historian explained.

The Monk, who was no longer laughing, tried to analyse the information. 'This makes sense when you remember that there were no negotiations before the attack was launched. Moreover, they attacked in the middle of the night, disguised as a merchant ship. Also, also . . . the killing of women and children. We know this because there is a news report in America that recounts how a woman pushed an American soldier's gun away, despite the fact that orders had been given not to harm the weaker sex.'

'Wow, this coming from a Monk!' the Psychiatrist exclaimed in amazement. He then continued to ask, 'So the Kuala Batu curse was a koro attack? What happened to Lieutenants Edson and Terrett? Did they only notice that they were sick once they were in Hawaii, on their way back to the United States?'

The Famous Historian answered. 'According to Lieutenant Edson, he believed that the curse that was making his penis disappear had been cast by the woman who fought against a marine in Tuko de Lima. She had muttered some sort of incantation in a foreign language.'

The Monk laughed. 'In Sanskrit?'

'This is interesting!' the Psychiatrist exclaimed, excited. 'But how do we know that it was koro? I still don't understand koro thoroughly . . .'

'In that report, it is called the "Jonnett sisters' sickness".'

'Jonnett Grant and Jonnett Clark were the two witches who were sentenced to death on Castlehill in Edinburgh in August 1590 for stealing penises,' the Psychiatrist quickly added. His face showed a keen interest.

'Only two men complained that their penises shrank after the attack in Kuala Batu, while the others, including Commodore John Downes, reported that they no longer had any sperm, or according to the term in Ayurveda medicine—'

'*Sukra Prameha,*' the Psychiatrist quickly finished the sentence for the Famous Historian.

The Monk interrupted the conversation. 'Eat vegetables. Control your lust. Stop eating meat. Drink warm water to kill viruses like Covid-19.'

The spectators who heard him burst out laughing, all at once. For a while, the audience was noisy. The Tycoon looked a bit lost as he did not understand what was funny.

The Second Pig appeared on the right side of the stage. Standing in the corner, he said, 'Do you know that it takes ten drops of blood to make one drop of sperm? One ejaculation requires eighty drops of blood. Ten grains of rice produce one drop of blood. It takes forty days of a healthy diet to produce one drop of sperm. Emmm, make sure your children do not masturbate.'

The audience became boisterous.

'But today, with the pollution caused by plastic waste, eating a lot of kote mamak does not increase sperm count.'

The pig walked to the back of the stage and disappeared, leaving the audience in stitches.

The Famous Historian added, 'All the marines who took part in the attack in Kuala Batu became infertile. Those who were still single at the time were cursed with the end of their bloodline.'

'The end of their bloodline . . .' the Psychiatrist looked frightened as he repeated the end of the sentence.

'So it was not koro then?' The Monk wanted to make sure.

'In the report about the expedition to Kuala Batu, it is also written that Po Adam was kidnapped and brought back to America. They believed that he was the only native who could remove the spell. When he was forced to reveal how to heal them, Po Adam recited six verses of a pantun, claiming that it was the cure for koro.'

The Monk was excited. 'Recite them!'

'Yes, recite them. Who knew that the cure for koro was in a pantun?!' The Psychiatrist joked.

The audience burst out laughing.

The Famous Historian faced the audience and declaimed:

'Javanese, Bugis and Moro
All Malay skins of various colours;
When you are stricken with koro
Find the crime that made you limp.

What to do with a rusty blade
It can be scrubbed with white vinegar;
What is the epitome of treason
It is putting one's race above all others.

In your pants what do you rub
In the night what do you see;
How is a race superior to others
It is forbidden by religion and not preached by the Prophet.'

'And this is the cure to koro?' the Psychiatrist, puzzled, asked.

The Monk giggled.

The Famous Historian looked at the Psychiatrist with a serious expression on his face. 'Yes, Po Adam said that this was the cure to koro.'

The lights went out. When they came back on, the Monk was sitting in the armchair beside the antique English Hexagon table. His mouth was moving as he muttered a spell.

After a moment, he spoke up. 'I told them not to consider their detention in this luxurious villa as an imprisonment. If we think that it is an imprisonment without reason, then we may get depressed and go mad. This is why I told them not to harm the Server. If he does not want to talk to us, never mind. He looks young. If you do not want to eat the meat he brings, then just leave it.'

The Monk inhaled deeply and looked at the audience as if he wanted to grab their full attention.

'So after a while, they agreed with me and started accepting that this detention was a time for meditation, a time to relax. In Max Heguy's words, "a time for reflexion".'

The spectators laughed again. Those who had not understood the previous jokes were now laughing with the rest, and the room was noisy.

'When you are a religious person, it is important to isolate yourself for a while from the noise and chaos of the world in order to aim for perfection. This is not a quote from Max Heguy.'

An actress appeared at the back of the stage. She was pretty, elegantly dressed, and she walked silently on the stage for a few moments. Some spectators sounded frightened when they saw that the actress wore ghostly white make-up on her face. The Monk pretended to ignore her. She finally walked up to him, stuck her tongue out and almost licked his left ear. The Monk was startled but quickly reassumed his calm.

'You're here again?'

'You don't want me to come?'

'As long as you are not here to haunt them and disturb their mind. They have found peace here,' the Monk said while pointing at his temple, 'and here', he finished while putting his hand on his heart.

'Who said I was disturbing anyone?'

'They are not the ones who killed you, Sistine. They are victims too.'

The elegant woman did not seem to care about what the Monk said as she started to laugh, before stopping abruptly.

'Don't overdo it! You should stop the koro epidemic. Many people are sick.'

The actress playing the part of Sistine laughed again. She walked up to the Monk, put her arms around his shoulders before linking her hands behind his neck as if she was feeling aroused.

'Are you sure you don't want to have sex?'

The Monk closed his eyes as if he was reciting something to repel the ghost who was haunting him.

'Imagine that you are deep inside me, your pubic hair rubbing against mine . . .'

The Monk kept his eyes closed.

'Your faith is strong.'

'Sistine, you should end the Muara Jambi epidemic. It is not fair to some of them.'

'How dare you speak about fairness?' Sistine grunted.

The Monk tried to convince the woman who remained adamant. 'Serlingpa did not teach Atisha Dipamkara Shrijnana this spell in order to be used indiscriminately.'

'The Suvarnadvipa spell is for bad people, to make them regret their actions.' Sistine was angry now.

'Don't hurt just anyone.'

'The Dictator was not a bad man?' The Tibetan woman protested. The Monk grunted angrily.

'What about the religious man who regretted his acts and helped the True Patriot? I returned his penis to him.'

'But what about the Editor-in-Chief?' the Monk asked.

The woman's shrill laughter reverberated. 'How did he treat his ex-wife? He was sexist.'

'What do you mean?' the Monk asked.

'Those who are racist, who are against women, who support colonialism, who deny justice—those are the men who can be infected.' The actress explained, or rather, enumerated a list. Then she left the stage, leaving the Monk speechless, his face full of incomprehension. He was lost in thought for a while, before standing up in front of the audience. In a loud voice that carried to the back of the theatre, he said: 'Lama Serlingpa Dharmakirti lived in 950 AD in Shri Suvarnadvipa, which is now known as Sumatra. He belonged to the Sailendra dynasty and became a famous religious scholar in Srivijaya. He built a temple in Muara Jambi. One of his famous disciples was Atisa. It was Lama Atisa who brought Buddhism to Tibet. He wrote a long poem in his book entitled *Bodhipathapradipa*, that contained Serlingpa's teachings. What did the master say about mankind? Serlingpa said that mankind can be divided into three categories, namely low, middle and high. Men of the highest category are those who seek eternal perfection while keeping in mind other people's suffering and making it their own. Men of the middle category are those who leave behind the pleasures and sins of this life but for their own peace of mind. Lastly, men of the lowest category are those who take what they want, look for pleasure and only care about themselves.'

The female ghost reappeared in a corner of the stage. 'Why do you blame me, Lama? The men infected with koro belong to the lowest category. They obtain what they want for themselves, they enjoy the pleasures of this world and live on earth only for themselves.'

'Hey, that is not for you to decide!' the Monk protested angrily.

'Hey Monk, don't think that you are the only one who has the right to know the truth! Why do religious men, like the Liverpool Mufti, always think that they know the truth?' The actress sounded furious.

'Atisa lived 150 lives before he became a monk and when he met the goddess Tara in the form of a young woman in the middle of a crowd, she told him: "Abandon all your desires, do not let desire control you, as this is the only way to uphold morals and virtue." This is why Atisa sailed through tempests and overcame many obstacles to meet Serlingpa, who was 150 years old at the time. Atisa stayed for twelve years in Muara Jambi to acquire the knowledge of *atma-para-samata-parivarta*. After Serlingpa asked him to move to a cold mountainous land, Atisa travelled to Tibet to spread the religion.'

The Monk fell silent. The woman as well. The theatre was quiet.

The lights were dimmed a little and the Monk continued in a sad tone of voice, 'Atisa had 100,000 slaves at his service. The palace was crowned with thirteen golden roofs, one set atop the other, and 25,000 silver ones. There were 25,000 pools and parks with seven bridges, all filled with beautiful plants. From the age of three until he met Tara, Atisa acquired a lot of worldly knowledge. Then, in a dream, she told him to learn love and compassion, as well as Bodhicitta from a Malay teacher, Lama Serlingpa.'

The woman appeared suddenly beside the Monk, as the lights resumed their full brightness.

'I did not acquire the knowledge about koro from Atisa alone. It is a knowledge that was transmitted by Serlingpa in his book *Durbodhaloka*, to threaten King Cudamaniwarman, who ruled Old Kedah, so that he would not become a tyrant, and if he or his descendants did lose their way, they would suffer the turtle curse from Muara Jambi, which you know as koro. You know, Monk, if the kings of Srivijaya became despotic, they were punished with koro. Koro is a reminder to seek perfection and not pursue lowly interests. But after Islam came, this curse became regarded as sorcery . . . and the population repeatedly suffers from calamities.'

The Monk remained silent. The woman as well. The theatre was quiet.

After a moment, the Monk broke the silence. 'I am tired of trying to reason with you.'

The woman chuckled. 'Koro is a way to control men who are full of lies. Especially if they have influence and power. Since the Srivijaya era, then in Malacca and Kuala Batu, and lately during Priapus' government, those who are cursed by koro are those who do not have manners, sincerity, love or compassion. It will always be so until the end of times.'

The Monk sighed and repeated, 'I am tired of trying to reason with you. Why did you kill the Editor-in-Chief? There are many types of feminists, but you are too extreme. You should stick to killing tigers. Get lost, go fight the weretiger!'

Sistine, excited, faced the audience. 'A ghost fighting against a tiger. Why didn't I think of this before?!'

The lights were extinguished, leaving the theatre in the dark.

Backstage, the Rookie Detective, who was the director of the play, was giving instructions to the actor who played the part of the Famous Historian.

'Did you see who is sitting in the audience?'

The actor, named Alvin Chin, nodded. 'Do you mean the Tycoon?'

The Rookie Detective stared at the actor. 'You are going to speak directly to him, got it?'

'He's got nerves to show his face here! Perhaps the moneygrabber wants to make a move on the Scientist?' Alvin, or the Famous Historian, had embraced a verse from the *Six Gurindam* and had even framed that verse and its response, and hung it on a wall in a corner of his house: 'If traders come plying their wares, of all their ruses beware'.

The Stage Director came and handed a *kompang* to Alvin. One theatre critic had commented on Alvin's skill at playing the kompang while reciting verses from the *Gurindam* during his long monologue (the actor playing the part of the Famous Historian was a Chinese man from Hujung Manani).

'Come on, we artists have a duty to remind people,' the Stage Director said.

The Rookie Detective patted Alvin's shoulder.

The stage was still dark.

The Famous Historian took his place on stage and as soon as the lights came on, he declaimed in a loud voice, 'Ode to the Martyred True Patriot'.

The spectators were attentive. The Famous Historian took a deep breath as he faced the audience, searching for the Tycoon and his son. When he found them, he locked eyes with the Tycoon. They stared at each other intently, like two ancient warriors at the beginning of a fight. The Famous Historian put the kompang down beside the armchair and looked at the audience again.

The spectators were all observing him. The cold air that blew from the air-conditioning units made the spectators shiver.

'Martyr Pertiwi, the True Patriot, once said: "The enemies of democracy are not always supporters of feudalism or narrow-minded religious figures; nationalists do not always flock together. The enemies of democracy can be traders, capitalists and moneygrabbing tycoons, who set their rules in the dark. The people rule, they break rules," the True Patriot said before . . .'

Silence.

Some spectators were wiping tears from their eyes. The Tycoon had lowered his head, silently cursing his son for suggesting that he put on a brave face and attend the performance.

'We did it, ladies and gentlemen. But we did it with blood and tears. Lotis, the Leader's Wife, and Pertiwi, the True Patriot, both hail from the small town of Kota Tahir, in the east of Hujung Manani. The town is important in the history of Hujung Manani because it is the birthplace of the "No More" campaign. Before Hujung Manani became a republic colonized by the French, it was an absolute monarchy. We must not forget that for three centuries, the country was ruled with unrivalled tyranny, until finally, warriors rose up in the form of two women. Nyemah and Piah, a mother and a daughter, who chose to stand and lead the people. Piah and her mother chose Tahir to launch the revolution against the monarchy.'

The spectators were attentive. The Famous Historian searched for the Scientist and his wife.

'Piah's mother was called Nyemah. She was an aristocrat from Hujung Manani who was rejected by her peers after she married a commoner. She fled after her husband, Tengku Mustafa, was killed and the popular movement they had launched, failed. Nyemah hid in the town of Tahir and when Piah was born, she left her miracle baby in the care of a medical doctor, Dr Afra. She told him: "I am a revolutionary and I will be killed. This baby, Piah Berkah, is a daughter of the revolution. Nobody knows that she exists. You must hide her." When she was pregnant with Piah, Nyemah made appearances to give strength to the people of Tahir. When Hujung Manani was still a republic, it comprised eight small regions. In the southeast it shared a border with a southern state of Malaysia. In its waters, the smallest island was called Gugup Island, and the most developed was Tiger Island. There is a famous legend regarding this island, *The Legend of the Tiger King*. It is an old manuscript which is kept in the Public Library of St Petersburg in Russia. The legend is about a queen who gave birth to a tiger. Several years later, when the old king died, the tiger became king, and was called King Tiger. When a group of Muslim scholars came to Tiger Island, they told King Tiger that he could turn into a man if a beautiful princess from a faraway land agreed to marry him. However, the princess must be a sacred princess able to bring *shafa'ah* to the people. To this day, the people living on Tiger Island are descendants of Arab and Tiger Malays. Some follow the Ba'Alawi Sufi order, while others follow the Ja'fari school of jurisprudence, but they all live together in peace and harmony.

'This is a very rare manuscript. When the True Patriot was the head of the government, she asked for copies of the *Legend of the Tiger King* from the Public Library in St Petersburg, which are now in the National Archives and in the Museum of Hujung Manani.'

The entire audience was focusing their full attention on the actor playing the part of the Famous Historian, giving him the strength to bring his character to life.

'Lotis' parents were not originally from Hujung Manani, although they lived in the region of Sari, near the town of Tahir. On the other hand, the True Patriot's family was native to Hujung Manani. In Sari, the population was dominated by people of Javanese descent who had migrated from Jogjakarta in search of a better life, several hundred years before. Most of them practised *kejawèn* or Javanism. Before the proliferation of plastic waste processing plants, Sari was the main producer of sugar. Sugarcane plantations were spread as far as the eye could see. Coffee was the second most important product. For instance, they supplied to the Star Back coffee chain. Finally, they produced cocoa. Apart from that, the town of Tahir was the cultural centre of Hujung Manani. For instance, the Tahir University of Human Sciences was renowned for its many graduates who became famous intellectuals. However, after the French colonized the country, the fame of Tahir as a cultural centre faded.

Tahir is not a very big town. A river called Pura River flows through the town. The short bridge that links the two banks of the river is called the Ababa Bridge. Before the fall of the Malay sultanate of Hujung Manani, the population of Tahir was less than 40,000 people. After French colonization, most of the inhabitants of Tahir were aged over fifty. The young population had moved to other towns or preferred to work in Malaysia, Singapore or the Middle East.'

The Famous Historian walked to the front of the stage, drew in his breath and looked straight at the audience. He did not say anything for a minute or two, letting the spectators stare back at him.

'Actually, several hundred years before French colonization, the French had already come to Tahir. They built four massive forts on each side of the town, as well as a tram system. Later, other small towns were connected to the tram system. There were twelve carriages. One of them was named Ben and it ran from the main station in Tahir to the towns of Gonoat and Bangi. Gonoat is located in the south, not far from the foot of Erupting Volcano. The countryside between the two towns is stunningly beautiful: a succession of greenery, mountains and beaches where the waves crash on a rocky shore under a sky that always remains a brilliant blue. As a French colony, the country made rapid progress. The French built two shopping complexes, which attracted many tourists. They were both located along the same street, Caliph Sod Street, named after the last king of Hujung Manani before he was ousted by the French. Luxurious hotels lined that street. Therefore, long before Singapore became a shopping paradise, Hujung Manani was already famous.'

The Famous Historian paused and took a few breaths. Alvin realized that the Tycoon was staring at him.

'Lotis' ancestors came from Java before they settled down near Bangi; they often travelled to Gonoat. They migrated after the bloody Nyemah March on the Ababa Bridge. The town of Tahir is located on the estuary where the Pura River flows into the Java Sea. It can be described as a port. However, the town has no intention to rival the Keppel shipyard in Singapore. In fact, Brutus Harbour only welcomes small boats and yachts, mainly belonging to Malaysian millionaires looking for some relaxation away from the noise and stress of the country. The *Equanimity* and the *Tranquillity* sometimes drop anchor there.'

Some spectators chuckled as other spectators whispered for them to be quiet.

'Hujung Manani has a population of Malay, Javanese and French ancestry, as well as a small number of indigenous people from Sari. They live quite far away at the foot of the mountains and some risk their lives by building huts on the slopes of Mount Bara. It is a dormant volcano, a popular tourist attraction in Tahir. Mount Bara is still not dead, however, and erupts once every few decades.'

The Famous Historian did not want to bore his audience. Raising his voice, he continued forcefully, 'What was the reason for Nyemah and Piah to choose Tahir as the starting point of the revolt against the monarchy? How did the fire from Tahir spread to the entire country? How was the flame of revolution lit and how did it consume the cities of Hujung Manani?'

He paused.

'Several years before, the population of Hujung Manani was suffering from a total lack of human rights. There was no democracy. All the decisions rested with one man: Emperor Sod. He cunningly used his ethnic identity as a Malay and his version of Islam to justify all his acts of despotism and oppression. In Sod's hands, Islam was not the religion which teaches equality, justice, generosity and unity. It was a selective form of the religion. For him, Islam and Hujung Manani owed their strength to him, yes, him, as the emperor. He was the representative of Allah on earth. And Islam was just one way of worshipping him. Emperor Sod then started to call himself Caliph. He even went as far as calling himself Amir al-Mu'minin Sod.'

Another pause. The Famous Historian then exclaimed: 'What kind of caliph was this? More like a demon! What Prince of the Believers was he, when he behaved like the devil? For instance, the Momok people who were indigenous to Hujung Manani, were victims of his cruelty. They were slaughtered. They were raped. They were enslaved. They were not allowed to live normal lives. Stories about Momok people being placed in ships and sent out to sea spread around. They were victims of human trafficking. They were sold as slaves in America. Throughout the mainland and the islands of Hujung Manani, there were stories about mass graves containing corpses of people who were treated like animals; the Momok people were treated like cattle. In fact, animals enjoy higher regard.

'The reign of Yam Tuan Muda Ali in Riau affected Hujung Manani. Emperor Sod chose to follow a hard version of Islam. Naming himself Caliph, then Amir al-Mu'minin, coincided with spreading terror in the name of Islam. Emperor Sod's soldiers were called the Wahhabi, because their general was named Wahab. Sod's army destroyed villages with tanks and shot people with bazookas. The bloody Padi War was unfolding again.'

Another pause. The Tycoon felt uncomfortable as he was forced to listen to the Famous Historian's long monologue.

'The Wahhabi invaded Tiger Island to look for Ba'Alawi followers. In the town of Tahir, they encouraged sectarianism. They went after anyone suspected of being different. Their main targets were the Malays from Hujung Manani because they were believed to practise the Kejawèn teachings. Emperor Sod's army started the repression by marking the doors of the inhabitants of Javanese ancestry with the letter Jim; just as they had done before to the Momok people, marking their doors with the letter Mim.

'Of course, it was impossible for the Malays of Hujung Manani to be totally free of the Javanese way of thinking. Besides the geographical factor, we know that the Javanese influence in this country is strongly embedded because Hujung Manani's ancient history was shaped by Majapahit's control over the country. During the Srivijaya era, Mahayana fought against Hinayana to conquer us. Then Islam fought against Buddhism. Then Muslims fought among themselves, vying for influence and power. When the Santri movement started to gain ground in Java, the Abangans who did not wish to change their way of living fled to Hujung Manani for safety. It took several hundred years for people to practise Islam properly. However, remnants of Abangan Javanese teachings are still strong everywhere. In fact, the brand of Islam practised by Javanese people in Hujung Manani is consistent with Kejawèn teachings. Remember that we follow both the Tareqat and the Ja'fari school of jurisprudence.

'Lotis' ancestors, afraid to be killed by the Wahhabi, gave their only son to a family of mixed French and Tiger Malay descent. This is how Lotis was eventually born. On the other hand, Pertiwi's ancestor joined the movement against the

monarchy started by Nyemah and later led by Piah Berkah. At
the same time, the French offered to help the Momok and the
Javanese Malays to oust the Wahhabi, after which many of these
French men became royal advisers. They accepted help from
the French without suspecting that they had a vested interest in
Hujung Manani. In fact, France was trying to rival the influence
held by Britain in the Malay Archipelago and by Holland in the
islands of Indonesia.

'The True Patriot's ancestor became Piah Berkah's assistant.
The French organized a congress against feudalism. They
approached Piah Berkah and told her that the tyrannical Malay
sultanate of Hujung Manani could not be overthrown without
foreign help.

'The True Patriot had often heard her ancestor recount:
"We joined that congress. I heard Piah's speech with my own
ears. I still remember how brilliant she was at giving speeches in
front of large crowds. The Momok and the Javanese Malays of
Hujung Manani must unite, she said. We must not look at the
Islam supported by Emperor Sod as a protection to get justice.
This is because religious leaders and Malay aristocrats are
synonymous. Religious leaders have a special status in the palace
and they use the narrative of the king as the representative of
God on earth as a slogan in order to protect the power of the
aristocracy. Even on their deathbed, these religious scholars
remind their followers to remain obedient and loyal to the
monarchy regardless of their bad governance, because they
have been chosen by God. Religious leaders of the Wahhabi
movement reinforced the lie. Hah, that was our first open fight!
We founded the Democratic Association of Hujung Manani to
fight against Wahhabi religious leaders. Our movement grew
until we were able to fight against the king. Then Piah became

the leader of the revolution. She was a brave woman. We took to the streets and held our positions for days."

He paused again. The spectators were animated.

'Forty days later, Emperor Sod fled to Malaysia and sought shelter there. He died in disgrace. This is the reason why we still resent the Malays in Hujung Manani. They found excuses to protect a tyrant—for what purpose? For the first time, Hujung Manani was free. But . . . But . . . We did not obtain total freedom at that time.'

Another pause. The audience could feel the revolutionary passion in the long monologue.

The Famous Historian raised his voice: 'There were traitors among us, who enabled the French to stay. On that day, Hujung Manani escaped from the mouth of the dragon and fell into the mouth of the tiger. The colonialists started to show their true colours. France wasted no time in seizing the opportunity. Wahhabi religious leaders held out their hands. When merchants, traders and businessmen dealing in plastic waste joined forces with colonialists and religious leaders, the people fighting against feudalism and colonialism were faced with a formidable enemy. We were tired after overthrowing the king and we did not have any strength left to face the cunning French.'

Silence.

The Famous Historian was overcome with sadness. Some spectators were also tearing up. The Tycoon, uncomfortable, inhaled deeply. The Scientist wiped the tears that were pooling in his eyes. The First Lady was sobbing quietly.

'The French colonized us for some time. As we all know, Piah Berkah was executed by firing squad. Her fate was similar to that of Jose Rizal in the Philippines. And then, we were blessed with a woman from her bloodline, a woman who came to lead us. We men are cowards. Without balls to fight the Leader. Her name was Pertiwi, the True Patriot. And tonight . . . tonight, we thank her for fighting. She was a true patriot, who fought for the country. Patriots must fight. Puppet leaders sell us in exchange for power. Pertiwi was the voice of the people. Our voice.'

Sobs could be heard.

'Piah Berkah's daughter married the True Patriot's grandfather. For a while, the opposition was more moderate. The French, with help from the Wahhabi, were able to hinder the freedom movement. Otto Ali, Pertiwi's grandfather, was a literary figure. One of his works, which is still relevant today, recounts how traders betrayed the country. It is entitled *The Six Gurindam*.'

The Famous Historian's scanned the front rows, looking for the Tycoon. The two men locked eyes and glared at each other.

'Hear my story . . .' he said as he seized the kompang and started to beat it slowly.

The sound of the kompang grew louder, as the beats started to form a rhythm.

The Famous Historian's gaze moved from the Tycoon to the Scientist, who was the current Leader. They were the guests of honour. The VIPs.

'Our ancestor, Otto Ali, wrote a gurindam in the Malay style, which offers advice from which wise people can benefit; this gurindam only comprises six clauses.'

'The poem starts like this:

"O my people, let me tell a story
That I wrote as I am unhappy

If this gurindam is disagreeable
It is because we fear for our people"

'Then the gurindam continues as follows:
    "This is wisdom for sovereigns
    Advice meant to benefit them

    Four enemies are detestable
    The population with misery they saddle"

'This is the first clause of the gurindam:
    "If a country wants to be in safe hands
    Do not let scoundrels ascend

    Scoundrels are of many types
    Know that they are all swines

    Some flatter the king
    To steal and sin with him

    Some behave like monkeys
    Oppressing people and taking their money"

'This is the second clause of the gurindam:
    "If a king forgets his manners
    He oppresses all his people

    If a king is dishonest
    The past is erased

    Do not abandon the country
    This is the reason kings go unruly

    If by wise men he is counselled
    A king can be modelled

If he is wilful he must be handled
If he cannot be guided he must be opposed."'

Now the audience was repeating the words of the gurindam.
It was clear that all the people of Hujung Manani knew it by
heart. The theatre was echoing with voices. And the Famous
Historian let the audience recite the verses of the *Six Gurindam*
after him. He could feel an extraordinary energy and strength
coursing through his veins. Every citizen of the country was
sharing the same fighting spirit. Pertiwi's absence was not an
obstacle.

The Famous Historian inhaled deeply and gazed at random
spectators, one after the other. The room fell silent. The
actor started striking the kompang again, accompanied by the
audience clapping their hands:

'This is the third clause of the gurindam:

"When religious men become full of themselves
We count on pious ones but they are all the same

When religious men behave like dogs
Along with the king they rob

When pious men a good example do not show
They do no good despite what they know

When pious men become pig-headed
They must be stopped or disaster will succeed

When behaviour is dictated by greed
The mouth opens to ask while the stomach is replete

When religious men turn into serpents
Everyone's reputation is damaged

If they abandon their religion
Their turban and slippers they must abandon."

'This is the fourth clause of the gurindam:

"History records the Malays' actions
A people careful to reject addictions

Addiction comes in many varieties
Some are addicted to smoking cannabis

Addiction comes in many varieties
Some are addicted to shameful feats

Some men are very vicious
Without restrictions they are ferocious

Some are violent toward others
They think the Malays are the chosen race

But how can the Malays the chosen race be
When they trample others without mercy

I say that violence must not be repeated
Angry behaviour must be abandoned

I say that the Malays are a gracious nation
They must act to avoid retribution"

'This is the fifth clause of the gurindam:

"If traders come plying their wares
Of all their ruses beware

If merchants are ruled by cupidity
They will ruin the country

If on the throne an earnest king sits
Treacherous traders want to take what's his

If traders obey commands
They bend to a hidden government
If traders have money aplenty
They care not for the country

If they are allowed their treachery
Evil merchants will sell out the country"

'This is the sixth clause of the gurindam:

"A country's enemies are many
Four among them always appear

If a country lives in harmony
Four categories are its enemy

If a king forgets his responsibility
The country will sink if they do not stop his activity

If religious men prostitute their wisdom
It will mark the end of the kingdom

If the Malays forget their humanity
Everyone will fall victim to their cruelty

If a country wants progress and prosperity
Beware of merchants' greed and cupidity.

"And thus ends the gurindam containing six clauses which I, Otto Ali, wrote in the year 1263 of our Prophet on a Thursday in the last week of the month of Shaaban at five o'clock in Hujung Manani.'"

The beating of the kompang stopped.

The lights went out. Some spectators clapped their hands.

The First Pig was on stage when the lights came back on and lit the entire stage. 'They all got it wrong,' he said. 'They are all trying to find an explanation. The koro curse came after the era of Sri Jayanasa. Serlingpa came even after that. The curse first appeared in the era of the Karang Brahi inscription, in 732 AD The inscription says—'

The Second Pig interrupted him. 'The inscription talks about those who conspire with rebels. It tells people to stay loyal to the king if they do not want to die in infamy. It goes like this: "And let all their evil deeds such as disturbing people's peace of mind, bringing illness to people, driving people to madness, using spells, using poison on others or on fish, using drugs, using love potions, forcing their will on others, and more, come to naught, and punish those who commit such evil deeds." The inscription and the curse came to be when the Srivijaya army was gathering to attack Java.'

The Second Pig pretended to be exhausted as he rubbed his protruding stomach, which caused the audience to burst out laughing. The First Pig seized the opportunity to glare at the audience as he said, loud and clear: 'The Srivijaya palace introduced Mahayana, which worshipped Buddha as a God, replacing Hinayana, which regarded the Buddha as merely a saint. How do you think Sri Jayanasa, the king of Srivijaya who supposedly worshipped the Siddh Yantra, an important religious ceremony, was able to act like a religious man and spread the Buddhist teachings of love and compassion among the violent population of Muara Jambi? He needed all the spirits and magic available to control the people. It was only by accepting the Buddhist religion and pretending to be its representative that he was able to pretend to be pious and threaten his people.'

'Where did koro come from?' Sistine asked as she appeared in the right-hand side corner of the stage. She stretched and played with the pigs. The audience laughed when the pigs pretended to be scared.

'In order to ensure that the principles of Mahayana were accepted by the people, Hinayana followers were treated as heretics. Any leader who practised Hinayana was threatened. Sri Jayanasa wanted people to believe that he could reach nirvana, despite his bloody behaviour. There was a lot of fighting and blood at that time, you know? It was not a time for peace and charity. The Lamas inherited the people's fears. In order to enforce the Mahayana, to assert his power, to wipe out Hinayana, which was the original form of Buddhism, Vajrayana, which was full of superstitions, was introduced. Have you heard of Heruka? A statue of Heruka was found in Srivijaya. He is depicted in the *Suddhamala* as follows: "Heruka is half-sitting on one folded leg in the *ardhaparanka* posture, over the body of a dead man. He is wearing human skin but his body is covered in ashes. His right hand is holding a shining *vajra* while his left hand is holding a long club called *khatwanga*. He is decorated with waving flags. There is a bowl made from a blood-stained skull.

He is wearing a sash and a necklace woven from fifty human heads. Fangs stick out of his half-open mouth, and his eyes are filled with lust. His reddish hair is standing straight on his head, making him even more frightening. *Aksobhya* figures decorate his throne and human bones are depicted in his earrings. His head is also decorated with human skulls. He teaches Buddhism and protects its followers from their enemies." This is the depiction of Heruka, a deity who is not just exciting, but terrifying.'

While Sistine was talking about the statue of Heruka, a large group of dancers walked from the back of the theatre up to the stage, where they spread out and started performing a dance imitating a brutal *tantrayana* ceremony by drinking blood. Other dancers, accompanied by eerie music, performed the *ksetra* ceremony, covering a corpse before burning it. Artificial smoke floated above the stage. Bright flames in several areas of the stage added to the surreal atmosphere. Everything contributed to create a ghostly feeling. One dancer was meditating, some were moving their lips as if they were reciting mantras, others drank blood and laughed madly, and some were burning prostrate bodies. Together, they symbolized magic, wealth, longevity, strength, immunity and oppression.

Sistine shouted. The dancers moved to the back. Shrouded in the smoke that still obscured the stage, the actress yelled: 'What was peaceful there? Worshipping Heruka was done to gain access to nirvana, to subjugate all other races in the world. Serlingpa taught all this to Atisa. Fortunately, Atisa was able to balance Hinayana and Mahayana, but at the same time the teachings of Vajrayana under the Mahayana system of thought started to spread wider and were enforced by the Srivijaya kings onto the people. Supporters of Hinayana were oppressed, considered to have gone astray, ostracized, hunted, kidnapped, killed, cursed, and so they lived in fear.'

The actress playing the role of Sistine twisted and twirled on the stage, truly embracing her character.

'A Sailendra princess was captured and brought to Srivijaya. She believed in Hinayana. The Srivijaya ruler wanted to force her to renounce her religion, worship Buddha instead, and denounce those who did not support Mahayana as Hinayana, or "using a lower vessel to attain nirvana". When the princess refused, she was considered disloyal to the king. She refused to have sex with him and was considered a rebel. She was accused of being in cahoots with Java. The princess was stripped naked, dragged to an altar and ordered to drink poison. As she was being burned alive, she shouted: "You will die with no balls! You will all die without balls! O karmmavasita. O datu. Drdhabhakti. Grant me Viryya."'

The few dancers who were still on stage moved as if they were floundering. One after the other, they removed their clothes until they were only dressed in a flimsy material that barely hid their body under the dim stage lights.

Sistine continued with passion: 'The ruler of Srivijaya, who was watching the princess being executed, suddenly said: "*Upasargga* (misfortune), what is this strong *vasikarana* (magic), my *shishna* (penis) has disappeared, my shishna has disappeared!"'

The dancers repeated, like a chorus: 'Shishna, shishna, shishna, shishna, shishna, shishna, shishna, shishna, shishna, shishna' before the lights suddenly went out, followed by the princess' shrill screams as she was dying in the fire.

The spectators were totally silent.

When the lights came back on, the Psychiatrist was sitting with the Famous Historian, facing the audience. They both had a frown on their face. The Famous Historian looked more dejected and depressed. They were clearly suffering from being held in captivity.

'I can't stand it! When the Server comes tonight, we catch him and use him as a hostage,' the Famous Historian said, sounding desperate.

The Psychiatrist, who was trying to keep his emotions under control, answered him at once, 'He is not alone, he has a policeman with him. And he's a trained policeman from the Special Branch himself. We would not be here if we were not useful to them. And I have already explained to you, the Dictator has gone mad. It's his wife who is in power now. We are waiting for a rebellion. I saw it with my own eyes, his penis has shrunk to the size of a date, er, a date is an analogy which is a bit too Islamic, er, let's say, a raisin. He has koro. Or panic caused by koro.'

The Famous Historian mumbled softly, 'There must be someone who can free us. I heard that Datin Lotis has friends in North Korea and she sends kidnapped people to Pyongyang.'

'Unfortunately, there is no Avenger here. Max Heguy can't help us either,' the Psychiatrist answered in a low voice, causing some spectators to laugh at the pop culture reference.

'What is happening out there?' the Famous Historian asked, still sounding stressed.

'Riots,' the Psychiatrist answered briefly.

'Riots?' the Famous Historian asked. 'What do you mean?'

'Benin,' the Psychiatrist added.

'Benin?'

'In 2001, in Cotonou, ten people were attacked by a mob that accused them of being sorcerers, or shamans, or Pak Lokan, or magicians, or wizards, or ghosts or traitors who used witchcraft to steal men's penises.'

The Shaman sitting in the audience chuckled, knowing that the words were addressed to him.

'And this caused riots?' the Famous Historian asked as the Psychiatrist seemed relieved that his fellow prisoner no longer looked disturbed by the change in the conversation.

'Yes, they believed that they could catch koro by shaking hands, or just by touching. So, some people panicked for no reason at the market, for instance. They feared that their penis would be stolen,' the Psychiatrist explained as he looked at the Famous Historian's face.

'Riots start easily. All you need is someone in a crowded place shouting "my penis is gone!"'.

From the sides of the stage, the pigs chanted in a soft voice: 'Shishna, shishna, shishna'.

Some spectators chuckled.

The Psychiatrist added: 'In 2014, in Burkina Faso, a mob killed a man accused of stealing penises in a restaurant. They brought him to a secluded car workshop and killed him. The police tried to protect several other victims, but people could not be reasoned with and they attacked the police station.'

The Famous Historian was shocked. 'How could they attack a police station?'

The Psychiatrist laughed like the demon Valak and the Famous Historian reacted with fright. Then the Psychiatrist pretended to have a seizure and when the Famous Historian started to panic, he emitted a loud shriek.

'It's not funny!' The Famous Historian was angry while the audience laughed. 'Some people were infected by koro after watching a Pak Lokan performance.'

'People will do anything if their penis disappears. They can storm a police station in a police state, or they can overthrow a ruler.'

The actors stopped talking. The theatre was quiet. The audience was silent.

The Famous Historian broke the silence. 'I'm bored of staying here. What are we waiting for? Why are they keeping us here? Does any of us, the Lama, for instance, know how to treat koro and heal the Leader? Then he might let us go free.' The Famous Historian's voice was breaking, showing that he was going back to his previous depressed mental state.

The Psychiatrist tried to make him feel better. 'If we had no use for the police or for the government, we would already have been killed, like they did to other victims of kidnapping before us. We would have been stuffed into a barrel and covered in cement. Or chopped up into pieces. Or blown up with C-4. They would not be looking after us and feeding us; putting us up in a luxurious villa like this one, fully furnished, even though we have no contact with the outside world. They know we can kill ourselves if we lose our will to live. And why should we live, after forty days without any news?'

'Is there any other villa like this one?' The Famous Historian ignored him, mumbling to himself.

'The Monk holds the key. You—why don't you talk to him, make him heal the Dictator?'

The Psychiatrist chortled. 'What did you understand about Kuala Batu? What did you understand about the curse from the Srivijaya era?'

'The curse?'

'Koro is not a real disease. The only sickness is here,' the Psychiatrist said as he pointed to his head.

'It's madness?'

'Yes, mental illness.'

Some spectators laughed.

'How many times must I explain? It is a mental condition, an illusion. Like hysteria. Like running amok. There is no medicine for it.'

'But you said that you gave the Dictator many types of medications.'

'Tranquillizers are not remedies. What did the Monk tell us? He said that in ancient times, when a man was under pressure because he believed that his penis had been stolen, he was treated with lilies.'

The Famous Historian laughed. 'Lilies? What for?'

'Red lilies with three leaves. They were used to treat depression.'

'The Dictator is depressed?'

The Psychiatrist tried again to make the Famous Historian feel better. 'Who knows, perhaps there are riots out there. Like in Benin, or in Burkina Faso. When I was kidnapped and taken here, I heard that the situation was no longer under control in Hujung Manani. The Kuala Batu curse, the Muara Jambi curse, koro, turtle fever, whatever you call it—perhaps it caused riots and who knows, perhaps the Dictator is no longer in power out there.'

'Who is keeping us here then, if there is no reason? They should let us go, let me go.'

'Perhaps it is the deep state.'

'The deep state? We have been kidnapped by the *deep state*? Who are they? People say that they are controlled by plastic waste traders.'

The Tycoon swallowed loudly.

'Arggh . . . What's the difference out there? Are we really free out there?' the Psychiatrist asked earnestly.

'We are all slaves to something. We are all imprisoned by something, even when we think that we are free. Some are confined by a religion, a culture, a belief or a principle. Some are trapped by material things. Capitalists, for instance, are bound by profit. We wear invisible shackles. Nobody can see them while we are still here, alive and enslaved. We should think about that, like Vladimir and Estragon did, when they were waiting for Godot.' The Psychiatrist's voice was loud and clear, aimed at the audience.

The spectators were quiet. The stage lighting was bright.

'We live in a country that imprisons us. We need to find the will to survive,' the Psychiatrist went on.

The Famous Historian started sobbing. 'But . . . but . . . Godot never came. Godot never came . . . and we don't know if their penis—if the Leader's penis will come back.'

'Forget about other people's penises. Mind your own penis. Look after yourself. *Kita jaga kita.*'

The audience burst out laughing.

The Famous Historian kept sobbing. 'Why is our fate determined by the Leader's short dick?'

The Psychiatrist comforted him. 'Do you remember how Islam arrived in Malacca?'

Between two sobs, the Famous Historian answered: 'Yes, the sultan dreamed that he was circumcised and met someone who introduced himself as the Prophet.'

'What is wrong with foreskin?' the Psychiatrist asked.

The spectators were amused and laughed loudly.

'He converted to Islam when Sidi Aziz arrived on the Malacca shore that afternoon from Jeddah. You mean . . . you mean the Malays became Muslims because of the sultan's penis? The Malays are Muslims because of a king's cock? Not because of awareness, not because they were drawn to the teachings of the religion, or to that preacher's morals?'

'We should have created a dessert to commemorate the event and named it "the king's cock". Hmmm, it sounds disgusting. The Sultan's Penis, that sounds more Arabic.'

The audience giggled as if they were being tickled.

The Psychiatrist waited for the spectators to stop laughing, his eyes fixed on the Famous Historian's face. 'You were telling the truth when you said that this was like waiting for Godot.'

The spectators laughed again.

The Famous Historian seemed to wake up from a dream, and he expressed shock at every sentence: 'What is the point of religion if it is all about cocks and not about the intellect? Faith should come from the mind, not from the cock. A cock, whether it is short or long, does not think and does not generate thoughts!'

He paused, took a breath and continued. 'Huh, saying cock instead of penis is more exciting.'

The audience burst out laughing.

The Psychiatrist added: 'From the Malays to Hinayana, Mahayana and then Vajrayana—it's always been about cocks and kings. It's the same in Hujung Manani. It's about Datuk Priapus Mappadulung Daeng Mattimung Karaeng Sanrobone's penis, about the Dictator's cock, and the cocks of his cabinet ministers. We are ruled by dickheads!'

'FUCK!' the Famous Historian exclaimed in anger.

The lights were turned off.

The audience laughed.

When the lights were turned on again, the audience was still laughing. In fact, even more spectators were laughing. On stage, there were two actors: a woman who was dressed to look like Datin Lotis, the Leader's Wife, and a man, stark naked, standing next to the low bookshelf displaying the two statues of the Fertility Goddess. When the audience realized that the actors were those who had played the parts of the pigs, they started laughing anew. Some spectators even rolled around on the floor in fits of laughter.

Datin Lotis waited for the laughter to die down before saying: 'Look, this is *bossku*, my boss. And your boss as well.'

The laughter started again, much louder this time.

'After the Pak Lokan performance shocked the entire country of Hujung Manani, Datin Lotis called the media to launch a new campaign following the advice given by several cabinet ministers.'

The naked actor playing the part of the Dictator did not make any effort to hide his penis. He stood and walked here and there, displaying the cellulite on his buttocks. The audience became rowdy. He waited for the laughter to calm down before opening his mouth, declaring: 'Okay, I don't have balls. The cabinet ministers don't have balls. The Liverpool Mufti doesn't have balls. The Director of the Special Branch doesn't have balls. The Head of the Religious Leaders' council doesn't have balls. More and more people don't have balls. We acknowledge the fact that we don't have balls. I believe that lack of balls is not an issue. I believe that we must embrace the lack of balls with a pure heart. The people should understand that this lack of balls syndrome is not an issue. We embrace koro. We embrace our lack of balls. It's not a problem.'

The audience went wild.

'Don't do anything rash. This is the time to adopt *wasatiyyah*. We have nothing to be ashamed of. Indeed, I want to tell all the men out there who don't have any balls that you are not alone. Don't be ashamed. Look at me today, look . . . look . . .' the actor said as he shook his bottom and his penis wobbled.

The audience burst out laughing again. The Scientist's wife covered her mouth with her hand as she laughed uncontrollably.

The actor playing the role of the Dictator shouted, 'Come on, gentlemen! In the name of plastic, let's get naked! It's normal.

Don't listen to accusations from the opposition! Don't listen to the claims made by people receiving funds from abroad! Don't listen to the Chinese! The Malays must stand up and shout together: *malu apa* bossku!'

The stage lights were extinguished, but spectators did not stop laughing. Behind the stage, the crew helped Justin Goh and Brian Chong get dressed.

Justin quickly said: 'I hope nobody filmed this with their phone.'

The stage director reassured him: 'We warned the spectators. We had people check that nobody filmed anything.'

Brian Chong appeared, dressed in his costume.

'Come on, let's put an end to this riot!' the Rookie Detective, who was the director, encouraged the actors.

The lights illuminated the stage.

The First Pig and the Second Pig returned to the stage, as the spectators got ready to watch the last scene.

Both pigs spoke in unison: 'We are just food. We are eaten by all, regardless of colour. Problems are created by men. This is because men think that colour is important.'

The First Pig turned toward the Second Pig and asked: 'How does it feel to get koro?'

The Second Pig answered calmly: 'It is like all your rights have been denied. You feel empty, weak, helpless, left alone on earth when everyone else has gone to Mars. You feel like you have lost the person you loved the most.'

The actors playing the parts of the Famous Historian, the Monk and the Psychiatrist walked to the stage from behind the curtain. The Famous Historian, panting, announced to the audience that he could see the Server in the distance.

'What we have been waiting for has arrived. What we have been waiting for is here.'

The Monk answered with one word: 'Godot.'

The Famous Historian snorted angrily: 'The Server! Perhaps we should force him to let us go.'

The Psychiatrist laughed. 'He is a policeman. He takes his orders directly from the Dictator. In Hujung Manani, the police are untouchable. Who can give them orders?'

The two pigs standing behind them looked around with excitement. Sistine appeared, swaying her hips as she approached the other actors.

There was a knock on the door. The Monk did not move but the Psychiatrist stepped back a little.

The door opened.

A small child entered. The spectators were surprised to discover the young actor. The child walked to the centre of the stage.

The Monk stared at him open-mouthed, while the Famous Historian looked puzzled. Then, like the others, the Psychiatrist wondered what was going on. The two pigs, functioning as comic characters, were whispering to each other. Sistine was the only character who looked calm, even though she did not make any movements to avoid drawing attention to herself.

The child announced in a clear voice: 'The revolution is over.'

'When did it start?' Sistine asked immediately.

The child repeated the same sentence: 'The revolution is over.'

The Famous Historian rushed forward. 'Who won? Who lost?'

The child did not turn his head. He kept looking at the audience as he replied: 'Does it matter, uncle?'

The Monk answered: 'Yes, it matters a lot. For my existence.'

The child shook his head.

The Famous Historian insisted. 'In the name of plastic, it is very important for history textbooks.'

The pigs nodded. The Psychiatrist advanced to the front of the stage, in the centre.

The child looked at them without changing positions and said, 'Go, you are free. You have your freedom. You have your independence.'

Sistine walked quickly to the middle as if she wanted to attack them, faced the audience and shouted in a high-pitched voice: 'Revolution!'

The lights went off.

The curtain fell. The spectators gave a standing ovation. The Scientist, who was the current Leader, and his wife were among the first to stand up and clap their hands with enthusiasm. The Shaman stood up quickly, followed by the Tycoon's son. After a while, the Tycoon also stood up, despite the uneasy feeling that gripped his chest.

The Tycoon whispered to his only son: 'Find a way to get back at these supporters of nimbyism'. Then, in an even softer voice, he continued, 'Find a porn actress who is willing to record that she had sex with the Leader's Jewish wife. We'll make a lesbian sex video clip.'

The Tycoon's son swallowed loudly.

The Tycoon was becoming angrier. 'Find politicians from Badang's camp who are willing to betray him. We are going to destroy their party. Find eleven guys who are willing to betray him. Eleven. Fuck reformation. Fuck democracy. Kita jaga kita.'

The Tycoon's son sighed.

The audience went on and on clapping their hands.

Backstage, the actors exchanged hugs.

Qu'allah Bénisse La Hujung Manani!

Once upon a time, there was a very poor old woman. She survived on charity, feeding off scraps spared by the people in her village. She was much too old to work and had to resort to begging in order to survive.

'One day, the old woman was on her way to the headman's house. She wanted to ask for a handful of red beans to make porridge. She hoped that the headman's wife—who was so elegant and beautiful with her hair bouncing over her shoulders—was not home so that she could just talk to the husband, who was more understanding.

'When the old woman reached the stairs to the kitchen, she called out but her hope died immediately. The wife appeared on the threshold annoyed, and chased her away with harsh words.

'How dare you show your face again?! Old hag, ugly, shameless hag!'

'The harsh words broke the old woman's heart. Dejected, she walked back home. In the middle of the night, she prayed to God, asking Him to change her life. She told Him that she was aware that people had to help themselves if they wanted their luck to change. But she did not know what more to do to get out of her misfortune.

'Her desperate cry for help was heard by three dwarfs. In the dark of the night, the dwarfs brought a magic pot to the old woman's kitchen. They also brought three magic red beans which would produce a full pot of porridge. All that was needed was to recite a magic formula to start the cooking.

'The old woman woke up in the dark and was very frightened. She thought that burglars had broken into her house. She hid and stayed very quiet. When the sun came up, she quickly went to her kitchen to check the source of the noises she had heard during the night.

'Imagine her surprise when she found a cooking pot full of delicious red bean porridge!

'The following night, she heard the same strange noises again. And the next morning, the pot was full of porridge, which was even more delicious than the previous one. The miracle happened every night.

'On the seventh day, the old woman could no longer control her curiosity. She plucked up all her courage and went to the kitchen. Imagine her surprise when she saw three dwarfs, no bigger than a thumb, cooking the porridge!

'At first, the dwarfs wanted to flee, but their size made it difficult. They decided to face the old woman. The oldest dwarf pleaded with her not to reveal their existence.

'She agreed not to tell anyone.

'The dwarfs warned her that if she revealed their secret, she would suffer terrible consequences.

'Week after week, the villagers were surprised to see that the old woman was no longer begging for food. The most surprised of all was the headman's wife, who used to take pleasure in humiliating her. She suspected that the old woman was keeping a *toyol* to steal food for her.

'Under continuous pressure to reveal her secret, the old woman finally confessed that she owned a magic pot.

'The headman's wife ordered her servants to seize the pot from the old woman's house and she ordered the woman to start cooking red bean porridge.

'The old woman was forced to obey. But when the pot was full, the porridge continued to bubble, spilling over the rim of the pot and onto the kitchen floor. The porridge soon filled the headman's house. The wave of porridge overflowed into the streets, flooding the neighbourhood, before covering the entire village.

'Porridge kept flowing and it became a huge flood. The old woman was desperate and complained to the pot, hoping that the dwarfs would hear her. She apologized for breaking her promise.

'"Until when will the pot shoot out porridge?"

'The pot answered: "*Sampai hujung* (Until the end)."

'The red bean porridge kept overflowing.

'"*Sampai mana?*" (Until when?), the old woman, desperate, contrite and ashamed, insisted.

'"*Sampai hujung.*" (Until the end.)

'"*Hujung mana ni?*" (The end of what?)

'The old woman learned never to break her promises again, and the headman's wife stopped being cruel. The flood of red porridge also touched the hearts of the villagers who had never before felt any compassion. But what can we do? From that day onward, the village was known as Hujung Manani.'

The story received a standing ovation. Pertiwi was the first to stand up, followed by Jesus. Benedict, who was barely six years old, smiled shyly on stage. Other parents stood up to show their appreciation.

This was at a storytelling competition in Benedict's primary school, located in a shabby neighbourhood in the suburbs of Paris.

Simone de Beauvoir, who was a member of the jury, turned toward Jean-Paul Sartre. They winked at each other, showing that they liked the story. Simone stood up and laughed, while Jean-Paul clapped his hands enthusiastically.

Benedict did not win the competition. But his name was destined to become famous in a faraway land. At the ends of the earth.

In Hujung Manani.

***

Three hours after the Pak Lokan performance was broadcast live on television to the whole country, five women ignored the curfew and took to the streets, bringing the revolution to the people. Here follows the detailed account which I, Faisal Tehrani, wrote, and which is kept in the National Museum of Hujung Manani, based on the testimonies of Professor Badang, Mother Pertiwi and Ashraf Wahidi:

3.29 a.m.

The Scientist woke up because a bright light was shining in his face. His wife was sitting close to the television set, staring at the screen.

'What is happening, darling?'

The woman looked intently at her husband. 'Honey, perhaps it's time for us to go back home.'

'Why?'

'Mother Pertiwi needs you.'

'What for?'

At the exact same time, the Tycoon was rushed to Hujung Manani Private Medical Centre.

No.

Not because of koro. Because of something much more serious and disgusting.

However, at the hospital, the emergency department was crowded with koro patients. While he was experiencing indescribable pain, the Tycoon witnessed a disturbing sight: naked men soaking in large tubs filled with cold water.

Every ten minutes or so, a male nurse poured ice cubes into the tubs. Hospital attendants were preparing more tubs in case more patients required them. One man was shivering with cold and mumbling incoherently. Outside the hospital, men who were afraid of being infected with koro were stripping completely naked and jumping into water.

Some jumped naked into tin mining ponds. Others sat in streams or open drains without thinking. In a village in Hujung Manani, a group of religious teachers shamelessly revealed their *aurat* and sat in filthy wastewater in an open drain. They held each other because they were cold. According to them, their actions were *harus* because they were under duress. The Liverpool Mufti issued a fatwa saying that their actions were *makruh* but still allowed if they had no other choice.

Many sat in fountains in parks and some poured water over their bodies on the streets in an attempt to cool down. Nobody knew who had started the rumour that soaking in cold water could prevent koro, but it seemed that the Pak Lokan performance had caused a nationwide koro epidemic, compared to the previous weeks when koro attacks had been sporadic. The national spread of the disease caused total panic.

The Scientist was watching television in Israel with stupefaction. The newsreader was saying that the men on the screen had wrapped some ginger with arum flowers (*Arisaema triphyllum*) in a piece of yellow-and-red cloth, which they had tied around their waist as an amulet.

The reporter also showed images of men attaching a sort of fabric around their arms. The news bulletin explained that the amulets contained calabash seeds (*Lagenaria siceraria*). The CNN reporter added that some victims of koro were taking cactus plants with basil leaves (*ocimum basilicum*). Men who were not infected with the disease yet applied lime leaves to their forehead, throat and earlobes. The television showed photocopy shops swamped by people trying to make copies of prayers and spells. There were many types of talismans. Places of worship were full, a clear sign that panic was gripping the country.

Another popular traditional remedy to avoid koro was to dip the entire shaft of the penis in cheese before drying it near a flame. What does cheesy cock taste like, I wonder? Apparently, coating a penis in cheese can repel demons.

The Scientist's wife told her husband: 'News reports like this only help the spread of koro and do nothing to educate people. This is a clear case of Munchausen syndrome. They believe it, so they invent the symptoms, which convinces doctors that they have koro. This is crazy, darling! Just crazy!'

'Koro is not a disease. It's a cultural landscape. A social, political, economic landscape! Only diseased countries get koro.'

'Racism, sectarianism, corruption . . . it all adds up,' the Scientist's wife asserted.

The Scientist was glued to the television screen. 'The koro crisis in Assam in India in 1998, lasted for eight weeks because the media kept reporting about it. Why has this disease spread so far and so fast? What did we miss?'

The Scientist's wife placed her hand on her husband's cheek. 'Last night, there was a live telecast of a Pak Lokan performance from the Leader's residence. They say, well . . . they say that several personalities were infected with koro after the main performer had a stroke on stage.'

'It was live?'

'Yes.'

'Actually, Pak Lokan is a strange type of performance,' the Scientist muttered. 'It is a traditional form of dance from Kelantan, which was banned when the Islamists seized power in the state. It is not part of Hujung Manani's culture and must have been imported by Lotis.'

In the midst of the prevailing panic at Hujung Manani Medical Centre, nobody could explain the stupidity of the situation that affected the country's male population. For instance, nobody publicly explained that the penis is an organ which can change size according to desire, temperature, or climate change. Patients could also experience variations in size due to depression, worry, stress, high fever or a combination thereof; or because of the use of certain drugs.

A female doctor looked at the Tycoon and asked the famous millionaire's son: 'Koro? Is it koro?'

The doctor thought that it was strange that the Tycoon had not called his private physician or sought treatment abroad.

'Please, Doctor, this is an emergency,' said the Tycoon's son, with worry on his face.

'Koro?'

'No.'

The doctor, without listening to the young man's denial, continued to grumble: 'It's normal to panic. But er, it only affects men who are not educated. Emmm, in 1967, the hospitals in Singapore were fully occupied with men who demanded to have their penises examined. They thought they were sick because they had eaten pork from unvaccinated pigs.'

The doctor who was not wearing a name tag, was having trouble breathing. Something smelled very bad nearby.

'It's not koro, doctor. It's not!' the Tycoon's son insisted angrily. 'I am sure that it's not koro. My father refuses to show his penis. But he has diabetes and was recently released from hospital. His penis smells.'

'Oh,' was all the doctor could say, 'and why should I look at his penis then?'

'It smells. There's something going on.'

Outside the hospital, more and more women were taking to the streets. The men, however, were busy dipping their dicks in cheese and generally obsessing over their penises.

4.29 a.m.

It was no secret that the Tycoon was the investor who funded the Dictator's political campaign.

The Leader had not been seen in public for over three weeks and all sorts of rumours were circulating. Usually, the Tycoon was able to handle anything that went wrong. For instance, currency fluctuations. Or unusual movements on the stock exchange.

Oftentimes, talk among businesspeople would also give clues. However, at the same time as the Dictator contracted koro, the cabinet lost control and the entire population of Hujung Manani was cursed, as the Tycoon was dealing with his own problems.

He relied on his son to look after the business and report any suspicious market behaviour, as well as to inform him of any political developments involving the animosity between the Leader and the opposition team led by the True Patriot. But now, his son had not updated him with the information that he needed to access, and he could not think straight because of his diabetes.

Almost at the same time as the Dictator had lost his mind, the Tycoon had collapsed and been taken to the VIP ward of the Hujung Manani University Hospital. He had fainted in his office when his blood sugar spiked. He stayed at the hospital for three weeks, during which his wife and his son refused to discuss anything regarding business or the political crisis that was gripping the country.

Even Datin Lotis' invitation to the Pak Lokan performance had not been delivered to him by his private secretary, upon the doctor's advice. To make a long story short, the Tycoon had been completely cut off from the outside world for three weeks, locked up in the VIP ward.

As soon as he was released from the hospital, his wife suggested that they go for a break in Malaysia, so they flew to Malacca.

There, several days later, their chatty maid let some information slip.

'Datuk Seri, did you know that there is an epidemic in Hujung Manani right now?'

The Tycoon immediately forced one his business managers to tell him the truth about the situation in Hujung Manani.

He was furious that he had not been told anything. He starting calling people on the phone and found out about all the strange incidents that had occurred in Hujung Manani.

He found out that there was a pig flu outbreak in a rural area of the country, which had broken out before the koro epidemic. He also found out that the former Editor-in-Chief of the *Hujung Manani Tribune*, one of the True Patriot's main supporters, had died of a heart attack.

He was shocked to hear that the Dictator had gone missing and that the political leadership of the country was in disarray. He became extremely preoccupied with finding out about how the koro epidemic that was surreptitiously spreading had now reached enormous proportions. One of his employees in Johor Bahru added that a preacher had gone missing, and when he reappeared, he was half-crazy and delirious.

When the Tycoon contacted the investigator who always did all kinds of dirty jobs for him, the man told him that the Leader was rumoured to have killed a woman who had also slept with many other cabinet ministers. The investigator also believed that the army was no longer loyal to the Leader, the police had no leadership, and they could be controlled.

While the Tycoon was supposed to be resting in Malacca, he lost his temper. He started yelling at this wife, his son and his staff for keeping him in the dark about such important developments. In his panic, the Tycoon forced his son to contact anyone he could from the True Patriot's team.

'We must change our allegiance. Hujung Manani could fall into the hands of the opposition. The True Patriot . . . That damn woman will cut us off! We'll be boycotted!'

His son, not convinced by the chances of success of that strategy, protested. 'But papa, do you really think that the True Patriot's team will accept our offer of peace, considering your long history of going against her? Do you think we can manipulate anyone?'

'Argh, you're stupid! Offer money! Offer money, do you understand? All political movements need money, right? We're not just anyone. We'll invite them to play golf.'

The son let out a silent curse.

'Also, arrange a meeting with the Head of the Religious Leaders of Hujung Manani. He is a Malay *silat* master. He is also the leader of the Right-wing Muslims Reject Mushrikin Alliance (MURMA). If Priapus falls and Pertiwi takes over, the shadow government should take action immediately. We must incite Muslims and Malays to fear that they will be in danger under Pertiwi's government. The Malays are overly sensitive about anything regarding Islam. They are not very smart.'

Thus, the Tycoon did not get any rest after his hospital stay. The only focus of his thoughts and his efforts was to handle all the issues that had been ignored during his isolation while he was being treated in hospital. That is why he had now been rushed to a private hospital. He was exhausted and had ignored his diabetic condition.

Two days ago, he had returned to Hujung Manani, ready to face the possibility that the True Patriot would call on the people to demonstrate in the streets. He suddenly passed out. He came to, but his blood pressure was 90/40, with a heartbeat of 130 bpm. His temperature was 40°C.

The Tycoon thought that he had caught koro because he was experiencing tremendous pain in his groin. His son called the family doctor, who was surprised by what he saw. He scolded the Tycoon: 'I can't believe that you didn't see the changes in your own penis! Didn't you urinate or defecate at all?'

Five days ago, when the Tycoon had resumed work, he had found a bump that looked like a cyst to the left of his crotch, but did not really pay any attention to it. He didn't inject insulin either. The family doctor was shocked when he discovered that the Tycoon's testicles had swollen to the half the size of a football. They were filled with a combination of fluid, blood and pus which was oozing out. The injured area smelled like a rotten corpse.

The hospital doctor now examined the Tycoon's genitalia and confirmed the report written by the family doctor. 'This symptom is typical of diabetic patients who do not follow their insulin treatment. It has become critical as it has reached the stage of Fournier's gangrene. This is an infection that attacks the genital and anal areas, and quickly necrotizes tissues.'

The Tycoon felt like dying.

'Did you bring the medicine that your previous doctor gave you?'

The Tycoon's son gave the list of medicines that he had brought with him.

'SGLT2; Canagliflozin, Dapagliflozin and Empagliflozin. Patients treated with SGLT2 are at risk of contracting Fournier's gangrene. Unfortunately, these medicines affect the genital organs and the urinary tract.'

The Tycoon looked at the doctor weakly. 'What are you going to do, Doctor?'

The doctor lifted the sheet covering the Tycoon's crotch, a worried expression on her face. 'Look, the penis is gangrenous. We need to remove the pus and the dead tissues to save your life.'

The Tycoon stared at the doctor and asked in a feeble voice, 'How is my penis, doctor?'

The doctor, who could no longer stand the putrid smell, answered briefly, 'There is a very high possibility that we have to remove it. It is rotten.'

The Tycoon lowered his head and tears filled his eyes. The doctor continued, 'The situation is critical. We call this "septic shock with multiple organ failure"'.

The Tycoon's son was nauseous but he pressed the doctor for more information. 'What are my father's chances, doctor? He has a lot of work to do in Hujung Manani . . .'

The female doctor remained polite as she replied, 'Sir, your father's chances of survival are only fifty-fifty. If he lives, he still risks getting a second or third infection. We also have to look at his kidney function to see if the kidneys are still working. And of course, there is also the possibility of depression.'

The Tycoon was now sobbing as he held to his son's arm.

The doctor only took a short breath before continuing. 'We need to stabilize the blood pressure. We need to support the affected organs. We need to control the sugar levels. I need to refer the patient to a surgeon who will remove the dead tissues. He also needs to clean the wound. We are going to start antibiotics immediately to kill the infection. After that, once the gangrened tissues have been removed, we will observe the wound and pray that it heals properly, and that there is no pus. Finally, we will ask a plastic surgeon to close the wound so that it looks neat. But at the moment, your father's penis looks very bad.'

It was while the Tycoon was writhing in pain that Lotis tried to contact him. The Leader's Wife remembered what her husband had told her when he was still lucid: 'If the General and the police turn coats, our only lifeline is the Tycoon. We protect all his profits from his plastic waste business, and he will not suffer any losses as long as he stays with us.'

However, the Tycoon was fighting for his life as the doctor was considering removing his penis. Therefore, the Tycoon's

wife told the Leader's Wife that her husband was focusing on
his penis too.

Lotis was quite surprised. 'The Tycoon is also focused on
his dick? What has happened to Hujung Manani?'

That was before the Pak Lokan performance.

In Israel, Professor Dr Badang Kuwau and his wife were
getting ready to return to Hujung Manani. One of the True
Patriot's assistants had called him.

'We believe that Dr Cakravantin, one of your former
students, has been kidnapped by Priapus' regime. We believe
that he was captured in order to treat the Leader's koro. We
also believe that the situation is critical and the True Patriot
needs you to make an appearance in the national media here to
reassure everyone.'

The Scientist took a deep breath.

'Koro is not a disease. It is a mental condition, which
manifests itself by an unfounded fear.'

He lectured the True Patriot's assistant, insisting that
someone must appear in public and explain that koro was a
psychosexual conflict. It depended on the patient's temperament.
It depended on his cultural beliefs, on his guilt due to his
religious background. Hujung Manani must know that only
those who were not educated could suffer from koro because
of their superstitions. Those who did not have self-confidence
in sexual matters were also susceptible to get koro.

'This disease is not in the penis, but in the mind; because
a man pays too much attention to his own genitalia. Someone
must explain all this to the people of Hujung Manani. We have
become the laughing stock of the world.'

On the other end of the telephone line, the assistant
answered: 'The person we need to do that is you, sir. We will
pay for all your travel expenses and your stay here. Someone will

pick you up at the airport as soon as you land. Perhaps we will organize a press conference at the airport.'

5.29 a.m.

The Scientist looked outside his window. It was still dark.

Some households were already awake. His wife Shulamit, feeling worried for him, pressed his hand gently. They were on their way to the airport. 'How do you feel, darling, about going back to Hujung Manani?'

The Scientist did not answer. Instead, he kept staring outside the window. It was still early in Jerusalem. A snowflake was melting on the windshield of the taxi. The Scientist held his wife's hand tightly in his and rubbed her fingers with his thumb.

'Hujung Manani is okay. As long as we don't go to Sayong Pinang . . .'

His wife rubbed his arm to calm him down. 'It's all gonna be okay. I feel that democracy will win. We're talking about a strong person here, not just anyone. She is the True Patriot.'

The Scientist thought about his life up to this point. So much had happened. He was an Indigenous man from Sayong Pinang in Malaysia who had migrated to Hujung Manani before landing in faraway Israel.

The airport procedures were smooth for Business Class passengers.

In the waiting area, the Scientist focused on writing notes about what the True Patriot's assistant had told him, and what had been reported in the news.

Why was Cakravantin kidnapped? He could not remember any student with that name. An unusual name. Perhaps he was Thai. Was it normal for the Special Branch to kidnap people in Hujung Manani? Why did the country deteriorate so much under Priapus' leadership? Why did people still want this kind of repression and tyranny?

The Scientist remembered Haji Ben Adik's face. It was replaced by a vision of Ungku, then of the Dictator. It was painful to think about Haji Ben Adik's cruel murder. They had become very close friends when his mother had married a member of the royalty in a neighbouring country. They had first met when they were in France, but their acquaintance had been limited to attending the functions held by the True Patriot and her husband. However, the situation in Malaysia had brought them closer together, albeit for a short time.

The Scientist was born in Sayong in the Hulu Sungai Selatan region.

As an Indigenous child, he almost did not get the opportunity to get an education. Fortunately, the name 'Badang' had drawn the attention of a Malaysian politician, who was visiting Sayong Pinang. He was still a child and had been given the task of offering flowers to the politician, a feudal custom that the Malays enjoyed. The minister had held his soft round cheek and asked him, 'What is your name?'

He had only uttered one word: 'Badang.'

The minister had laughed and answered, 'Wah, are you as brave as the legendary warrior? Do you eat ghost vomit? I am Orang Kaya Nira Sura from Seluang.'

The minister put his hand in the area between Badang's legs and whispered, 'Oh, you're quite big! The real Badang! Come to my house. I have an apartment in Mont Kiara. We can go to Port Dickson on weekends and pick up litter from the beach for charity events. Or we can have ginger drinks at the Hard Rock Café.'

Badang still remembered how everyone present burst out laughing. As for him, he was so scared that he vomited behind the stage. It was surreal because the minister had been making vehement speeches upholding Islam in front of the Indigenous people.

Five months later, Badang was holding a fish-trap in the Linggiu river, where the other Badang had fished a long time before, but the fish were eaten by ghosts, when his father came looking for him. The old man was out of breath from running. 'The minister who visited before is offering you a scholarship to study in Kota Tinggi.'

Badang did not waste any time thinking about it. He considered the act of groping as payment for the scholarship. He liked science and excelled in the subject.

His rapid academic success enabled him to continue his studies in France. There, he met Benedict, or Haji Ben Adik. As a Malaysian citizen, he was quickly accepted by Pertiwi, who also came from the same region. Even Dr Jesus considered him his son. But then, his friendship with Benedict was not as close when he moved to Hujung Manani.

6.29 a.m.

After the Subuh prayers, there were already 100 women marching in the streets of the capital of Hujung Manani. There was hardly any police control. The army's warning that they would send tanks to suppress any protest or demonstrations remained an empty threat, considering the fact that there were no uniformed units on the streets. Consequently, the number of demonstrators grew.

Most of the women who took to the streets were pushing strollers, but there were no babies inside. The strollers, strangely enough, contained television sets.

Many rumours had been circulating since hysteria had gripped the country as a result of the failed Pak Lokan performance. The official media of Hujung Manani featured clips of an interview with the Leader, his wife and several cabinet ministers. It was clear that the interview had been recorded a long time ago. Demonstrators became fed up with the Leader's propaganda, unplugged their television sets and brought them to the streets.

The propaganda had become ridiculous. In an interview, the Youth and Single People's Affairs Minister told CNN news that reports about koro were malicious and were a conspiracy conceived by the West against the East. 'I am like a father to you. So I know. In Southeast Asia, like Pigafetta wrote, we pierce our penis with metal pins, wheels, spurs, or hooks, so that when we have sex, it gives more pleasure and when it jingles, it produces a pleasant music. Don't insult us by saying that our penis is shorter or shrinking because of a disease which nobody knows where it comes from.'

At about 5.00 a.m., before the time for Subuh prayers, the Liverpool Mufti appeared on television (unfortunately, most television sets had been stolen by women and brought to the streets) and issued a fatwa. 'I wish to stress to the pubic—er, the public—after observing the current situation and examining all the evidence together with the National Fatwa Council of Hujung Manani, that we have discussed the issue and arrived at the conclusion that it is haram to take part in any unlawful activity aimed at overthrowing the Leader. For women who demonstrate in the streets without their husband's permission are considered *nushuz*, and if they are not married and demonstrate in the streets without their father's permission, they are disobedient and it is haram. Considering the men's situation in Hujung Mani—er, Manani—who are facing *mihna* and tribulations, a trial sent by Allah since they have lost their dick—er, their penis—and their testicles, it is compulsory for women to stay at home and give priority to preserving men's honour. It is haram to let our country, Hujung Manani, lose its reputation, and any shameful action to oppose a government which protects Islamic law is also haram. In the name of Allah, the Leader is performing *tawaf*, and you are being disobedient to Allah by organizing demonstrations. In the name of Allah, any attempt to cause trouble is haram. We, religious leaders, urge women to look after their aurat. Verily, the aurat refers not only to the parts of the body which must be covered, but also to their honour, which must be protected and not exposed to the public eye, such as by going to demonstrate in the streets. We ask those who have been led astray by the invalid opposition campaign led by Pertiwi the Bastard to stop their support because it is haram. It is haram for a Malay Muslim woman like Hajjah Pertiwi to become the leader of this country. Haram. Haram. Haram. What will happen when she menstruates and makes a mistake when making a big decision about the country because she is having her period? We urge the people, especially Muslim people, to get clear and true information from time to time from the local news bulletins and not to believe any haram foreign news reports which have been manipulated by the French and are trying to destroy our Muslim government. It is absolutely haram to conspire with Christians and Jews. Haram. Haram. Haram!'

In response to the long-winded and empty fatwa, the True Patriot's assistant urged the population and especially women, to take to the streets to protest against any type of interdiction or condemnation.

'O women, daughters of Nyai Gede Pinateh, daughters of Dang Sirat, daughters of Nai Gede Wonogiri! We tell you that it is halal to take your television sets to the streets. It is haram to watch news which is unfair to women. Prejudiced news. Women are power. Women are the law. And power is women. The law is women.'

Thus, the strollers carrying television sets became a symbol of protest against the fatwa and propaganda.

At the same time, the Tycoon was in an operating room. Five surgeons were removing dead tissues from his penis, cutting away rotten flesh and removing pus so that it would dry faster.

The swollen, bleeding and damaged penis looked like it could still be saved.

The Tycoon was unconscious. There was no news from the Leader. Hujung Manani was entirely in the dark. The dark-skinned Youth and Single People's Affairs Minister was the only one who tried to maintain the Leader's government. Interviews with other ministers had stopped.

7.29 a.m.

Ashraf Wahidi (who had also once been known as Adele), the famous handsome preacher who had suffered mental problems a few weeks before, appeared on Indonesian television with his wives, Bahiah Burduri Binti Satdin, Bibiana Layolet Binti Abdullah and Hindun Nurul Wati Binti Haji Galak. The religious celebrity was calm and faced the camera with confidence.

'I urge the people, and in particular Muslim people, to unite and protest against falsehood. I regret to tell you that Hujung Manani is facing an important test. We are at a crossroads. The time has come for us to make reforms. I humbly declare my support for Mother Pertiwi, the True Patriot, and her opposition team. I intend to use what little influence I have to do good. In truth, Hujung Manani has a lot of potential, and we should not let our country fall into the hands of criminals, whether they are religious men looking after their own interests, supporters of feudalism who want to restore the throne to the descendants of Emperor Sod, or capitalists who are only looking to increase their wealth.'

Ashraf Wahidi paused. He remembered when he was Adele—his legs spread apart, raped by the Liverpool Mufti in front of Abu Bakar Baghdadi. His heart was filled with sorrow.

'Let us march in the streets, and follow the same steps together. I declare that I repent of my sin of being a conservative fundamentalist orthodox patriotic nationalist extreme Malay, and I am taking to the liberal path in full awareness. Let us save our country and while the men have not yet healed, we need to follow wise female leaders like Maryam, Asiah, Khadijah and Fatimah; they were the mothers, wives, sisters and daughters of virtuous men, who can lead mankind.'

The Scientist and his wife were queuing up to board the plane when they happened to see Ashraf Wahidi on the television screen of the waiting area.

'Who is that man, honey?'

The Scientist shrugged his shoulders. 'There's a lot we don't know since we moved to Israel.'

On the plane, as he sat comfortably in his seat with a glass of orange juice, resting his aching back, the Scientist thought about his past.

The plane took off from the runway and flew against gravity.

Over fifty years ago, he was in the South and was invited by the Palace there to research why urban men in the South were experiencing a low sperm count.

The Palace was afraid that the situation could affect the ongoing campaign to increase the size of the population. Badang had already made a name for himself in Malaysia and Singapore as a reproductive epidemiologist. He had become famous after helping a member of the royal family of a rich state in North Borneo, who had a low sperm count.

For his meta-analysis, Badang worked with a group of scientists, including several epidemiologists. They took samples of sperm from 43,000 men of various ethnic groups, ages and backgrounds, and found out that in 1973, the sperm count was ninety-nine million per millilitre but that now it only amounted to forty-seven million per millilitre. If the trend continued, the population of the South could become extinct. If the symptom became global, the entire human race was at risk of extinction.

When he discovered that the level of testosterone in men started to get affected in the womb, which had consequences in adult life, he was contacted by the Palace, who told him that they had heard of a strange case of cryptorchidism, in which the testicles which did not descend into the scrotum, grew instead in the abdomen near the kidneys.

At the time, several research assistants who were from the South advised him, 'Don't contradict the Palace. Just do what they ask. It's not worth fighting. It is better to remain calm and act normal. Everyone knows that the Palace does not react well to criticism and rejection.'

Badang was asked to treat a Very Important Someone who was suffering from testicular dysgenesis syndrome, which accounted for a low sperm count, among other symptoms. At the time, he was free to come and go as he pleased, including in and out of the Palace. At the same time, Haji Ben Adik asked for his help because his mother had been taken to the South against her will. Of course he was shocked because to him, Pertiwi was a mother, a personality—a goddess, even—since they had met in France.

'My mother has to get out of there. We will hide in a school in Indonesia with Nahdatul Ulama's help. My mother has come to her senses now. We plan to get her out of the South. We will smuggle her out by the Kim Kim River but we need someone over there. Someone like you, who can go inside to get her.'

'How will Mother Pertiwi trust me?'

'Our password is Nike. Just say Nike, and she will trust you.'

'Nike?'

The True Patriot's successful return to Hujung Manani caused a diplomatic crisis between the South and Hujung Manani, for a while. And Badang immediately became a suspect. He was held in captivity for about six months until his Jewish wife launched the campaign 'Where is Badang?'

Pressure from Tel Aviv, then from its ally, Washington, as well as London, forced the South to release Badang. When he returned to Hujung Manani, he suffered from depression after learning that Haji Ben Adik had been murdered. Immediately afterwards, he migrated to Israel and built a career as a scientist there.

At the beginning of the Dictator's rule, he returned for six months to visit the True Patriot. During his stay, he continued his research with the team of scientists to identify the reason for the decrease in sperm count which had spread from the South to Hujung Manani. Moreover, that research had been funded by the Dictator, who did not have any children.

The Scientist's research found something which was worrying. A sharp drop in sperm count occurred in men who suffered from stress, were smokers, or were obese. But now that it looked like a disease which could cause infertility, a more scientific explanation was required. Badang had a shocking hypothesis: the industrial revolution had happened. The oil industry had come up. The chemical industry had come up in the twentieth century. People had accumulated all types of substances and poisons in their body, disrupting their hormone system, including the levels of estrogen and testosterone. When chemicals disturb hormones, they are called endocrine disruptors.

The Scientist found that both Hujung Manani and its neighbour in the South had developed a large plastics industry. Factories that processed plastic to make it softer, used phthalates, while those that processed it to make it hard and solid, used chemicals like bisphenol A or BPA. Both phthalates and BPA are endocrine disruptors.

The Scientist's research concluded that men who had phthalates in their system produced less testosterone and therefore their sperm was of poorer quality. Male foetuses exposed to phthalates through the reproductive system also became 'less virile'.

The Scientist then published his research and revealed that BPA could be found everywhere in Hujung Manani, including water bottles and food containers. Phthalates were used in the foil wrappings of pills and supplements, oil, detergent, paint, playdough, pharmaceuticals, textiles, toys, nail polish remover, liquid soap and hairspray. It was used to process food products such as milk, yoghurt, condiments, soup, eggs, fruit, vegetables, pasta, noodles, rice and drinks. In brief, it was impossible to avoid phthalates. Even more frighteningly, the endocrine disruptor was genetically transmitted from father to son, causing the sperm count to keep decreasing with each generation.

Unfortunately, the Scientist's findings, just like most studies conducted by honest researchers for the benefit of mankind, were ignored, refuted and ridiculed.

The Scientist became a laughing stock. The Tycoon, who was the King of Plastic, could not let him destroy his source of revenue. He fought back with his usual weapon: money. As everyone knew, the Tycoon was financing the Dictator, and he increased his financial support with one clear message: Love Plastic. Immediately, the Dictator stopped subsidizing research projects.

The capitalist's demands, supported by money, made politicians turn their back on the people. This is why capitalists and politicians are the devil's friends. Religious men, in turn, declared that the use of plastic was harus.

A long time ago, the *Six Gurindam* had predicted what would happen:

'If a country wants progress and prosperity

Beware of merchants' greed and cupidity'

The Scientist refused to give in to the pressure exerted by the Leader and he publicized the results of his research. He believed that a good scientist had a duty and a responsibility towards mankind.

However, capitalists and politicians do not care about humanity. All they care about is profit and power.

When the clash became increasingly ruthless and hostile, the Scientist had to retreat. He decided that he should not have to sacrifice himself to fight a battle that he could never win. He returned to Israel and offered them his expertise, because the Jews were willing to listen to him, whereas the Malays preferred to remain backward.

Since then, the Scientist had never set foot again in Hujung Manani. Being in the plane flying towards Hujung Manani felt completely surreal to him.

8.29 a.m.

The number of demonstrators had increased to a large crowd, and most of them were women.

In a sixteen-storey condominium facing the main road in the heart of the capital, the owner of the apartment hung the flag of Hujung Manani with the symbol of a trident at the window, so that it could be seen from outside. At first, only two or three residents had done so. A few hours later, almost all the condominium units had a flag hanging from their balcony or window.

The crowd of demonstrators pushing strollers was overflowing on the sides of the street.

What were they doing?

In order to avoid being accused of breaking the law, the women were carrying tiffin carriers. A famous French photographer took a photograph of a woman pushing a television set in a stroller, while a woman holding a rainbow-coloured tiffin carrier stood beside her. The photograph became instantly famous, and appeared on the front page of many newspapers around the world.

Foreigners could see that the Dictator's government was coming to an end and would be over soon. The atmosphere in the capital of Hujung Manani, which for weeks had been tense and rife with conflicts brought about by the confusion caused by koro, turned festive. The women took to the streets as if they were going for a picnic. There had been no reactions from cabinet ministers, the General, or the police, as if law enforcement had suddenly stopped in the country.

The Pak Lokan performance that was televised the night before had clearly put a stop to everything, as if the world had become paralysed in Hujung Manani, without any explanations. It was a puzzling situation because one could only see women in the streets, wearing all types of garments. Some were wearing *kebaya* blouses that were all the rage in the 1960s. Others wore the traditional *baju kurung* from Johor, T-shirts, or blouses. Some women covered their hair, others did not. At first, one could only see women with brown skin, but after a while, one could notice that the colour of their skin ranged from a very light tan to a very dark brown. There were also some Indigenous women. Right after the dawn prayers, the women looked like bored housewives, but near the beginning of office hours, elegant ladies started boycotting work and those who should have been in offices, were now in the streets as well.

A few demonstrators were dressed in costumes representing a penis covered in cheese.

CNN called it the 'Women's Revolution'. Al Jazeera named it the 'Koro Revolution'. At 8.29 a.m., the demonstrators flooding the streets numbered 500,000, most of them concentrated around a square in the heart of the city. The women who joined later brought with them posters, manila cards, banners and placards with the True Patriot's face or quotes from her speeches.

Where were the men? Were they under a spell since the Pak Lokan performance the previous night? Where was Datin Lotis? And where was Priapus the Dictator?

9.29 a.m.

The police headquarters were agitated. Since the loss of the powerful Director of the Special Branch the previous night, the police had no direction and no clear leadership. The Chief of Police of Hujung Manani, an old man who was no more than a puppet put in place by the Dictator, did not know what he should do. The presence of the media, and in particular the foreign press, who were camping outside the police station, was stifling and made him panic. The Chief of Police called the Assistant Director of the Special Branch to come meet him.

'Where is the Director of the Special Branch?'

'As the Mufti said, the last we heard, he was on a flight to Bangkok with the Leader, on their way to Jeddah in Saudi Arabia to . . . er . . . perform the minor pilgrimage; they received an official invitation from the Saudi prince.'

Why would they go to perform the pilgrimage during a crisis? What were their priorities? However, the Chief of Police did not dare ask. He accepted the situation without questions.

'Did he leave any message before he left?'

The Assistant Director tried to remember, but there was no message. However, he was used to making up stories. 'The Leader just said to make sure Lotis can keep singing. She likes to sing. Make sure she can sing Rick Astley's songs.'

'Huh?'

The Chief of Police had trouble believing what he was hearing. 'They left in secret, and the media don't know? They left us?'

The Assistant Director remained silent. He could not verify anything.

'Where is Datin Lotis? Who is the most senior minister after the Leader?' The Chief of Police could not hide his confusion.

'Since when do we have a senior minister? The most senior person after the Leader is his wife, and after that the Director of the Special Branch—'

'And after that? The General?' the Chief of Police asked, completely stressed. 'Lots of bitches are marching out there, and CNN is calling it the Women's Revolution—what is the General going to do? What is he waiting for? Can we find out from him? But, argh . . . first of all, we need to find out about Datin Lotis, did she go to Jeddah too?'

The Assistant Director of the Special Branch, perplexed and uncomfortable, bit his bottom lip.

'We don't have any information about the Leader's Wife, sir. But she didn't go to Jeddah. She disappeared right after the Pak Lokan performance last night.'

'She disappeared?'

'Yes, when we took the Director of the Special Branch and the Leader to the emergency airport, we checked the official residence and couldn't find Datin Lotis anywhere. Except, employees at the house said that they had seen something . . . er—'

The Chief of Police was impatient and interrupted him abruptly, 'Saw what?!'

'A tiger, sir, or something like that, in the garden of the Leader's official residence. The tiger left and ran into the bushes in front of the house when we frightened it.'

The Chief of Police sat down heavily in his chair. For a moment, he was speechless.

'Declare a state of emergency. Send the police to get demonstrators off the streets immediately.'

'We've already done that. There's many of them, sir.' The Assistant Director looked overwhelmed.

'Many of them? They're just stupid bitches. Whores and tramps! Can't we beat them? Make sure that this country is in order and get me the General, now!' All of a sudden, the Chief of Police lost his temper and grew determined. He could not believe that he had to deal with such a bad situation.

The Dictator had run away and his wife had become a tiger?

What kind of story was that? Was this some sort of bad soap opera?

But when he thought about what had happened in the last three or four weeks, including the koro riots, everything seemed liked fiction. He felt like he was living in a satire.

'This is real life, this is not a satire about living under an authoritarian power. And who said I was just a puppet?' the Chief of Police snapped roughly.

The Assistant Director of the Special Branch nodded. And immediately contacted the General.

10.29 a.m.

The protestors who had gathered outdoors under an increasingly hot sun, started putting up tents. Various groups of demonstrators preferred to have fun. They danced the zapin, accompanied by a *gambus* and the beat of the kompang, on a temporary stage set up in the centre of the square. Teenage girls sang the words of the *Six Gurindam*.

The most hilarious were the participants who sang '*Hatiku Luka Lagi*' ('My Heart Bleeds Again') by Black Dog Bone, an extremely famous song in Hujung Manani.

In another part of the square, a woman wearing a naqaab to cover her face was giving a lecture about John Hawkins and slave trafficking from Africa to Europe.

'They burn entire villages, capture us and sell us in exchange for ginger and guns. In Hujung Manani, we are treated as commodities for the benefit of plastic mongers. When our men suffer from koro because of this tragedy, they put the blame on us. We must punish the capitalists and the leaders who conspire with them!'

In another part of the capital of Hujung Manani, where increasingly large numbers of women were assembling, there was a different type of political lecture.

'Ever since we were fooled by capitalists into becoming labourers, we have been covered in smoke and dust. We carry five tons of coal every day, we weave and sew fabric night and day, and we are not allowed to think. All we can do is work, work, work. We forfeit our health, our children and the capitalists compete among themselves, swallowed by banks like Willy Rust. Capitalists have enormous appetites, which they satisfy with help from giant bank consortiums. They have taken away our freedom, and now we have no more opportunities. If capitalists can work together to form a cartel to exploit us, are we going to let them tear us apart and destroy us? Are we going to let the government and the capitalists behind it, oppress us? Kita jaga kita!' The woman addressing the crowd was wearing a hat featuring an arrangement of penises covered in cheese.

In a different area, a tall woman wearing a kebaya blouse and a scarf loosely draped around her head, was haranguing about a hundred women who had gathered around her. 'We are being treated like fools in order to give respectability to shady businesses, to give respectability to corrupt bosses, to give respectability to bankers, to give respectability to cartels, and to the leaders who benefit from them. Then they use God's name. They use the Prophet's name. As a result, we end up having Islamic capitalists! Or Islamic cartels that keep operating just like before. In order to subdue us, religious men are paid to protect the capitalists. Capitalists, politicians and religious leaders work together to keep oppressing us and taking advantage of us. We have become slaves! In Hujung Manani, we have become slaves! That was true under the emperor; it was still true under the French colonizers, and now we are slaves under the Dictator. Can't we trust the True Patriot?'

At that moment, several police helicopters appeared in the sky, flying low over the capital, and dropped pamphlets that flew to the ground like giant snowflakes.

The demonstrators rushed to grab them, like children receiving gifts from the sky.

The pamphlets were printed with an order: 'You have two hours to vacate the city and go home before cleaning begins. Your husbands and children need you at home. Your kitchens are waiting for you.'

The pamphlets were quickly ridiculed. One female labour leader took to the stage and shouted to get attention. 'Dicks dipped in cheese are trying to threaten us! How stupid they are! Listen, men, to how Aristophanes proposed to end the Peloponnesian war in Greece in the fifth century BC. He wrote a play called *Lysistrata*. What did Lysistrata say to Myrrhine and Calonice? Do you want to end this tyranny? Do you want to kick plastic traders out of our country? Do you all want to enjoy freedom?'

The women who were listening to her shouted their agreement with enthusiasm. They cheered each other.

'What did Myrrhine answer?'

Some women shouted: 'We will do it! We will do it! Even if we have to pay with our life for it!'

The speaker who was holding the loudspeaker laughed, before encouraging the crowd again: 'Lysistrata said that we have to cross our legs. We must not open our thighs. We must not have sex with men. And we will force the men of Hujung Manani to listen to us.'

One demonstrator shouted: 'When there's no dictator, we can have sex. Cross your legs, don't spread them!'

Her words were repeated, over and over again.

'Cross your legs, don't spread them!'

'Revolution!'

The crowd broke out into a rendition of the national anthem, *Q'Allah bénisse la Hujung Manani*.

11.29 a.m.

Over 10,000 policemen from the Tactical Units were rushed to the centre of the capital. They shot tear gas and rubber bullets, and armoured cars rolled over the demonstrators' tents.

One woman yelled in an effort to stop an armoured vehicle: 'Have you no shame? Shameless stupid males! Women are in the streets to fight for your safety too, and for your children; and you stand in front of us, shooting at us, ready to kill us. Go to hell and damn you jerks! You have no dicks! You have no balls!'

The police kept attacking.

Some women were injured. Some fell.

12.29 p.m.

'I am going to go out onto the streets,' the True Patriot declared. 'I no longer have a choice.'

The True Patriot had several assistants, who now looked at one another. Age, safety, health—those were all important factors against that idea.

Her private secretary protested: 'There has been blood, Mother . . . There's been blood.'

'I remember reading somewhere that spring cannot be stopped by cutting a flower.'

'Some women have been injured by armoured vehicles, Mother.' The press secretary also tried to stop her.

'I have lived for almost a hundred years. Are they going to run me over?' The True Patriot knew what Bertolt Brecht had written, 'General, your tank is a powerful vehicle, it smashes down forests and crushes a hundred men. But it has one defect: it needs a driver.'

The True Patriot's staff members squeaked, exchanged worried looks and sighed. Some of them scratched their head.

'I am going into the streets. Who is coming with me?'

It began.

1.29 p.m.

The General glared at the Chief of Police. They locked eyes, without blinking or flinching.

The General had been summoned by the Chief of Police.

'Please have a seat.'

'We all know that Hujung Manani is in the midst of a crisis. Until now, everything had been working because of Datuk Priapus and for him. But now we must face the current situation without him or the Director of the Special Branch. Moreover, yesterday, you were at his official residence watching the Pak Lokan performance. We, the police, think that we should work together with the army in order to restrain the demonstrators and the rioters.'

The General took a deep breath. He had not slept all night. The incidents that occurred during the Pak Lokan performance had caused unrest in various places. All he could think about was his only daughter. Where was she? His heart started to beat faster.

'The women, the younger generation, those who use reason, they all reject Priapus and Lotis. Father, you must do the right thing; the honourable thing.'

'Which is?'

'Take the side of the truth. Don't side with falsehood, with plastic,' his daughter had tried to convince him.

'Plastic?'

'Mom died because of plastic. Everything is about plastic. Many people in Hujung Manani have discovered that they have stage 4 cancer because of plastic. And plastic brings us back to the Tycoon. To Priapus. They have turned our country into the world's dumpster! Western colonizers throw their rubbish in our country. How could you take the side of murderers?!'

The General remained speechless. He thought about the inscription carved on the Stone Well. Could the ancient spell really come true?

The Chief of Police, who was savouring the little bit of power he had, waited for the General's decision. Why was he wasting his time?

'Datin Lotis,' the General finally said.

The Chief of Police felt a wave of anger. 'Everybody knows that she is not human.'

The General was stunned. He remembered that his daughter had once told him: 'That woman is evil, she is not human. She hunts tigers with greed. She thinks that she is Amoghapasa Avolokiteswara from the Srivijaya era, wrapped in a tiger skin. She needs seven things to rule forever. One, a horse to ride, that's Priapus. Two, gold, which is covering her body. Three, a minister, and we can see that she controls the entire cabinet. Four, an elephant—Hujung Manani represents the elephant which kneels before her. She also needs the chakra—all the spells that she uses so that our important organs, such as our brains and now men's penises, do not grow. She already has a tiger. All she needs now is a general so that she possesses all seven *saptaratnani*, or the seven jewels that a ruler must have.

She is an ancient witch who violated the purity of Amoghapasa Avolokiteswara who was a *cakravantin*, a fair world leader. She is not a saviour, father. She is an evil sorceress from the past who has come to our time to stop the emergence of the world's saviour.'

'How do we fight this curse?' the General had asked. His daughter's face appeared again in his mind. 'Only a ghost from the past can fight and destroy her.'

The General returned to the present. The Chief of Police was still facing him with anger on his face. 'She's not human. She's not human. She's . . .'

In his heart, the General said 'the devil' but the words died before reaching his mouth.

The Chief of Police left the sentence hanging without finishing it. The General mumbled. The Chief of Police lost his calm. 'Since she's not human, we'll let her be destroyed by something which is not human either. But Hujung Manani will crumble if we leave the country in the hands of another witch: Pertiwi.'

The General was startled by the Chief of Police's suggestion.

'It is safe to say that this country has been cursed. The Leader is no longer in-charge. Lotis has disappeared.'

The Chief of Police was carefully trying to suggest that they should join forces in order to take over the leadership of the country.

The General understood that the Chief of Police was offering him the government of Hujung Manani. It was not unusual for a country in crisis without leadership to fall into the hands of the army and the police; it had happened in the past.

The General stood up, walked to the window and looked outside. Far away in the city, among the sea of people, a woman was speaking with passion about a coin which has two faces, race and religion. She was saying, 'A dictator has two faces, a racist one and a religious one.'

That woman speaking was his own daughter, who had joined the demonstrators.

The General turned to the Chief of Police. 'Have you ever heard the word *siruvnik*, from the Hebrew word "*siruv*", meaning refuse?' The General was looking for words to convince the Chief of Police. If he failed to persuade him, Hujung Manani could end up being torn apart by civil war. He went on: 'This is a crucial time'.

'In 2002, Yigal Bronner led several hundred Israeli soldiers and was willing to go to jail for refusing to be sent to occupied territories in Palestine. They fought with only a letter as a weapon, sir. The contents of that letter were surprising. It is called the Combattants' Letter.'

The Chief of Police, who had never been anything more than a puppet, blinked and remained silent.

'The letter said: "We shall not continue to fight beyond the 1967 borders in order to dominate, expel, starve and humiliate an entire people. We hereby declare that we shall continue serving in the Israel Defense Forces in any mission that serves Israel's defense. The missions of occupation and oppression do not serve this purpose, and we shall take no part in them." Bronner said that he refused to become an emotionless robot who aims and launches missiles from a tank. The soldier, who wished to stand for what is right, was not alone. He wrote: "Our protest will be recorded in the history books, for all generations to see." So General, before you shoo me away, perhaps you too should begin to think.'

The Chief of Police exhaled. Before the General could continue, he said: 'This is not patriotic at all.'

The General nodded. 'Do you know that the operations in
Gaza between December 2008 and January 2009 resulted in more
actions by siruvniks? It was unpopular and it will always be deemed
unpatriotic. Sir, the lives of others are as valuable as our own.'

The Chief of Police calmly looked at the General. He stood
up, a million emotions in his chest, and shook hands with him
before walking to the door. 'They are just women, sir. We can
rule this country efficiently, by joining forces.'

The General wanted to reply, 'you are wrong, they are not
just women,' but the General spoke in a sharp tone of voice:
'This is koro. It makes you unable to control women'.

2.29 p.m.

Between thirty and forty victims of kidnapping who were
still alive were released, and they walked into the main mosque
of Hujung Manani. Ashraf Wahidi, the famous preacher, was
there to welcome them. The atmosphere was highly emotional
for the families of the former prisoners.

However, some relatives had to face a different reality: not
all the victims of kidnapping had been released. Some were still
unaccounted for.

Foreign journalists covering this development interviewed
the persons released, group by group. One of these groups was
formed by the Rookie Detective, the Psychiatrist, the Famous
Historian and a Monk, whose disappearance had drawn the
attention of the Dalai Lama himself.

The Famous Historian revealed that they had a hypothesis
to explain the koro phenomenon that infected the men of
Hujung Manani. With his friends, they believed that the patients
seeking treatment in hospitals and clinics were suffering from an
illness that was not located in their penises but in their minds.

Hujung Manani had to be healed. The country was the victim of a humiliating madness, with the men going crazy while the women fought against authoritarianism.

The Famous Historian asked to meet the True Patriot to explain the meaning of a pantun, which said that when you are stricken with koro, you must find what made you limp:

'Javanese, Bugis and Moro
Different colours for the Malay skin;

When you are stricken with koro
Find the crime that made you limp.'

'What does this pantun mean?' a journalist asked the Famous Historian.

'The crime it refers to is "putting one's race above all others", while "How is a race superior to others? / It is forbidden by religion and not preached by the Prophet" clearly indicates that koro is caused by racism. Racism is a mental disease that infects society. The symptoms of the disease are panic and fear, which we translate as koro.'

On the streets, the riot police were striking women with batons, shooting tear gas, and hitting the protestors with anything they could get their hands on.

Despite the violence, the number of people in the streets did not decrease, but kept growing.

3.29 p.m.

The True Patriot arrived at the Hujung Manani Airport. No, not to go abroad. To greet the Scientist and his wife, who were going to land soon.

As soon as the immigration formalities were completed, the Scientist and his wife were taken to a private waiting room where the True Patriot was waiting for them. Without hesitation, the airport management authorized the meeting and the first press conference to be held by the True Patriot since the fall of the Dictator.

For the first time, when the Scientist kissed the True Patriot, the population of Hujung Manani was stunned to see a septuagenarian kiss the cheek of a nonagenarian.

Very few people knew about the relationship between Pertiwi and Badang. That the True Patriot considered him as her son. And for a while, Badang reminded Pertiwi of her son Benedict. They hugged. Then the True Patriot put her hand on Badang's cheek and wiped his tears, while he gave her his handkerchief.

'Kacau keledek, my sweet darling,' the True Patriot whispered as she ruffled the Scientist's white hair while he kissed the back of her hand.

The seventy-seven-year-old man tried to control his emotions. 'After this, we'll go look for kacau keledek together.'

They hugged as they let the tears roll down their cheeks.

For a moment, nobody could understand what they were saying to each other. It sounded like a secret code. Most people had no idea what kacau keledek was: a traditional delicacy from Johor, which was no longer popular.

The press conference started.

A moderator started by asking the numerous representatives from the press to find a seat and not remain standing, although the space was crowded.

'The True Patriot will try to answer as many questions as possible, but we ask that you do not make the situation difficult. There are many journalists here today and I have to admit that security is not very tight, and there are still riots going on out there. The situation in Hujung Manani is still chaotic. So I ask you to sit down because we will ask anybody standing to leave the premises. If you want to ask a question, please raise your hand and someone will pass you a microphone. When you have a microphone in your hand, you can ask your question.'

The True Patriot began the conference which was broadcast to the entire world.

'Salam everyone. Salam One Hujung Manani. Greetings of peace from Hujung Manani. Salam to all. I thank Professor Badang, the first Nobel Prize recipient in the field of medicine in Hujung Manani, who came from Jerusalem with his wife. We greatly appreciate his presence here at this time.'

The room was quiet. Everyone was giving her their full attention.

'We believe that early this morning, the third leader of Hujung Manani, Datuk Priapus Mappadulung Daeng Mattimung Karaeng Sanrobone, left the country for Riyadh in Arab Saudi in order to seek medical treatment.'

Confused voices rose. The reporters who heard for the first time the sensational piece of information that the Dictator had fled the country, came to a simple conclusion.

'However, we will not make any suppositions at this time, since the police are still repressing protestors in the heart of the city and we do not know who is in power. In other words, who is ruling Hujung Manani at the moment? We know that the parliament has been suspended for a while now. We also know that the cabinet has not been in charge ever since the beginning of the koro breakout, about a month ago. I will not speak about koro. I will ask Professor Dr Badang to answer all your questions regarding this matter after this.'

The press conference became orderly again. The people who were in the waiting room were aware that they were witnessing a historical event, which made the hair on the back of their neck stand with excitement.

'Therefore, my friends and I will join the protestors marching from Kota Tahir to the Hujung Manani Square in two hours. This is a protest. A declaration. It is a lesson I learned from one of my comrades, MLK, who marched from Selma to Montgomery. Anyone can join us. I mean that anyone is free to join.'

The waiting area which had been turned into a hall for the press conference became noisy again. It sounded like bees buzzing around the queen in the hive.

'I want to remind everyone that Hujung Manani is still exposed to various threats, coming from both inside and outside the country, and I also want to ask the authorities, who depend on guns and bullets, to stop any form of violence toward civilians, whether they are in the square or marching with me in the streets.'

All eyes were fixed on the True Patriot.

'What are we trying to achieve with this 25 kilometre march? We want to show that together, we reject Priapus' rule. We will hold a vote. If enough people march with us to the square, we target 1 million people. If 1 million protestors march with us, we will declare that Hujung Manani has returned to the people. I will set up a temporary government before we hold free and fair elections to choose a government by the people, for the people. We expect the process to take about two years. I want to create a unity government in the meantime.'

For the first time, the True Patriot was speaking plainly, directly, without metaphors, without hidden stories, without allegories—she sent a clear message.

The True Patriot looked at the moderator, signalling to him that she was done. She passed the microphone to the Scientist.

'Salam, One Hujung Manani. I have been asked to talk about koro. I will keep it very simple.'

Most people did not know Badang and had never had the chance to hear him talk. Now, for the first time, they listened carefully to the local Hujung Manani man who was globally famous.

All the journalists in the room were paying attention to him. Many were wondering why he had been invited from so far away to answer questions about a country that he had left a long time ago.

Nobody understood yet.

'Koro is an imaginary illness which is related to emotions and not really connected to the male physical organ. It is an illness rooted in culture. It is a symptom, a sort of signal, telling us that there is something wrong with our culture. If some of us are infected, it means that our society is sick and needs to change. I believe that koro is about our way of thinking. That is, thinking with our lust instead of our reason. I ask men to remain calm and to let women lead the country in this difficult time. Then, if women wish to continue ruling the country, it is not a problem . . .'

The moderator allowed questions from the room. A journalist from Radio Television Malaysia (RTM) was the first to get the chance.

'Professor Badang, was the koro disease caused by plastic? As you know, Hujung Manani and Malaysia have both become dumping grounds for plastic waste from Western industrial countries. Should the products from countries whose economy is based on plastic be reassessed? Finally, did the koro disease occur because of racism? There have been claims to that effect . . .'

The Scientist glanced at the True Patriot. The famous lady nodded, indicating that he should respond. 'That question is for you, my kacau keledek.'

The Scientist looked at the journalist from RTM. 'I will not refute the fact that various disabilities and problems affecting men in Hujung Manani are caused by plastic. I conducted thorough research on this subject in the past, but the results were ignored. In order to determine whether koro involves plastic, I would have to conduct more research. But at the moment, there is no scientific evidence to this effect, because koro has been identified as a disease rooted in culture. We do not deny that racist—and perhaps also sexist—men are exposed to the ancient koro illness, but I can confirm that it has nothing to do with witchcraft. As far as I am concerned, any plastic other than The Plastic People of the Universe, is a risk that we must be aware of.'

The few people who understood the Scientist's joke, laughed.

The True Patriot interrupted. 'Countries that smuggle plastic illegally into our country and dump their plastic waste here have signed the Basel Convention. They must pay for what they discard. We are going to return their plastic waste.'

A journalist from Brunei was allowed to ask the second question. 'I am addressing my question to the True Patriot. For your information, the Mufti has declared that it is haram to get involved in the ousting of a leader by using illegal means; his conclusion is that it is "haram, haram, HARAM". Can you comment?'

The True Patriot took her time before answering. She pushed a lock of hair behind her left ear, so that it would not fall on her cheek. Then she said: 'Haram? When a poet remains silent in a conspiracy, the pen that writes a verse is like the boom of a cannon. When a mufti remains silent in a conspiracy, disobeying his verdict is like a small reward from God on the summit of the mountain of sin. Haram? I call for civil disobedience. Civil disobedience! Meet me in Tahir, and let us march with the people to the Square in Hujung Manani. Qu'Allah bénisse la Hujung Manani!'

4.29 p.m.

The Mufti was interviewed by the television station of Hujung Manani and he nervously declared, 'Liverpool is exciting. Who watched TV yesterday? Praised be Allah Who only belongs to Muslims, may He be praised for all the blessings and gifts He bestows on us and that we can never repay. Peace be on the Prophet and his companions, and those who follow the true path until the Day of Judgment. Damned be the Shiites, the LGBT, the liberals who have been tarnishing our faith since the Abbasid Caliphate. I watched the European Champions League match a few days ago between Real Madrid and Liverpool. At first Real Madrid led with a 3-0 aggregate, but when they played at Anfield, their main players like Muhammed Serlah and Robert Elnino were benched due to injury, and victory switched to Liverpool with a 4-0 aggregate. Thus, the final decision was a 4-3 aggregate. One of the *ibrah* that can be learned from this is that overconfidence can be our downfall. This is forbidden in Islam. Perseverance and a strong determination can, *inshallah*, change destiny. A spirit of unity and team-building based on *tawhid* are the best ways to reach *hayya ala falah*. Never giving up or quitting will result in perfect jihad.'

The journalist who had asked the question was speechless. What did Liverpool have to do with . . . cocks?

Nobody could understand what the mufti was saying. That being said, the Right-wing religious conservative group believed that his words were sacred and holy, and that whoever did not take them seriously, was being disrespectful. If it was a woman who denigrated him, it was harus that she be raped; if it was an effeminate man, the rule was that he could be killed.

When the mufti's words reached the ears of Childish Gambino, who was on tour in Kuala Lumpur, the artist said, 'This is not *ijtihad,* not a fatwa at all, and not *amar makruf* and *nahi mungkar.* This is Hujung Manani!'

5.29 p.m.

Around 200,000 protestors had gathered at the Kota Tahir bridge to join the march to Hujung Manani Square. If they were not stopped by the riot police, they would arrive in the capital before midnight. Most of the participants were empty-handed, but many carried all sorts of banners, displaying quotes from the *Six Gurindam* or from the True Patriot's message. There were also slogans against the use of plastic and pictures showing women crossing their legs, indicating that there would be no sex with men who opposed the demonstration. The demonstrators came from all ethnic groups. More importantly, the message from celebrity preacher Ashraf Wahidi had been heard, and there were a number of men who were clearly not concerned by the koro epidemic and had found the courage to join the 25 kilometre march.

The media from many foreign countries were providing wide coverage and reporters were lined up along the road from Kota Tahir to the capital of Hujung Manani.

Would the Chief of Police have the nerve to strike the peaceful protesters? Nobody could predict what would happen.

A few demonstrators were wheelchair-bound. Some came with children who were holding balloons. A large number of them were holding flowers. Hawkers took the opportunity to sell street-food all along the road, and some even sold kacau keledek.

The protestors were full of enthusiasm and the crowd that stood on the sides of the road cheered them on and clapped their hands in support. Villagers gave them boxed drinks and food (packets of rice).

When the rally left Tahir and approached the town of Asahan, a police force which was much smaller than the number of protestors, was waiting for them with batons, shields and tear gas.

The True Patriot, sitting in a wheelchair pushed by the Scientist, told the protestors not to be afraid. 'I ask you not to fight, even if they shoot tear gas at us. We will fight by not fighting.'

At the junction leading to Asahan, two police trucks were parked, but they let the protestors pass by without provocation. A child gave a frowning policeman a balloon shaped like a pig.

As they marched, the participants talked, and sometimes they sang. After walking for ten kilometres, they stopped to rest. They opened their food containers, talked and joked with the people who lived nearby who came to greet them.

The people who lived along the road offered the use of their toilets and they spread woven mats in their courtyards for the protestors to rest. Makeshift tents were pitched everywhere.

The progression continued as some people stopped walking and others moved along as they chose. The power of the people cannot be stopped, whether they choose to support Real Madrid, Chelsea, Manchester or Liverpool. The march now counted over 600,000 people.

The noise made by the marching crowd echoed in the air. There was a multitude of odours, from cooking spices to perfume to the sour stench of sweat. But all those smells combined did not stink as bad as the pus oozing from the Tycoon's dick.

A group of Momok people from Sari (who are now nearly extinct) formed the rear of the procession, holding stems of wild ginger measuring the length of a forearm. Their chief walked in front of them, accompanied by young women carrying winnowing trays with several types of rice grains on their head. Several young men were carrying cow hides and hitting one another playfully. They also threw a yam stem which was as thick as a thumb and almost two feet long at each other or hit each other's behind gently with it.

This unusual behaviour drew the attention of the journalists, who kept taking pictures. One of the foreign photographers from the National Geographic was engrossed in capturing the Momok people's uniqueness. A man came out of the group; he looked educated and explained, 'This is a traditional custom called *adat berpuar* to drive away ghosts before planting rice. We combined it with the custom of fighting with a yam stem, which is another way to drive away ghosts.'

'Are there really ghosts here?' The foreign photographer's tone of voice was unintentionally provoking and even insulting.

'Eh, haven't you heard? There's a rumour going around. People say that Lotis, the first lady, is a weretiger disguised as a woman. If she's in the crowd here, she will be frightened away by our customs.'

'Ah, so this is an old belief?'

The educated Momok man answered with a smile. 'This is the problem with Westerners. You measure everything in terms of old or new. You differentiate between modern and traditional. You call it witchcraft. We call it occult science. It is an invisible science which helps us live our lives.'

In the new Hujung Manani, advocates of traditional customs like the Momok people and believers in science like Badang will cooperate and encourage each other, inshallah. *Amin.*

In the middle of the crowd, the Scientist was standing on the roadside, surrounded by journalists and onlookers. The True Patriot looked at the protesters as she sat with Shulamit in front of a tent, which had been pitched by villagers.

There were security guards standing near them, scrutinizing the surroundings. Every few minutes, a demonstrator asked the True Patriot for a photo and an autograph, and the guards had to hold the crowd back and bark at them.

'Mother, what does kacau keledek mean?' Shulamit finally had the chance to ask.

The True Patriot chuckled and stared at Shulamit's face. Then, she caressed the woman's wrinkled cheek.

'He never told you?'

Shulamit shook her head.

Two grey-haired ladies were now the heroines in Hujung Manani.

'I wish I was still young and strong like you,' Pertiwi added lightheartedly.

'I am seventy-two years old.'

'I'm much older than you.'

The True Patriot sighed as she thought about the past.

'I wish Benedict was here . . . He would be here, at our side, in the front row, fighting against those who are greedy for power.'

Shulamit saw her husband Badang laughing with a group of reporters and demonstrators.

'This will be an act of civil disobedience which will be remembered. This is my goal . . .'

'This march?' Shulamit asked, although she had understood what Pertiwi meant. She had been looking for the right words to say.

'Do you want to come back to live in Hujung Manani after this, Shula?' The True Patriot's question exploded like a time bomb.

'Live here for good? We are Jewish.'

The True Patriot smiled in response. She continued: 'Hujung Manani doesn't have many options for leaders and statesmen. There are a lot of money launderers and sex addicts, for sure. But I don't know how many people are trustworthy.'

Shulamit did not know what to say. Could she endure settling down in Hujung Manani?

'Think about it, love.'

Shulamit kept silent. She was uncomfortable around conservative people. If Hujung Manani became more open, she was willing to do it, because in Israel, the conservatives embracing Jewish supremacy were growing in power, stifling Jews of colour like her.

'Badang risked his own life to help me escape when I was held captive in the South. The king of that country was reckless. He would strike anyone without warning. When Benedict asked for Badang's help, he did not hesitate. I was locked up in the palace, as a sort of hostage from Hujung Manani; like Tuah imprisoned Teja; like the sorceress imprisoned Rapunzel. The Tycoon had been investing a lot of money in the plastic waste industry in the South and Hujung Manani. He did not want to incur any losses. And my ex-husband was a capitalist criminal who worked as his middleman in the South. Large areas of land were taken from the people and turned into landfills for plastic waste shipped from Canada, Australia, France, Germany and the United States. The king of the South made a huge profit from this business. The First Leader knew how to convince Hujung Manani to accept plastic waste—using me. A woman is the door between a country and the rest of the world, Shulamit. He deceived me and the people of Hujung Manani were made to believe that the South was their friend. This made it easy for the Tycoon to do business. No politics and no country administration are safe from the corrupted minds of three types of people: capitalists, religious leaders and hardcore nationalists who sell the country in the name of race and patriotism. Benedict discovered all that. His father was from Africa, a continent that has been exploited by capitalists for much longer than Hujung Manani. Badang comes from Sayong and he is doing well, but his dignity is always being tested. Fortunately, at that time, he had access to the palace. He had been hired to conduct a pseudoscientific study.'

'Pseudoscientific?'

'Yes, there's real science and pseudoscience. Real science encourages mankind to reach new horizons, but pseudoscience is nothing but a tool for kings, men of power and capitalists, just like these evil people use fatwas and religion.'

Shulamit gazed at her husband who was engrossed in conversation.

'In the South, he is known as "the Scientist". Argh, you know, every time a scientist discovers a new threat posed by a product and tries to save people's health, another scientist is paid to conduct research and cover up the existing damage. Badang was being used like this. He comes from Sayong. From the South. He could not refuse. We shared the same fate, we were both being held hostage. But Badang knew, he swallowed his pride and became stronger, and with this strength he obtained freedom and possessed the power to negotiate. So they assumed that he was willing to be dishonest. He pretended to play along with this farce for several months in order to convince the royals in the South. In particular, my ex-husband, who needed the lie in order to cover up his greed. Remember, the Tycoon was behind all this.

Because they trusted Badang, he managed to convince the palace guards in the South that I should be tamed first. One of the ways to do that was by spoiling me with my favourite sweet treats: kacau keledek, a traditional delicacy only prepared in certain parts of the Malay world.'

Shulamit was fascinated. 'Oh, so this is the secret behind kacau keledek?'

The True Patriot chuckled. 'I haven't finished my story, honey. Badang hid messages about our escape which was being planned by Benedict in Hujung Manani and Gus Dur in Indonesia. The notes were hidden inside the kacau keledek that was brought to me. That was how we communicated.'

Shulamit burst out laughing and the True Patriot smiled back at her.

'I have been calling him kacau keledek ever since. My sweet Benedict was killed and Badang was detained in the South for helping me run away. Fortunately, I managed to contact the Malaysian leader to ask him for help. As an elder, he intervened quickly.'

Shulamit was impressed.

'So that was the beginning of the Plastic Revolution, which is still going on today?'

The True Patriot's assistant approached her. 'A poet from Malaysia is offering to recite some poems at the square.'

'Who?'

'Zarinah Shim.'

The True Patriot laughed. 'Look at artists and writers, Shula. When we are in trouble and need their help, they do nothing. But when we are about to win, or we have already won, they show up to write our narrative. Tell Zarinah, Sri Ayo, Enon, Taha . . . and the others—we do not write when it is safe, we write when it is right. She's too late.'

Her personal assistant jotted something down. 'A female leader from a neighbouring country called. Her name is Yeo Bee Yin. She wanted to wish you good luck, and congratulations for refusing the use of plastic. Also, for taking a tough stand against the dumping of plastic waste in this country.'

The True Patriot smiled.

The Scientist was walking quickly toward them, a worried expression on his face.

'A reporter told me that there were no riot police on the way to the city. But they are arresting a lot of protestors at the square and there are a lot of policemen at the city gate.'

The True Patriot looked first at Shulamit and then at Badang. 'Come on, kacau keledek, let's finish what we started. I owe this to Benedict.'

Shulamit rose to her feet, full of energy, and whispered to her husband, 'We will live here after this.'

Badang frowned. 'But . . . you're a Jew.'

Shulamit kept smiling. 'Come on, kacau keledek . . .'

The Scientist pouted with his full lips.

'Come on, everybody! We have a big task ahead of us.'

The sea of people was still swelling, determined to reach the capital of Hujung Manani.

6.29 p.m.

Z Good's anger rose as he watched the live reports from various news bulletins.

He was most enraged by Wahidi, who claimed to have been reformed, or rather TRANSformed, and was calling on men to support the revolution launched by women. He was truly irritated. He had just finished jerking off when he saw Ashraf, or Adele, on the television, looking like he had changed and joined the opposition.

He changed the channel.

There was a foreign news channel talking about the Koro Revolution, another which referred to it as the Flower Revolution because it was led by women. Another yet called it the Plastic Revolution, because it was driven, among other factors, by the awareness to reject the use of plastic and the plastic waste industry, which was the primary industry of Hujung Manani.

Z Good was enraged by the thought that his sex slave, his delicious wife, whom he had used for a week, was a man. He felt extremely stupid. 'I can't believe that I fucked a guy, a pansy posing as an ustaz.'

All he could think about was revenge. He wanted to fix what was happening. He could not begin to imagine a new government that would reject Islam. He could not stand to think that Islam would be insulted and threatened under the True Patriot, who did not even wear a veil on her head. He could not imagine that he could endure living under a government led by a leader who was liberal, or even worse, a female.

He was disgusted (yet thrilled) that he had slept with Wahidi, who pretended to be a sexy woman. When he heard the news that koro apparently affected men who were racist, sexist, or sectarian, he was amused, because hey—he was all that but he did not get koro.

He believed that if someone really had faith and stayed on the true path without straying, he would be safe. Like him!

The endless visuals of the march and demonstrations on TV really bothered him.

The posters of Abu Bakar Baghdadi and of the football-mad mufti hurt his eyes. They fuelled his rage. He knew that he had to put an end to all that nonsense. He had to put an end to that ignominy so that the dignity of Islam remained intact. He could not contain his disappointment and humiliation.

'I've got to get rid of these obscene creatures. People like Wahidi defile Islam, while I work and do my best to defend Islam.'

At that moment, he became possessed. The Devil controlled him. And he conceived an evil idea. What about what he possessed, the chemical knowledge he had acquired? This was the time to put it into practice. If they wanted so much to go to hell, he should give it to them and the song 'Fire' boomed in his head, as The Crazy World of Arthur Brown sang, 'I am the God of Hellfire' over and over again.

7.29 p.m.

The General announced in a statement that the army of Hujung Manani would not attack civilians and that he was supporting the True Patriot.

He said, 'We will not turn our guns against ourselves. We call on the police to do the same.'

At that time, I, Faisal Tehrani, arrived in the capital of Hujung Manani at the invitation of the True Patriot, to read poetry at the square, later that evening.

8.29 p.m.

There were sightings of an injured tiger wandering near the estuary of the Hujung Manani river. When the Momok people cheered loudly and made a lot of noise as they threw their magic sticks at it to chase it away, the tiger jumped into the river and swam across to the border between Hujung Manani and the South.

Nobody knew for certain where the tiger came from or why it had appeared suddenly.

In modern legends written afterwards, the monster would be described as a temptress who later married an influential man from Hujung Manani. That woman would go down in history as the centre of many scandals.

9.29 p.m.

200 police trucks tried to stop the huge crowd of demonstrators from entering the city. At the square, over 500,000 protestors had gathered, filling every space available. People still kept arriving. On the road entering the city, the march had paused because there were too many people everywhere.

The True Patriot abandoned her wheelchair and, accompanied by the Scientist, she walked up to the three rows of policemen blocking her way. The young men stood straight as they stared beyond her.

The True Patriot took the right hand of one of the policemen, who started looking guilty. The media representatives and the photographers captured the momentous incident.

The True Patriot addressed the young men who were blocking the road. 'My dear grandchildren, your strength has no equal. You are still young. I am older than your grandmothers. I dream of death so that I can be with Jesus. So that I can be with Ben. Raise your batons and strike me, so that the angel of death may come for me quickly.'

The policemen stared at the True Patriot. As they tried to control their emotions, their nostrils flared.

'You say *Allahuakbar*, I also say Allahuakbar. You say the shahadah, I also say the shahadah. You want to defend Hujung Manani, I also want to defend Hujung Manani. Yet you come from a village to hit our heads with your batons?'

Slowly, one of the policemen relaxed his rigid stance, stepped closed to the man beside him, and immediately the three rows of policemen parted in the centre to let the True Patriot, the Scientist and his wife through. The rest of their party followed after them.

The breach became wider and wider as the police barricade was swamped by the crowd.

In the blink of an eye, the police surrendered. And the march overcame the obstacle that had been put in its way to stop it.

10.29 p.m.

The True Patriot arrived at Hujung Manani Square, where she was greeted by the several hundred thousand-strong crowd composed of citizens of various races, sexes, faiths and backgrounds. They all cheered: 'Long live Pertiwi!'

At the same time, Z Good was getting ready. There was an ominous thought in his mind.

He had trained for a long time and was ready for revenge. All he needed was a reason. One kilogram of the mother of all evils. The father of all malevolence. He had learned from a member of Boko Haram, who was a PhD student in an Arab-owned college in Hujung Manani. It was not that difficult. He just had to oxidize aldehyde to produce carboxylic acid by using liquid chlorous acid. The reaction uses 50 ml of acetone as a solvent and produces a yellow side reaction which contains toxic chlorine dioxide.

When 30 per cent of hydrogen peroxide is added, the solution loses its yellow colour, for there is elimination of the side reaction. While focusing on the chlorine dioxide, and while waiting for the yellow colour to disappear, Z Good added another 50 ml of hydrogen peroxide. The resulting reaction produced TATP when mixed with acetone.

Now, it was an explosive. The mother of all evils. 40 grams of the mother of all evils.

This is what Adele had found when she was held captive in Z Good's house.

11.29 p.m.

The True Patriot was scheduled to speak to the crowd in one or two hours from now. I, Faisal Tehrani, had finished reading poetry.

What I didn't know was that Z Good had prepared a solid dry material which had crystallized. It was now a highly sensitive white powder which could easily explode if exposed to heat, friction or any mechanical movements. He was planning to blend into the crowd. Nobody would care to check the powder that he was carrying. He only had to make sure that it could explode, and it had to be as close as possible to the evil, sin-loving old hag. So that he could be proud. He believed that he would become a legend. He believed that he would become famous. His name would be recognized. History books would praise him.

In heaven, he would be greeted by tight virgins—angels who would always be wet for him and willing to spread their legs for him. They would not have to be tied to a bedpost. His semen would be plentiful and he would always be ready to shoot cum ropes.

That was a beautiful picture of heaven. A delicious heaven. A heaven, in his mind, full of pussy; and his cock would always be glistening wet.

Z Good smiled as he rubbed his cock. Before going out to do jihad, he took the time to masturbate.

12.29 a.m.

The General appeared on television again with the official announcement that the Leader of Hujung Manani had left the country and that the date of his return was not known.

'I also declare that the army has taken over the leadership of the country for the time being, and we are prepared to work together with the Mother of Democracy, the True Patriot, to restore democracy and human rights in the country. I also announce that the Chief of Police is under arrest for the crime of treason, together with a number of cabinet ministers. The army is actively looking for all the parties who have been conspiring with the Dictator.'

The General's official announcement was greeted with loud cheers and applause by the demonstrators. It was the largest gathering to protest against oppression and injustice in Southeast Asia.

The True Patriot asked the Scientist to represent her in a meeting with the General. Negotiations should start at once. All the more if they were to reach a compromise. At that moment, Badang was confirmed as Pertiwi's right-hand man.

1.29 a.m.

The number of demonstrators that flooded the centre of the capital kept growing and the largest square in the country could no longer accommodate so many people.

In an interview with a foreign television station, a woman explained, 'This is democracy. This is what school textbooks call "from the people for the people". You can see how many of us are here to show our support to the new government.'

Men who were not suffering from koro started to arrive at the square.

The crowd at the square sang 'Anak Kampung' as they performed the Sumazau dance.

2.29 a.m.

The Tycoon's surgery went well. They did not amputate his penis, only removing the skin covering the male organ. He was still in a coma and unable to witness the historic events that were taking place. He could always watch a documentary or a stage play about the Dictator's fall later.

On the television screen in the waiting room of the VIP ward, the Tycoon's son read the words written on one of the banners held by the demonstrators:

HUJUNG MANANI WANTS THE WEST TO TAKE BACK ITS PLASTIC. SUE PLASTIC CRIMINALS.

He was also going to witness a shocking and unspeakable event.

3.29 a.m.

The True Patriot arrived.

She was going to speak.

The Scientist and his wife were prevented from approaching the centre of the square by the large number of demonstrators.

Badang was bringing a clear message from the General: Pertiwi would lead Hujung Manani until fair and clean elections could be held in two years. A unity cabinet would be formed until power was returned to the people.

The country would be rebuilt.

The country would be cleansed of corruption.

The country would be cleansed of all plastic waste. All of it.

4.29 a.m.

Datuk Priapus Mappadulung Daeng Mattimung Karaeng Sanrobone appeared on television in a neighbouring country. He looked distressed, exhausted and panicked. As if reading a script, he declared that he was performing the pilgrimage in Mecca.

'Alhamdulillah. I am happy to be in Mecca. The last time I came here was during the fasting month. I never fail to fast in the holy land. Actually, I want to tell you a story. I was granted Lailatulqadar on the twenty-fifth night of Ramadan. I was circling the Kaaba. When I raised my face, I saw seven doves flying around the Kaaba. Ya Allah, I felt very lucky. One of the doves pooped and its droppings fell on my right cheek. Then, a big Arab man shouted behind me: "Don't wipe off the droppings. Rub them carefully and lick them with your tongue to get their blessings. It is very rare for birds to circle the Kaaba

on an odd night during Ramadan." I did exactly as he told me.
He also interpreted this event as a sign that Hujung Manani was
facing a challenge but that it would return to the hands of a
leader who loved his religion and his race. After this strange
incident, I went back to the Sheraton—eh, the Hilton—to sleep
on a soft bed, and I dreamt that I met the Prophet. Inshallah, I
will return to Hujung Manani. The country that I love dearly. I
will return to sing "Tomorrow Never Comes", one day.'

5.29 a.m.

'It was only yesterday, it seems, that we were told we could not
be here. That power was staring down at us in anger.

'This morning, I want to tell the Square of Hujung Manani,
this morning I want to tell the capital of Hujung Manani, this
morning I want to tell the entire country, and our neighbours
too, and the entire world: we did it! We did it!

'Yes, we broke the shackles of race. We broke the shackles
of feudalism. Bribing us with *Qur'an* stands and mosques will
not subjugate us. Bribing us with bells and churches will not
subjugate us. Bribing us with incense and temples will not
subjugate us. It is not easy to make us bend. But we did it! The
holy books that we read have inspired us to reject corruption
and defend human rights.

'I know that you will ask: "How many more times must we
do it? How much longer must we oppose the government? How
much longer until all the enemies of mankind are vanquished
and welfare is restored?"

'How much longer? Not much longer, because we shall all
die, including the Leader and his wife. The world is not eternal.
How much longer? Not much longer, because every seed of
evil which is planted will grow into a thousand evils which

will destroy them. How much longer? Not much longer, since soldiers with their guns were not able to stop us.

'This morning, we are gathered, united by our desire for freedom. For liberalism. So that we are not manipulated. Freedom from exploitation is a liberal strength that we will preserve. Secularism protects all religions, and democracy is real and concrete.

'My sisters, we are here this morning with one purpose . . .'

The True Patriot looked at the crowd. It was a sea, an ocean of people.

In front of the stage, for some reason, she saw Hassan and beside him, Jesus and Benedict.

A satisfied smile spread on her lips. 'I see nothing but beauty.'

The True Patriot locked eyes with Z Good, who appeared out of nowhere. 'I see nothing but beauty.'

Pertiwi continued the sentence that had remained hanging: 'In the name of Allah, one purpose: revolution is just a process, and not a final goal.'

Her final words echoed: 'I see nothing but beauty . . .'

Silence.

Beauty.

Glossary

Maqasid al-Shari'ah   A branch of Islamic law that determines whether something is in the public interest or not.
Shahid   Martyr in Islam.
Keris   A type of Malay dagger.
Tabayyun   An Arabic word meaning explanation, clarification, elucidation.
Mamak   Used to refer to a person of Indian Muslim descent.
Ustaz   A religious teacher in Islam.
Mat rempit   A biker who participates in activities such as illegal street racing, bike stunt performances, petty crime and public disturbance. They openly rebel against authorities, as they run past roadblocks, ride the wrong way in traffic or hit police officers with their bikes.
Latah   A nervous illness affecting women who, under the effect of surprise, cannot control their speech or behaviour.
Kun faya kun   An Arabic expression used to illustrate God's power. It means 'Be! And it is'.
Ukhti   The Arabic word for 'my sister'.
Masha'Allah   An Arabic phrase that is used to express a feeling of awe or beauty regarding an event or person that was just mentioned.

Lelaki ini Meaning 'this man'. It is the title of a song by Anuar Zain.

Astaghfirullah An expression of guilt or shame.

Ong Good luck.

Pak Lokan A traditional dance performance in which the main performer, Pak Lokan (meaning 'Mr Clam'), imitates the movements of a clam and enters a trance.

Silat gayong A traditional Malaysian martial art.

Tok Short form of *datuk*, meaning grandfather, used as a mark of respect for an elder person.

Dato Grandfather.

Keling A derogatory term used for Malaysian Indians.

Kote mamak Literally meaning 'Muslim Indian's penis', this is a flowering tree. Its scientific name is *Cassia grandis*.

Kompang A Javanese musical instrument resembling a tambourine.

Berkah Grace, blessing.

Shafa'ah A divine intercession.

Kejawèn Or Javanism, refers to a Javanese religious tradition which is an amalgam of animistic, Buddhist and Hindu aspects.

Amir al-Mu'minin Can be translated as Commander of the Faithful, or Prince of the Believers.

Gurindam A form of traditional Malay poetry.

Suddamala A classical Javanese text.

Kita jaga kita Or 'we look after each other', was the slogan used by people who provided assistance to others in need without waiting for the government to act during the Covid pandemic in Malaysia.

Bossku Meaning 'my boss', is a nickname ex-Prime Minister of Malaysia, Najib Razak; used after he was ousted in 2018.

Wasatiyyah   Meaning 'balance' or 'moderation' was a concept introduced by Prime Minister Najib as the direction of his government.

Malu apa bossku   Meaning 'there is nothing to be ashamed of', first appeared in a tweet by PM Najib, claiming that he was innocent from accusations of kleptocracy. It has since become a meme.

Toyol   A very small ghost who steals for his master.

Aurat   Refers to the part of the body which must remain covered, i.e. between the navel and the knees for men.

Harus   Encouraged according to Islamic law.

Makruh   Not sinful, but one is rewarded if they avoid it.

Datuk Seri   The highest state title conferred by the Ruler.

Malay silat   A traditional form of martial arts.

Orang Kaya   An aristocratic title.

Badang   A legendary Malay strongman.

Nushuz   The act of being disobedient to one's husband.

Mihna   An ordeal.

Tawaf   Circumambulating the Kaaba seven times while praying.

Zapin   A traditional dance in Southeast Asian countries.

Gambus   A sort of Arab lute.

Kacau keledek   A delicacy from Johor made with sweet potato (keledek).

Salam   Peace

'One Malaysia'   A concept introduced by former Prime Minister Najib Razak to promote national unity.

Ibrah   A lesson.

Tawhid   Means believing in Allah alone.

Ijtihad   In Islamic law, the independent or original interpretation of problems not precisely covered by the *Qur'an* or the *Hadith*.

Amar makruf and nahi mungkar   Commanding what is just and forbidding what is wrong.

Allahuakbar   God is the Greatest.

Shahadah   The statement of faith.

Sumazau   A traditional dance of the Kadazan, the largest indigenous group of Sabah. Its graceful dance moves mimic the eagle in flight.

Lailatulqadar   Translated into English as the Night of Decree, Night of Power, Night of Value, Night of Destiny, or Night of Measures, it is the night when the *Qur'an* was first revealed to Prophet Muhammad. Its exact date is unknown but it is believed to be on an odd-numbered day during the last ten days of Ramadan.